A Knight on Duchess Square

The Silver Duchesses
Book 1

by

Meara Platt

ARE YOU SIGNED UP FOR DRAGONBLADE'S BLOG?

You'll get the latest news and information on exclusive giveaways, exclusive excerpts, coming releases, sales, free books, cover reveals and more.

Check out our complete list of authors, too!

No spam, no junk. That's a promise!

Sign Up Here

www.dragonbladepublishing.com

Dearest Reader;

Thank you for your support of a small press. At Dragonblade Publishing, we strive to bring you the highest quality Historical Romance from some of the best authors in the business. Without your support, there is no 'us', so we sincerely hope you adore these stories and find some new favorite authors along the way.

Happy Reading!

CEO, Dragonblade Publishing

Additional Dragonblade books by Author Meara Platt

The Silver Duchesses Series
A Knight on Duchess Square

The Silver Dukes Series
Cherish and the Duke
Moonlight and the Duke
Two Nights with the Duke
Snowfall and the Duke
Starlight and the Duke
Crash Landing on the Duke

The Moonstone Landing Series
Moonstone Landing (Novella)
Moonstone Angel (Novella)
The Moonstone Duke
The Moonstone Marquess
The Moonstone Major
The Moonstone Governess
The Moonstone Hero
The Moonstone Pirate

The Book of Love Series
The Look of Love
The Touch of Love
The Taste of Love
The Song of Love
The Scent of Love
The Kiss of Love
The Chance of Love
The Gift of Love
The Heart of Love

The Hope of Love (Novella)
The Promise of Love
The Wonder of Love
The Journey of Love
The Dream of Love (Novella)
The Treasure of Love
The Dance of Love
The Miracle of Love
The Remembrance of Love (Novella)

Dark Gardens Series
Garden of Shadows
Garden of Light
Garden of Dragons
Garden of Destiny
Garden of Angels

The Farthingale Series
If You Wished For Me (Novella)

The Lyon's Den Series
Kiss of the Lyon
The Lyon's Surprise
Lyon in the Rough

Pirates of Britannia Series
Pearls of Fire

De Wolfe Pack: The Series
Nobody's Angel
Kiss an Angel
Bhrodi's Angel

Also from Meara Platt
Aislin
All I Want for Christmas
Once Upon a Haunted Cave

CHAPTER ONE

Duchess Square, Mayfair
London, England
June 1820

"BERRY, IS HE out there?"

Lady Berengaria Thane grabbed the porcelain vase sitting atop the small table beside her parlor window before it toppled as her friend, Miranda, and Miranda's niece, Gwenys, elbowed their way past several other friends who were peering out the window to see *him*.

"Eek!" Gwenys cried. "He's taking off his shirt!"

"Cover your eyes," Miranda scolded. "You are too innocent to look upon that shameful man."

Berry thought she and her friends were the shameful ones for gawking at this fellow, who appeared to be in a position of authority amid the construction work going on at her neighbor's residence.

But who could blame them?

"Aah! He's flexing his muscles!" her friend Arabella cried.

Dear heaven.

Had all her friends gone mad?

"Ladies, the tea cakes are out," Berry called to them to gain their attention, to no avail. "Ladies!"

Sighing, she set her rescued vase atop her pianoforte for now.

The Ladies Tea Society to which Berry belonged was supposed to meet at a different member's home every Thursday afternoon, but meetings had been held at her home on Duchess

Square every week for this past month because of *him*.

"Is he out there today? Let me see!" Margaret, a newly arrived friend, asked as she sprinted across the parlor to join the others.

"Would anyone care for a tea cake?" Berry called out again, and then sank onto her floral silk settee to await the meeting's start.

A booming noise from next door shot her to her feet again.

This was intolerable.

First the constant noise as her new neighbor, a mysterious gentleman by the name of Mr. Knight, reconstructed a perfectly fine townhouse that had belonged to her dear friend, Lady Fiona Shoreham, who was now Duchess of Durham. Then to have his builders put on a display of their muscles... Well, their attention was mostly on that one spectacular man who seemed to be the hardest worker, and it had been brutally hot all week.

There was another loud boom that startled them all and had them leaping in fright.

"What are they doing?" Miranda asked, finally turning away from the window to address Berry.

Berry frowned. "I don't know. Extending the back wall of the townhouse, I think. Fiona often mentioned her desire to do the same but never got around to it. It was the first thing that oaf of a new owner did upon purchasing her home. I am going to put a stop to all that banging. How are we ever to hold our meeting if we cannot hear ourselves talk above the din? I'll be right back."

She marched out of her townhouse and stormed next door just as a massive beam came tumbling off the roof and almost struck her.

"Who in bloody blazes let you back here?" the man they had all been gawking at roared as he scampered down the tall ladder with the agility of a cat.

A big, dangerous cat, for he strode toward her with a look so savagely angry that steam could have poured from his ears.

Dear heaven.

His body appeared to be carved from granite.

Endless muscles stretched tautly across his tanned skin. He had a thick head of raven-black hair that needed a proper trim and piercing gray eyes as cold as honed steel. The dark blotch that seemed to wrap itself around his upper arm turned out to be the depiction of a dragon.

Yes, she could see this man breathing fire down on unsuspecting innocents.

"What are you doing to this beautiful house?" she shot back in defiance, having to peer upward to meet his incensed gaze, for he was tall as well as brawny. "I am trying to hold a meeting of my Ladies Tea Society, and we cannot hear ourselves speak because of all the noise you are making."

He rolled his yes. "A bloody tea society? This is why you barreled into my back garden and almost got yourself decapitated?"

His garden?

Goodness, what a haughty oaf to refer to it as his when they all knew it belonged to Mr. Knight.

He turned away to call for one of his workers to bring him his shirt.

"If you are so keen to have your meetings," he said, as he tossed the shirt on and covered his flawless body, "then why not hold them elsewhere?"

"We rotate turns, and this is my turn," Berry said, blushing because she had just told a falsehood and felt quite guilty about it.

He knew it, too.

He saw through her because she could not hide her expressions, and that harmless, tiny fib showed right on her face. But it was not a complete lie. They did rotate turns, and how dare he doubt her word on that?

But it wasn't her turn today, or any of the past Thursdays this entire month.

"You couldn't simply have switched places until the worst of this construction was over?"

Yes, she could have.

She ignored the question because she could not bring herself to tell him another fib. But he was as much to blame as they were. Did this oaf have to look so spectacular even with his shirt on? The expanse of white linen only made his shoulders appear broader and his torso more magnificently sculpted.

"The lot of you have been gawking at me all month long," he grumbled. "Every time I look up, there are more faces peering at me from your window."

Berry tried not to blush again, but how could she deny it?

"We were curious about the construction."

Again, this was only a half truth.

He had the impertinence to arch an eyebrow, questioning her veracity.

Should he not harbor some of the blame? They would not have been looking if he hadn't been out there dazzling them with his glorious muscles. "If you weren't such a big clot, we wouldn't—"

He picked her up by her armpits and carried her out of the garden.

She gasped and grabbed on to his shoulders. "What are you doing? Put me down!"

But gad, he smelled good beneath that sheen of sweat on his skin. Had he bathed with sandalwood soap? Because there was a wonderfully earthen scent with citrus overtones about him.

"I demand to see Mr. Knight!"

"Then you should have gone to the front door and asked his butler to let you in." He plunked her down on the front step.

"I did knock, but you were making so much noise, his butler could not hear me."

He grinned. "Yes, Bonham is quite deaf."

"Then how is Mr. Knight to know when people come to his door?"

"He isn't, and he doesn't care."

"That is outrageous!" How could dear Fiona have sold this

property to that *nouveau riche* scoundrel? "Will you be working on Mr. Knight's house this Saturday?"

"Who wants to know?"

This man was seriously infuriating.

Berry tipped her chin up again. "I do."

"And who are you?"

"As I am sure you know by now, because you do not strike me as a man who misses much of anything, I am Mr. Knight's neighbor, Lady Berengaria Thane," she said, just as another boom drowned out the mention of her family name.

"Berengaria? That's a mighty big name for a little thing like you."

"My friends call me Lady Berry."

"Sweet," he muttered, casting her a look she could have sworn was mocking. His silvery eyes seemed to dance with amusement.

"But you shall refer to me as Lady Berengaria."

He nodded. "Yes, Your Highness."

"Curb your arrogance or I shall demand Mr. Knight discharge you."

The glint of amusement disappeared.

Oh dear.

He arched a dark eyebrow and crossed his arms over his massive chest. "Excuse me?"

She let out a deflated breath. "I won't really. Forgive me, that was rather insolent of me. But I am at my wits' end. You see, I am holding a charity affair at my home this Saturday on behalf of St. Brigid's Orphanage, as I do every year. You cannot be pounding your hammers and tossing down giant beams while I am trying to coax donations from my guests to keep the orphanage funded. How are we to resolve this, Mr...." She waited for him to introduce himself.

He sighed. "Gideon will do."

"Mr. Gideon. I—"

"Just Gideon."

"All right…Gideon. Is there a solution to this dilemma?"

He surprised her by actually giving the question a moment's thought. "St. Brigid's, you say? You could invite Mr. Knight to your charity event. He would halt the construction if he were invited."

Her eyes widened. "Would he consider it? Or will he consider me rude and grasping, and think I only want his money?"

"Yes, to both."

"He would accept? But also think me rude and grasping?" She shook her head. "Please tell him that donations are desired but not required. Any small token is appreciated. I shall send him an invitation as soon as my meeting is over. If he wishes to learn more about the orphanage, I would be happy to show him around the place."

"It won't be necessary. Mr. Knight knows it well."

Her eyes widened. "He does?"

Gideon nodded and pointed to the men working in the back. "We all do. Every one of us came out of St. Brigid's."

Berry did not know why his remark brought tears to her eyes. "That is wonderful, Gideon. My father would be so proud."

"Will he be in attendance?"

"No, he died many years ago. My mother, too. I was orphaned at the age of eight."

He frowned lightly. "What did you say your family name was?"

"Thane. I am the daughter of Lord Archibald Thane and granddaughter to Lord George Thane. My grandfather founded the orphanage and my father carried on his work. Upon *his* death, the duty fell to me. It is expected that every generation of Thanes will keep the orphanage funded to honor my grandfather and protect the children brought there. I—"

"Send your invitation, Lady Berengaria. Mr. Knight will attend," he said with a surprising depth of feeling.

"And will he bring his wallet?"

The cold steel of his gaze turned warm and mirthful as a slow smile spread across his face. "Yes. With his wallet, Lady Berengaria."

She nodded and was about to return to her residence when this man called Gideon suddenly took hold of her hand and drew her back. "One more thing…"

"Yes?"

He picked her up by her armpits again and planted a savagely tender and scorchingly wild kiss on her lips. "That is for all the orphans your family has saved at St. Brigid's."

He set her back down and strode away.

Berry put a hand to her tingling lips as she glanced up at her parlor window.

She counted seven faces plastered to the glass. All of them wide-eyed.

Had her friends seen what just happened?

CHAPTER TWO

"HE KISSED YOU!" Gwenys shrieked, and rushed to her side the moment Berry returned home still slightly dazed from that thoroughly improper kiss that had every bone in her body melting.

The other ladies now surrounded her, all atwitter.

"How was it?" Alice asked, grabbing her hand and giving it an excited squeeze.

"Was it nice?" Mabel asked, turning Berry to face her.

"The brute! You ought to have slapped him," Maude Harcourt intoned, for she was quite the stickler for decorum, and what Gideon had done was utterly shocking and not to be condoned. "That would have put him in his place."

"And what do you think he would have done had I slapped him, Maude?"

The prudish spinster fidgeted. "Well, you could have at least *looked* angry."

"No, I could not," Berry said as her friends now took their seats and she began to pour the tea. "He told me the most extraordinary thing."

"What did he say to you?" Miranda asked, almost toppling out of her seat in anticipation.

"All of those workers, including himself, were raised at St. Brigid's. *My* orphanage. And isn't it wonderful they are all productive members of society and working in honorable trades?

My father and grandfather would be so proud."

Arabella smiled at her as she reached for a slice of buttered bread. "How wonderful. And does this not say something about Mr. Knight, too?"

Berry nodded. "Perhaps he is not as arrogant as I thought. I am going to send him an invitation to Saturday's charity affair. I think he will attend."

Miranda had just scraped some sugar off the sugar cone and now looked up. "Truly? That will cause quite a stir, but I'm glad you will invite him. After all, he is my neighbor, too. Perhaps not right next door, but you and I and Mr. Knight all reside on Duchess Square, do we not?"

Maude pursed her lips, looking as though she had just sucked on lemons. "Fiona really ought to have sold to a respectable spinster of means instead of a crass oaf off the streets."

"I think Mr. Knight was also raised at St. Brigid's, so I would hardly refer to him as an oaf off the streets, Maude. Perhaps this is why Fiona thought he might make a good neighbor for me. That is quite a strong bond between us, don't you think?"

She snorted. "You are best served encouraging Viscount Hawthorne's courtship. Now, he's a real gentleman."

"A viscount with a desperate need for deep pockets," Gwendolyn Carstairs, another of Berry's neighbors on Duchess Square, remarked. "He is interested in Berry's trust fund, not Berry herself. Although you are lovely and kind and he could very well fall in love with you."

Berry did not believe the viscount would ever love her, although how could she know what love looked like? In all of her eight and twenty years, soon to be nine and twenty, she had never been kissed with true passion—except for Gideon's surprising kiss today, but that did not count.

How could it? He had kissed her passionately on behalf of the orphanage. Not for himself.

In many ways, his was the nicest kiss she had ever received, because it was given with a sincere abundance of feeling.

Was this not how kisses ought to be given? From the heart. With depth and meaning.

Since the noise from next door had finally died down, they moved on to attend to their business matters. Their weekly meetings over tea were not merely to relate the latest gossip but to discuss causes and do something about helping the downtrodden.

The next few hours flew by, and it was soon time for her friends to take their leave.

Berry gave each one a kiss on the cheek, even sour Maude, who was really quite nice but had such a dreary outlook on everything. If the sun were shining, she would remark upon how annoyingly aglare it was. If the weather were cool and overcast, she would complain about being frozen and found dead in her bed by morning.

Berry had taken it upon herself to coax smiles out of Maude, and was delighted when she got a smile and a hug out of her now. "Berry, keep your windows closed or all the dust stirred up by Mr. Knight's construction will seep into your lungs and give you a fatal disease."

"Thank you, Maude. I shall do my best not to breathe."

Miranda's niece, nineteen-year-old Gwenys, threw her arms around Berry. "What an exciting afternoon! I cannot wait until next week. Do you think he will kiss you again? Do you want him to? I certainly would. Do you think he would kiss me if—"

Miranda dragged her away. "Gwenys, if I catch you anywhere near that man I shall haul you off to the wilds of Scotland and keep you locked away until you turn fifty."

"Aunt Miranda!" Gwenys whined as the pair marched off for home, which was merely across their small square.

Arabella kissed Berry's cheek. "I had better hurry home to await my dear Hubert. He is such a creature of habit and would be utterly lost if I am not home to greet him."

Berry thought it was quite nice the way Arabella and her husband were around each other. They sincerely enjoyed being in each other's company. They adored their children and adored each other.

Once all the ladies had gone home, Berry sat alone on her settee while lost in thought.

Her butler approached. "Lady Berry, shall I clear away the table now, or do you wish me to wait?"

"Oh, yes. Please do it now, Melton. I shall get out of your way. I ought to look in on Mrs. Garland, since she was feeling too poorly to come out of her bedchamber today." The genteel, elderly lady had been hired years ago by her father's trustee, Lord Berwick, to live with Berry and serve as her chaperone and companion.

The arrangement served both of them well, since Mrs. Garland had been raised in the better circles of London Society but had fallen upon hard times, and Berry was considered too young even now to live on her own without raising eyebrows.

"And I have an important invitation to write."

"Very good, Lady Berry."

She scurried upstairs and quietly entered Mrs. Garland's bedchamber.

"Cora," she whispered to the maid attending her, "how is she?"

"No fever, m'lady. But the poor thing is quite fatigued. I fear it is old age and not any disease that is wearing her down."

Berry felt a pang of regret. The passage of time seemed to be stealing everyone away from her.

But Mrs. Garland would be well cared for here. Berry could do no less for her after all the years of her kind devotion.

Since she had no intention of waking the woman from her peaceful slumber, Berry went downstairs to her study to write Mr. Knight's invitation. The invitation cards were engraved with all the details, so she had only to add a short, personal note to him.

Once done, she thought to hand it to Melton to deliver next door, but then changed her mind.

He and her housekeeper, Mrs. Bolton, were busy clearing away the mess from the parlor. And anyway, should she not make the friendly gesture toward her new neighbor? They had St. Brigid's in common, and that ought to put them on immediately friendly terms.

Well, Maude would consider it highly improper to deliver the invitation herself, as would most of the *ton*, Berry supposed.

"Honestly," she muttered, walking out the door with the invitation card in her hand. She had led an exemplary life, never taking a toe out of line. To make anything tawdry out of this friendly gesture would show her accusers to be the rude and petty ones.

She marched up Mr. Knight's front walk and knocked at his door. When no one answered, she pounded until her fist began to throb.

His butler finally opened it.

"May I help you?" he asked, his eyes opening wide in obvious surprise.

The man looked a little dusty, no doubt from all the construction swirling around him. He probably served as butler, caretaker, and night watchman while the entire back of Mr. Knight's house was being torn out to expand what had once been Fiona's music room.

This explained why he was not wearing proper livery. His uniform would be ruined while he worked amid this mess. Obviously, no decent staff could be kept here just yet.

"You must be Bonham. Yes, I came to deliver this invitation for Mr. Knight."

The man cast her a blank stare.

Honestly, why hire this man who appeared slow and was obviously deaf, as that Gideon fellow had mentioned in passing? Not to mention, she had resorted to pounding on the door with the full force of her fist to get him to hear her. Thieves could break in and steal whatever they wanted, and this man would never know it.

Well, few outsiders ever walked onto Duchess Square, but they might if they realized how poorly watched this house truly was. She hoped having a warm body seen patrolling would be enough to keep most bounders away.

"An invitation!" she said louder, trying not to show her frustration as the man continued to gaze at her with a look of utter bewilderment.

Hopefully, the work would end soon and Mr. Knight would move in with a full complement of sharp-witted servants.

She craned her head to peek inside, just out of curiosity.

Ugh, what a mess. The place was simply not livable yet.

"It is nice to meet you, Bonham," she shouted again.

Good gracious. That fellow, Gideon, had mentioned Mr. Knight's butler was deaf as a post, but this was beyond description.

"I am Mr. Knight's neighbor, Lady Berengaria!" She smiled, pointed to herself, and then to her house, which looked quite lovely as the fading sunlight shimmered upon the lintels and roof coping, and warmed the stonework. "I have an invitation for him," she shouted again as she shoved the sealed card into his hand, hoping Bonham knew to forward it to his employer with all due haste. "For a Saturday party. It is important he receives it today. In time for Sa-tur-day!"

When the man did not appear to understand—goodness, he had such a confused look about him—she shouted the instruction again. "Important! Mr. Knight! Today!"

"Yes, m'lady," he said with a smile. "I'll see that he gets this invitation at once."

Berry breathed a sigh of relief and smiled back at him. "Very good."

She turned and walked away, hoping this had not been a wasted excursion. When she glanced back to reassure herself, she saw the man still standing at the door, watching her with that utterly bemused look again.

Oh dear.

Deaf and possibly senile.

Should she say something to Mr. Knight when they finally met?

After all, he could place Bonham in another position within his household. And was it wise to use Bonham as his watchman when thieves could throw a party in this place and he would not hear a thing? She resolved to alert Melton and her staff to keep an eye out for strangers lurking about Duchess Square.

Having addressed this concern, she hurried home and scooted up to her bedchamber, where her lady's maid, Harriet, was waiting for her. "Oh, m'lady! There you are. Hurry up. Lord Berwick will be along at any moment to escort you to the theater."

"Yes, yes. It won't take me but a trice." Berry hastily slipped out of her tea gown and undergarments with Harriet's assistance, wet the cloth by her basin and ewer on her night table, soaped it with a fruity-scented soap—because she was Lady Berry, after all—then quickly scrubbed her body.

She dried herself off and donned her robe while Harriet fashioned her hair in a more ornate, upswept style suitable for the evening. Once done, Harriet held up the gown she was to wear, a lemon silk that she now put on. To complete the outfit, she had gloves and silk slippers in the same yellow hue.

"Diamonds or pearls this evening?" Harriet asked, pulling out Berry's jewelry box.

"Pearls, I think."

Harriet arched an eyebrow. "Are you sure? Diamonds are quite the thing and will go better with this gown. Pearls are fine for quiet dinner parties or afternoon wear."

Berry laughed. "All right, we shall go with the sparkly gems."

She selected a simple diamond heart necklace and diamond studs for her ears. Instead of a tiara, she chose diamond star clips for her hair.

"Your choices are rather understated tonight," Harriet remarked.

Berry shrugged. "I know, but I am not of a mind to be dripping in glitter this evening."

"Well, you look beautiful as always."

Berry heard voices in the entry hall, so she grabbed her lemon silk wrap and hurried downstairs to greet Lord Berwick, her father's best friend who had been appointed trustee of the fund established for her under her father's testament. The dear man had been like a father to her these past twenty years.

"Berry," he said with a beaming smile as she walked forward to greet him, "don't you look lovely. Come along, my dear. Lady Berwick awaits us in the carriage."

They arrived at the Covent Garden theater and settled in the Berwicks' box shortly before the curtain went up.

She and Lady Berwick enjoyed looking at all the ladies and commenting on what they were wearing. They often made a game of it, tossing snide remarks at times, although arrogance and pettiness were not really in their nature. But what was the point of a night out at the theater if one could not people watch and opine on the garish tastes of others?

Lady Winslow, for example, and that ostrich feather she wore on her head.

"I think she put the entire ostrich on herself," Lady Berwick remarked. "It is in danger of laying an egg."

Berry laughed. "Oh, she is looking back at us, and now leaning over to whisper to her friend, Lady Gorse. I'm sure they are remarking on my gown, declaring I look like a canary, for I am all in yellow."

"Nonsense, my dear," Lady Berwick said, always one to come to her defense. "It is the lightest shade of yellow and quite elegant. Perfectly suits your complexion. You look quite lovely tonight. Lady Gorse is overdone, as usual. Rings on every finger and bracelets running up her arm. I'm surprised she can lift her arms."

"Lady Mosby is going to blind someone with all those diamonds she is wearing," Berry said, taking her turn. "They'll need to toss a blanket over her once the play starts to keep her from distracting the actors."

Lady Berwick laughed. "I fear they will think the same of me. I am too done up."

"No," Berry insisted. "You are perfect, as always. I am the one who is subdued and felt like dressing myself down this evening."

"Why, my dear?"

She let out a breath. "I don't know. I have been feeling out of sorts lately. Mrs. Garland has not been well."

"Yes, I know," Lady Berwick said with sincere concern.

"And here I am enjoying a pleasant night out. But it isn't only Mrs. Garland that has me sad. It is all this." Berry waved her hand across the theater. "Here we all are in our diamonds and sapphires while others are struggling to fill their bellies."

"Oh, my dear." Lady Berwick patted her hand. "You do more than your share to help those in need. You cannot take on all the burden of it."

Berry did her best to shrug off her malaise because she did not want to ruin Lady Berwick's evening out.

Perhaps it was that kiss she'd received today. She was still tingling over it.

"Oh heavens. Oh my," Lady Berwick said, suddenly grabbing Berry's arm. "Will you look at those beautiful ladies? Have you ever seen two more stunning creatures?"

"Where?" Berry followed the direction of Lady Berwick's gaze to a box on the opposite side of the theater where a tall, slender blonde and an equally tall and slender brunette, both of them dressed in the height of fashion, were now taking their seats.

She gasped.

It was not the ladies she was staring at but the man now taking a seat beside them.

Gideon. Mr. Knight's construction man.

"How on earth?"

"What is it, my dear?"

No, it simply was not possible. She had to be mistaken.

"Lady Berwick, who is the man with those exquisite ladies?"

Unfortunately, the play started just then, and she did not receive an answer.

Was it Gideon? Had he noticed her?

Was he looking at her?

She turned to glance at him and saw him looking straight at her, his steel-eyed gaze boring into her.

Then one of the women touched his arm and he turned to her.

Would he be kissing either of those women tonight?

CHAPTER THREE

"YOU TOLD HER I was deaf," Gideon Knight's good friend, John Bonham, humorously accused him, dropping into a chair in Gideon's study at the Musket Club and tossing him a look of reproof. "She almost blew out my eardrums while shouting instructions in my ear about your invitation to her bloody charity tea."

Gideon looked up from his desk where he had been reviewing documents, and grinned at this man he'd known for ages, one of the few he trusted. "You could have simply told her the truth, but instead you played the dunce when she came to the door to hand you the invitation. Where were you when she came around that first time to complain about the noise?"

"Chasing a mouse in the kitchen. Whatever possessed you to tell her I was deaf?"

"I had to come up with some excuse for your rudeness. You know I almost killed her when she marched around back into the yard. That board I was hammering slipped loose and almost struck her on the head."

"That would have made a lasting impression," Bonham said wryly. "Are you going to attend her affair?"

Gideon nodded. "Yes."

"Why? It will be filled with her boorish friends who would sooner scrape their muddy boots on you than smile at you. And all she wants is your money."

"No," Gideon said emphatically, "Lady Berry isn't like that."

Bonham arched an eyebrow. "Oh, *Lady Berry*? Have you gotten that cozy with her already? When have you had the chance to bed her?"

"I haven't," Gideon said, casting his friend a warning look. "Nor do I intend to. She's respectable."

"Since when has that stopped you?"

Gideon did not know why he was so rankled by their conversation when Bonham was right about his behavior.

This was what he always did with ladies of his acquaintance. If they caught his fancy, he tossed them a look. They always responded. He bedded them.

Once he lost interest, he gave them a pretty trinket and never looked back.

"You retired early last night," Bonham remarked. "Left me sleeping on a rickety cot in that big, dusty house while you stayed up reading a book here at the club. Jasmine and Chloe gave me an earful when I arrived a few minutes ago. They said you took them to the theater and that was all. Not a kiss or request to join you later. You simply handed them over to Pudge to escort them into the gaming hall and retired up here. Are you feeling unwell?"

"What are you, my mother?" Gideon growled back, obviously irritated, since neither of them had mothers and would not know a mother's touch if it bit them on the arse.

"Well, you had two beautiful women on your arm. Two courtesans to whom every man in that theater would have given their right arm for a night of pleasure, and all you did was watch the play."

"'To whom every man'? What are you suddenly? An Oxford professor? Who gave you permission to keep track of my sexual exploits?"

"Or sudden lack thereof," Bonham muttered. "Have you decided to become a monk?"

Gideon rolled his eyes. "Who is teaching you to speak like that? *Lack thereof*? *To whom*? Now you are sounding like one of those nobs we both detest."

"It is your diction coach, Miss Wright. She happens to be giving me diction lessons, too. I have also been taking lessons from your dance instructor, Miss Feswick. You and I have been friends and business partners for years. Our ventures are doing well, so why should I not put some of that blunt to good use? Aren't you doing the same?"

Gideon nodded.

"Better than spending it on drink or a tart," Bonham continued. "Why shouldn't I learn to pass as an elegant gentleman? We have become more successful than anything we dreamed possible. Those years when we hoped to get jobs as clerks are long past. Why are you frowning at me, Gideon? If they are our enemy, then why do you want to be like them?"

"I don't want to be like them. I hate their arrogance and entitlement. Who are they, anyway? What makes them better than us? It is nothing more than the luck of their birth," Gideon said with unmasked bitterness. "What would they be without their advantages? I have no intention of ever being like them, but I want to rub their noses in my success. Stick it in their pasty faces and make them green with envy. I'll show them who's the better man."

"You can toss the wealth of England at them and they will still revile you. And if you want my opinion—"

"Which I don't. Enough, Bonham. I mean it. I have work to do."

"Shuffling through those papers?"

"Yes, this is what comes with building our assets. Contracts, ledgers, reports."

"More like Julius Caesar building his empire. And what about the house construction? Why did you send the boys away? They are close to finishing up that back expansion. Shouldn't they be working on it?"

"They'll resume work on Monday," Gideon replied. "Lady Berry needs to set up for tomorrow's charity tea, that fancy gathering she is hosting, and does not need the distraction of our hammers. As you said, the work is almost done. Little more left than cleaning out the yard and putting in the glass doors."

"You'll still have to furnish the house."

"Yes, in time." The place was empty save for a cheap desk and a few old chairs he had brought over from one of their gaming hells. He'd purchased some cots from a military auction, and these were what he and Bonham slept on whenever they were there. However, Bonham was the one mostly sleeping there lately. Gideon had spent most nights in his private quarters here at the Musket Club because as their wealth grew, so did his responsibilities.

Bonham worked just as hard supervising all their clubs and maintaining their prime condition. He managed supplies, hired the right employees, and repaired whatever needed fixing while Gideon handled much of the more academic work. That included scouting new ventures, negotiating contracts, and investing their profits.

The amount of work they each had to put in just to stay abreast of all that was going on with their assets was mounting steadily.

This club had become Gideon's headquarters of a sort. It was the elite gaming hell he and Bonham operated, one among several such establishments they owned in London. This was also where Gideon bedded courtesans and bored wives of the nobility whenever the urge struck him.

He was never going to bring any of them to his house on Duchess Square.

With his having started out life as a tossed-away, homeless boy covered in ash found wandering the London streets and brought to St. Brigid's to be given a home and a chance to make something of himself, that house was his dream fulfilled. That beautiful residence on Duchess Square was the first thing ever purchased completely for himself.

His alone.

Yes, his once impossible dream. His sanctuary.

"I'll have to engage a decorator."

"I'm sure your Lady Berry will be able to recommend one."

Gideon shrugged. "Maybe. Now get out of here. I have work to do. But have Cook prepare a hot meal for you before you head back to Duchess Square. And be polite to Lady Berry if she stops by again."

Bonham laughed as he rose. "Are you suggesting I ought to stop behaving like an arse and stop teasing her with my deaf act? You're the one who started it."

Gideon chuckled. "She is deliciously gullible, isn't she? All right, let's see how long it takes her to catch on to the ruse."

Bonham shook his head. "You are a bounder, and she is such a sweet thing."

"I know. Thane's daughter. And isn't she as pretty as an angel? Green eyes that sparkle and dimples when she smiles. She also has a soft heart."

"Don't you go breaking it, Gideon," Bonham warned as he walked out.

The rest of the day passed quietly for Gideon.

He worked through much of the tedious pile of documents he had put off sifting through while caught up fixing his new townhouse. But as night fell, he washed, dressed, and then walked downstairs to play host at the Musket Club. This was their crown jewel, the place where he and Bonham had built their wealth, this elite gaming establishment that catered to the Upper Crust.

Joss Fraser was the canny Scot who worked as floor manager for them. Gideon and Bonham had placed trusted men to manage each of their establishments, but in many ways the Musket Club was the hardest to run and required their best man. It took a sharp mind and a bit of intelligence to handle the elite, who were *not* used to paying their debts in a timely fashion.

"Viscount Hawthorne's here again," Joss muttered as Gideon entered the gaming salon.

"Is he winning or losing tonight?"

Joss glanced at the viscount and shook his head. "He's about even so far, but he's downed two scotches in thirty minutes. He'll start losing soon."

Gideon nodded. "Have Pudge see him to his carriage before his losses get out of control. Anyone else we ought to be concerned about?"

They all needed to keep alert to pickpockets and card sharps who were attracted to this particular club because the moneyed set spent their evenings here.

"That beady-eyed bloke over in the corner. Pudge is watching him closely."

"Good. And the ladies?" He knew which ones came from privilege and were regulars because they liked to gamble. He also knew who the courtesans were and allowed them entry with limitations. Ladies like Jasmine and Chloe were permitted to remain so long as they merely spoke to the gentlemen gambling here. After all, they were entitled to find benefactors for themselves.

But he was not running a cathouse, and any lady showing up to make a quick coin would be discreetly and immediately shown the door. Not even his copper hells had rooms upstairs for such goings-on.

Lady Berry suddenly came to mind, her shimmering green eyes and tumble of strawberry-blonde curls making him yearn for something better.

But what could be better than what he had now? He had never known his mother. He did not need a wife.

Bah!

He had no idea why thoughts of Lady Berry kept popping into his head. She was no tart, of course. She was not even classically beautiful.

But gad, she was pretty. A little tightly wound and buttoned up, but soft as a kitten. Few women ever stole his breath away, but she was one of them.

He'd wanted to bed her the moment he set eyes on her.

He never would, of course.

She and her family had saved many girls from that sort of life, and he had every respect for her. Her kindness and compassion were admirable, and he would always honor her for it.

No, Lady Berry was not to be touched…much as he ached to do so.

The Musket Club was lively tonight, and Gideon now turned his attention toward making certain the patrons were well attended and not being taken by cheaters.

He retired shortly before dawn, knowing by all the activity that this just might have been their most profitable night ever. He and Bonham made a habit of giving their workers a little extra on a good night.

But he also gave thought to something else, something concerning St. Brigid's. Why should he not start setting aside a little extra for the orphanage, too?

Perhaps he would take Lady Berry up on her offer to tour the place, since he hadn't been back there in over a decade—in truth, almost two decades—and he was now curious.

Well, all to be taken under consideration. He was too tired to think clearly just now.

Gideon had never required more than four or five hours of sleep, so he was fully refreshed by the time he awoke on Saturday morning. The hour was just coming on nine o'clock. Still early for everyone else who had worked the club last night. But he had a pile of documents to get through before he set out for Duchess Square and Lady Berry's charity event.

After ordering coffee and scones brought up to him, he spent the morning tabulating last night's receipts. Once done, he rode with Joss to each of his other clubs to take account of their profits.

The invitation to Lady Berry's afternoon tea was for two o'clock.

He returned to his private quarters at the Musket Club around noon, and ordered a light repast brought up because he suspected Lady Berry would serve her guests those minuscule, dainty buttered breads and tiny cakes that would leave him starving for a decent meal.

As of three months ago, he had acquired a valet. Somewhat of a valet, he supposed. Horace was another of those lads coming out of St. Brigid's who had found his way to Gideon. Trying to figure out where to place him had not been easy, for the lad was not brawny enough to work at the door, nor was he particularly streetwise and able to spot a thief.

But it turned out he had the ability to spot true elegance by the cut of one's clothes. Then and there, Gideon decided he needed a valet.

He washed up and then called Horace in to assist him in dressing. The lad bustled in with his garments freshly pressed and set them out on Gideon's bed. "Gray for afternoon tea," Horace said with confidence.

Gideon usually wore dark colors but did not question the lad's advice.

"And this cravat will go perfectly with your jacket. See how it also picks up the gray steel of your eyes with its patterned swirls? And how that gray is softened with just those hints of rose."

"Horace, I don't give a rat's arse. Leave my cravat alone already. Just tie it around my neck, stick a fancy pin in it, and let's be done."

"A bit impatient today, are we?" Horace said, laughing. "Lady Berry will melt when she sees you. You have the outward look of a gentleman, but inwardly you are a seething cauldron of seductive allure. Powerful, dangerous, and always naughty. Ladies cannot resist that combination."

"For pity's sake, Horace." Gideon arched an eyebrow and groaned. "I am not going there to seduce her."

"If you say so. Make note of what she wore and you must tell me."

"Forget it."

"You *must*. There is no one more stylish or refined than Lady

Berry. Every boy at the orphanage adored her and every girl wanted to *be* her."

"Fine, if it means that much to you." He and Bonham were not total dullards to fashion. They had spent years watching the elegant set attend their teas and musicales, for they had grabbed work wherever they could, willing to take on the most menial tasks to earn a few coins.

Even when they were young lads still in the care of the orphanage, he and Bonham would think up ways to make money. They used to slip away on occasion and beg on the street with soot on their faces and tin cups in hand.

But now, they watched these pampered elite gamble, some of them quite recklessly, took a cut of everyone's winnings for themselves as per their club rules, and held most of them in contempt for the vapid way they lived their lives.

And despite those elite having done nothing to better themselves or society, he and Bonham were the ones considered beneath contempt. They had spent years watching that privileged set walk by them with their noses in the air.

The carriages were lined up around Duchess Square when he arrived and presented his invitation to Lady Berry's butler, Melton, who surprised him by casting him a gracious smile. "Good afternoon, Mr. Knight. Lady Berry will be pleased to see you. This way, sir."

Gideon followed the man through the parlor, noting its elegant décor, and out into the immaculately groomed garden. A dais had been set up along the side wall that served as the elegant stone separation between her home and his. Tables surrounded by delicate wrought iron chairs filled up most of the grassy areas. Her roses were in bloom and just in time to show themselves off to greatest advantage, because nothing had been blooming last week. She probably timed this annual event to present her garden to spectacular effect.

As he feared, there was nothing to eat but rabbit food. Tiered platters of sweets and savories had been placed in the center of each table. He could have devoured everything on those tiers and still been hungry.

Footmen strolled among the guests, offering champagne, coffee, or tea.

Melton announced him.

Gideon had spotted Berry amid a circle of her friends, and saw her immediately perk her ears at the mention of his name.

He watched as she excused herself and made her way toward him. But her smile slipped the moment she saw him. "Gideon? Did Mr. Knight send you in his place?"

Her eyes were as green as the grass beneath his feet and her hair was the loveliest shade of blonde, golden and almost amber because of the hints of red. Her gown was the palest dusky rose, and had layers of some sheer fabric over the silk so that she looked like a flitting butterfly as she walked toward him.

"Knight!" Lord Berwick said from behind Berry. "Glad you could make it. Berry hoped you would."

She frowned as her gaze darted from Gideon to Lord Berwick and back again.

Then her eyes grew wide as saucers. "Wait…you? *You* are Mr. Knight?"

"Yes, Gideon Knight. One and the same."

She put a hand over her mouth and gasped. "Do you mean to say that my friends and I have been—"

He grinned.

Yes, they had been staring at him every Thursday afternoon for a month.

"Oh, Mr. Knight." A blush shot across her cheeks and she groaned. "Do forgive us."

Lady Berry was the most adorable woman he had ever met. Not only was she kindhearted, but pretty as a button, and those green eyes of hers far outshone any gemstones.

"Of course. Forgiven and forgotten. I was the one at fault. I ought to have introduced myself to you earlier."

Lord Berwick regarded him curiously. "Was there a misunderstanding between you and Berry?"

"Not at all. She mistook me for hired help the other day. Nothing serious."

"You?" Lord Berwick laughed and shook his head. "Well, it is all cleared up now. Do join us at our table. I have been meaning to talk to you about those warehouse investments of yours, and several other matters."

Berry again looked from one to the other. "I did not realize you were acquainted."

Lord Berwick nodded. "Several years now. Knight's a very clever young man. Sharp mind. I invested some of your trust fund in one of his warehouse ventures about two years ago, and it has done very well. Just a small investment, Berry. You know how cautious I am."

"You are a marvel," Berry said, giving Lord Berwick a kiss on the cheek. "I don't know what I would do without you."

"My dear, you exaggerate. Talk later, Knight. Don't forget. Now where is that champagne?" He excused himself and walked off in search of the footman carrying that tray.

Left momentarily alone with Gideon, Lady Berry cast him a delicate smile. "I have saved you a seat at our table. Lord Berwick was most emphatic about it. I hope you don't mind sitting with us, Mr. Knight."

"I would be honored."

"Not that we shall have all that much time to talk to each other, since I will be hopping up and down, going from table to table. But you will find Lord Berwick and his wife to be delightful company. My neighbor, Lady Miranda Lawson, and her niece, Gwenys, are also seated with us. You'll like them. Oh, I suppose they are your neighbors now, too."

"I'm sure I will find them delightful."

She cleared her throat and cast him an earnest look. "You need not feel obliged to participate in the auction or the endowment pledges. I am glad you are here and hope you enjoy the afternoon."

He was in danger of drowning in the exquisite pools of her eyes.

She cast him another smile, excused herself, and darted off to greet some more new arrivals.

He and Lord Berwick had been doing business together for several years now, just as his lordship had indicated to Berry. They had developed a friendship over the course of those years, but he was not on friendly terms with any of Berry's other guests.

A few he recognized from his gaming hells. They were not about to acknowledge him, although they were not above sneering at him. Had they purposely gone out of their way to walk by him for the express purpose of putting him down?

He did not care what any of them thought of him.

But he did care about Berry's attempts to raise funds for St. Brigid's. Would his presence hurt her efforts? He ought to have considered this before accepting her invitation.

Well, too late now. If it did become a problem, he would make up any shortfall in her donations goal.

As he stood in contemplation, someone rudely bumped his shoulder and spilled a little champagne onto the cuff of his shirt sleeve. "Viscount Hawthorne, I am surprised to see you here."

The man was already drunk and stumbling. Or had the toad knocked into him on purpose? Was he looking to cause a scene?

"No more than I am surprised to see the likes of *you* here, Knight," he said with undisguised venom. "What are you doing here?"

"Same reason as you—I was invited."

Hawthorne narrowed his beady eyes. "And by what trickery did you obtain an invitation from my betrothed?"

"Your betrothed?"

What in blazes?

"I was not aware you were engaged to marry," Gideon said, trying to curb his temper as he withdrew his handkerchief and blotted the spill on his cuff. "Surely you cannot be referring to Lady Berengaria."

Hawthorne finished his champagne and then grabbed another off the tray of a passing servant before looking over at Berry. "Of course I am."

"Lady Berry? You and she are betrothed?" Well, Gideon would have to put an end to that courtship, assuming it was true.

But how could it be? There was no way on this green earth that Lord Berwick would allow Hawthorne to sink his fortune-hunting claws into Berry.

"We are *soon* to be betrothed," Hawthorne clarified.

Gideon breathed a sigh of relief. The clot hadn't proposed to her yet. He could not imagine Berry's accepting him.

Lord Berwick would nip it in the bud if she did. The man had good sense and was obviously protective of Berry.

Gideon moved on, ignoring Hawthorne as the man began to toss accusations about his being cheated at the Musket Club. A lethal look from Gideon silenced him quickly, but the clot seemed to be following him around and looking for more opportunities to cause mischief.

Was his animosity due to the gambling debt he had accumulated? Or was this mostly about Berry?

Gideon ran an honest club, and Hawthorne ought to be thanking him and Joss for containing him and keeping him from digging a deeper hole of debt for himself.

Regarding Berry, Gideon had made no move on her. Nor would he ever.

Perhaps it was that the sluggard did not like the idea of an outsider intruding in these Society affairs.

Well, he did not like Hawthorne, either.

Nor did he expect to make a habit of attending these suffocating affairs. This was the first and probably the last time he would ever be invited.

He settled at Berry's table to chat with the Berwicks and the Lawson ladies, Miranda and her niece, Gwenys, who proved to be quite genial.

Gwenys was to make her debut next year, although she was

of age and could have made her come-out this year. But she could not stop gawking at Gideon or giggling every time he turned to her in conversation, so he thought Lady Miranda was wise to keep her niece off the Marriage Mart for a little while longer in order to gain sufficient maturity.

Berry returned, gathered the papers she had left by her plate, and then took a deep breath. "Here we go. Wish me luck," she said, casting him a dimpled smile.

She did not need luck. Gideon knew she was going to charm everyone.

He listened attentively as she gave her speech and then began her appeal for donations.

Hawthorne stood up and pledged one hundred pounds that Gideon knew he did not have. The wastrel viscount would renege on his pledge when it came time to collect. The man made Gideon's blood boil, and he had to curl his hands into fists to keep calm when Berry cast the wretched boor a breathtaking smile and thanked him.

Others stood up next, some handing over banknotes on the spot and others pledging donations to be delivered to Berry before the end of the week.

Since many of the gentlemen frequented his clubs, Gideon knew the ones who would honor their pledges and those who would not. Fortunately, most would. But there were a few bounders like Hawthorne who would disappoint Berry.

Not that it mattered.

Gideon was determined to make up any shortfall.

Berry next moved on to her small auction, thanking those who had donated items for it. He was happy for her when the auction proved a success.

He was also surprised by the number of guests who participated. Well, not *all* of them were insufferable fools. It appeared most genuinely wanted to help out a good cause.

Also, Berry knew what she was doing. She was not only honest and sweet, but also intelligent.

He thought of her as a rose in her garden, one that had beautifully blossomed under the capable guidance of Lord Berwick, a decent and honest fellow. Berry's father had put his trust in the right friend to care for his daughter.

It took Berry the entire afternoon to reach her goal, but in between her speeches and coaxing, there was more food and entertainment.

Still not enough food to feed a rabbit. Or an ox like him, Gideon mused.

An orchestra began to play, and there was a small dance floor erected for those who wished to dance.

Gideon knew better than to ask Berry. To be seen with her was bad enough. To be seen *dancing* with her would damage her reputation and hurt her future charity undertakings.

Hawthorne had no such hesitation, and asked her to dance. She did not appear pleased, but reluctantly agreed.

The snake cast Gideon a triumphant sneer.

Gideon was ready to smash his fist into Hawthorne's nose.

Lady Miranda happened to be seated beside him and grabbed his arm when he started to rise. "You do realize he is purposely riling you."

He sighed and eased back in his chair. "Yes."

"If you hit him, it is Berry who will be hurt most."

"I know. I was merely going to intimidate him, not actually lay a hand on him."

Lady Miranda cast him a stern look. "It is all the same. Whether you hit him or not, he will have won. Isn't it the height of hypocrisy? We all detest Hawthorne, and yet most of these guests would consider him a better match than you for their daughters."

"Lady Berry's guests have made that quite clear. Hawthorne was not the only one to snub me."

"I'm sorry for it. You seem to be a decent fellow. Lord Berwick thinks very highly of you."

"Then I am honored," Gideon said, for he thought very highly of Lord Berwick as well.

"One other thing, Mr. Knight," Lady Miranda said, once again taking hold of his forearm when his gaze darted to Berry and Hawthorne dancing.

"Yes?"

She and her niece grinned at him. "We are not sorry we made Berry hold our tea society meetings at her house this past month so we could watch you shirtless. But she absolutely refuses to tell us what is that dark patch on your upper arm. Is it something wicked and dreadfully shocking?"

He laughed and shook his head, appreciating that some of Berry's friends were nice. "It is a dragon tattoo, that's all. No significance other than an old man came around to my club, obviously frail and hungry, but too proud to beg for food. So I had him draw the dragon on my arm. He comes around weekly now, and I pay him for every worker of mine who decides they need one, too. He's quite the artist and can draw anything requested. One man had a sea battle drawn on his back—frigates, cannon bursts, sails catching the wind, and roiling waves. Not sure what the point of it was, since he could not see the master-piece. But that old man surely was proud of his work."

"That is remarkably kind of you," Gwenys said.

He shrugged. "I know what it means to be hungry and desti-tute."

Lady Miranda smiled at him. "It seems our friend, Fiona, chose the perfect buyer for her home. She must have seen that kindness in you and known you would make a good neighbor for us."

"I hope that proves true," he said, and meant it, for these ladies on Duchess Square were proving kinder and more accepting of him than he'd ever expected.

But any feeling of warmth soon faded as Hawthorne and a few of his boorish friends passed by him again and tossed cutting remarks.

Again, he cared not a rat's arse what they thought of him. But he did not want his continued presence hurting Berry's charity cause.

When he rose to leave, since this afternoon affair was nearing its end anyway, Lord Berwick drew him aside and insisted on his staying. "Please, Knight. This is important to me."

"All right," Gideon said with a nod, and waited patiently while Berry bade the last of her guests farewell.

She had an exceptionally sweet smile for each of them.

That smile. Would she bestow one on him, too?

He did not know why he ached for it.

He stepped forward once the last of the attendees had gone.

"Oh, you are still here," Berry remarked, a little surprised.

"Lord Berwick asked me to remain behind. Do you know what this is about?"

"No, not a clue. I wonder what he has in mind."

As her staff began to clear away the tables, Gideon escorted her into her study, where Lord and Lady Berwick were awaiting them.

Lord Berwick had taken possession of the donations pouch and was busy tabulating the receipts as they walked in. "You did very well, Berry. In fact, you exceeded your target."

Her eyes lit up as she took a seat in one of the cushioned floral chairs beside Lady Berwick. "Really? I hoped I would. I tried to keep count as I went along but the task was in vain. I was constantly distracted."

"Not all of the pledges might be honored," Gideon warned, moving to the side and propping his shoulder against the hearth mantel. He had made note of those who could not be trusted, and knew there would likely be about a five-hundred-pound shortfall.

Lord Berwick nodded. "How much do you think I ought to deduct from the total?"

Gideon gave him his estimate.

"Ah, then that might leave us a few pounds short of our goal."

"I'll make up any shortfall," Gideon said. "In fact, here." He reached into the breast pocket of his jacket and withdrew a bank draft he had written out before arriving. The sum happened to be in the same amount as his estimated shortfall, but this was mere coincidence. Five hundred pounds had felt like a good number to donate as a start. He was ready to give more as needed over the course of the year.

Berry's expression turned tender when he handed the draft over to her. "Thank you, Mr. Knight. This is very generous. You did not need to give me anything."

He shook his head. "There is no better cause for me, as you know. St. Brigid's is where I was raised. Where many of us survived and thrived because of your family. This is only the start. Never hesitate to come to me if more is ever required. But I do have one request."

She was already nodding without having heard him out. "Yes?"

"My donations are to remain anonymous."

She stared at him in surprise. "But why?"

"Two reasons. The first is that I have a bad reputation and wish to maintain it."

Her eyes, those lovely, sparkling orbs he was going to dream about tonight, widened. "You cannot be serious."

"Oh, but I am. Not everyone I deal with is as honest and decent as Lord Berwick. Some are only kept honest through fear of what I might do to them if they ever tried to cheat me. If word gets out that I am contributing to charities, they might believe I have gone soft and seek to take advantage." He folded his arms across his chest. "Lady Berry, no one takes advantage of me and gets away with it."

"Oh." She put a hand to her throat. "You hurt people?"

"No, I never have done. But this is precisely because they fear me and no one will dare put me to the test."

"Would you *ever* hurt anyone?"

"I don't know. Never a good person, for those I will protect. But as to the bad ones? Depends on how bad they are and whether they are trying to hurt an innocent. Who would you rather see harmed? The innocent or the vicious attacker?"

"The attacker, of course. Well, it appears you have a soft heart for some things."

"For most things," he corrected her. "But when one deals with bad people, it is always wisest to appear more dangerous than they are."

"I shall honor your request. If you wish to be thought of as an angel of vengeance or retribution, I shall not give you away. What is your second reason for maintaining anonymity?"

"You."

She blushed. "Me?"

He nodded. "You would have brought in more donations from your friends and acquaintances had I not been here today. While many might not say it to your face, they resented my presence and resented you for inviting me. More than a few went out of their way to give me the cut direct. If they were to learn I was one of the orphanage's benefactors, they might break off any association with St. Brigid's. They might go so far as to distance themselves from *you*."

She tipped her chin up. "My true friends never would."

He sighed. "You would be surprised how few true friends one gains over the course of one's life. Lady Berry, everyone adores you. Let's keep it that way, shall we?"

"All right," she said with a bob of her head. "I understand your reasons and will honor them. But I want you to know that you have my sincere gratitude, and I am not ashamed to consider you a friend."

Bollocks.

She was going to turn him soft as pudding.

"I am honored," he replied. "But do not consider me a friend. It serves you no good purpose and can only damage your reputation. However, if you ever have a worry or need my help in anything, you have only to ask. Please, never hesitate."

He now turned to Lord Berwick and contemplated the reason

he was asked to stay on. "I think this is why you brought me here, isn't it? Hoping that I might quietly watch over Lady Berry now that we are neighbors."

Lord Berwick nodded. "Yes, in part. But there's more. Berry's father trusted me to look out for her, and I hope I have done my best."

"No one could have been kinder or shown more care than you and Lady Berwick," Berry insisted. "Not only have you been a trusted guardian, but a wise friend, advisor, and trustee."

"Yes, and this is my concern. The trustee situation, my dear. Lord Wilkins was to be my successor, but he is ailing and cannot possibly manage your funds. So, who is to succeed me when I am no longer able to perform my duties? Lord Wilkins wishes to resign immediately. My solicitor is drawing up his resignation as we speak. The terms of your father's trust allow me to appoint a successor trustee. I wish to designate Mr. Knight."

Gideon was rarely ever caught off guard, but this threw him. He was certain Lord Berwick had only meant to give him some of those charity funds to invest.

But all along, Lord Berwick had meant to give him Berry.

Blessed saints. He had not seen that cannonball coming at all.

This also meant he would be given responsibility for St. Brigid's, since the Thane family had been the orphanage's life support for generations.

"Obviously, Berry no longer needs a guardian. It is the matter of her trust fund and the management of St. Brigid's endowment. I can think of no one more capable or trustworthy than you, Knight. Please, this is very important to me. Berry is as dear to me and Lady Berwick as our own daughters. I hope to have many more good years ahead of me, but let us be realistic. I am older than Lord Wilkins. I must protect Berry, and that means having the best man to look after her when I am gone."

Berry began to cry. "You must not speak like that, Lord Berwick. Indeed, you must go on forever. I would be lost without you."

Gideon wanted to reach out and take her in his arms, but that was a bad idea. He was already too attracted to her and this was dangerous.

Lady Berwick hugged her, and then Lord Berwick came around to the front of the desk and took her in his arms. "There, there, my sweet Berry. I am not going anywhere just yet. And you will always have my dear wife and daughters for family."

Lord Berwick looked over at Gideon and cast him a pleading look.

Bollocks.

Double bollocks.

He could not refuse the man.

But how would it look if he were taking care of Berry?

Well, he was only meant to look after her finances. No one had to know he would also be watching over her like a hawk and chasing away snakes like Viscount Hawthorne and other assorted vermin. Perhaps it would be all right.

She also had a woman by the name of Mrs. Garland that Lord Berwick had hired as a chaperone and companion for Berry years ago. A genteel lady of Berry's stature could not live alone without being looked upon with censure. But Gideon understood Mrs. Garland was also getting on in years. Miranda and Berry had just been talking about how the old woman stayed mostly in her bedchamber now.

Berry could not reside alone.

So, who would take over as companion to Berry if something happened to Mrs. Garland? Who would be in charge of interviewing and hiring her replacement?

Lord Berwick was right. Gideon needed to take charge.

Who else would better protect Berry?

He gave the nod. "Have your solicitor draw up the designation and my acceptance. I'll sign whatever you need."

CHAPTER FOUR

"Y OU HAVE AGREED to be Lady Berry's guardian?" Bonham asked incredulously, dropping into his usual chair across from Gideon's desk within his study at the Musket Club around noontime. Several days had passed since Berry's charity affair, and Gideon had gone to the Thane family's solicitor just this morning to sign the necessary documents.

"Her *trustee*," he clarified, recently returned and now filing the copies he had been given into a secure drawer. "I am to be the successor trustee, that's all. She isn't an infant and does not need me to be her nanny. However, if Hawthorne or some other fortune hunter starts sniffing around her, rest assured, I will make them regret it."

Bonham nodded. "I have to give it to Berwick. He is an excellent judge of character. I'll wager he's been following your progress for years, perhaps as far back as when we were living at the orphanage. You were hard to overlook."

Gideon snorted.

"I did not think he would look outside his elite circle for a suitable replacement, but I am glad to be proven wrong. You are the best man for the task. I heartily approve Lord Berwick's choice."

"That remains to be seen, doesn't it?" Gideon said with a shrug. "But I will give it my all. Lady Berry deserves no less from me."

"By the way, she knocked on your front door again this morning."

"She did?" Gideon looked up from the pile of papers on his desk that he needed to review before the end of the day. "Why?"

"She brought me some fresh scones and coffee."

"Gad, she is such a little kitten." Gideon could not suppress his smile. "Why in blazes did she do that?"

Bonham shrugged. "She noticed I was alone in that big house, guarding it all by myself, not a cook or other servant in sight. She was concerned you had abandoned me there with nothing to eat."

"Dear heaven, is this girl for real?" Gideon muttered.

"She is quite the do-gooder," Bonham said with a chuckle. "I told her the glass doors would be going in tomorrow. That's the last of the structural work to be done. Next is painting and decorating. Have you done anything about that?"

Gideon leaned back in his chair and groaned. "No."

"I thought not. You ought to ask for Lady Berry's help. I know she wants to give it, and I think she is very good at this sort of thing. She understands elegance. That is the way to show up those fancy nobs. It is not about shoving your wealth in their faces. They will only mock you for it. No, you need to be subtle and show them that an orphan out of St. Brigid's can match them in refinement."

"Is this your idea or Lady Berry's?"

"She may have mentioned it to me over coffee."

Gideon was surprised. "So, the two of you conversed? Does she no longer think you are hard of hearing?"

"Oh, she still thinks I am deaf as a post," Bonham said, once more chuckling. "Honestly, Gideon. She's just...so adorably gullible. I know I will have to tell her sometime soon, or else I will truly go deaf. My ears are still ringing from this morning's conversation because she was shouting her opinions and ideas into them the entire time I showed her around the house."

Gideon's eyes widened in surprise. "You gave her a tour of

my house?"

"Yes, why not? She's been there many times. Have you forgotten that she and the Duchess of Durham were good friends? To be honest, she offered some very helpful advice." Bonham winced. "Of course, she shouted all of it into my ears."

Gideon gave a hearty burst of laughter. "She is going to hate us when we tell her the truth."

"I'll confess it, if you want me to."

"No, not yet. I'll tell her myself in my own good time."

"Just do it before my ears start bleeding."

He shook his head and laughed again. "All right, but you must admit it is fun. Harmless fun. Since I am encouraging this prank, I'll shoulder responsibility for the consequences."

"You had better." Bonham shrugged. "But I'm sure she'll forgive you. She has a heart of gold, doesn't she?"

"Yes."

Which was what worried Gideon. She was a lamb who needed protecting from all the wolves out there. It could be said that he was the most dangerous of all. Not merely a wolf but a fearsome black dragon, as was now imprinted on his skin.

He was dangerous, but Berry should never fear him.

She was his to protect.

And protect her he would.

The more serious concern was that Lord Berwick getting too old to look after her would have those *ton* vultures sensing it and starting to circle her.

Mrs. Garland was already of no use, merely a warm body residing with Berry for the sake of respectability. It seemed the roles had been reversed for months now, Berry assuming the task of caring for her.

"I think I will invite Lady Berry and Lord Berwick to dine with me at the Denby Arms this evening. I know Berwick wants to involve me as soon as possible in matters concerning the orphanage fund. I can ask Lady Berry's opinion on decorating at that time."

"What about Jasmine? Or Chloe? You haven't gone near them since meeting Lady Berry. Weren't they supposed to attend some *demimonde* salon with you?"

"Let Pudge escort them. Or let him guard my Duchess Square property tonight, and you take the ladies to that party. Test your diction on the upper-class nobs who will be there."

"Not a bad idea. I think it's time I tried my hand at passing as a gentleman. Fine. I'll escort them. I'll need proper evening attire."

Gideon motioned toward his bedchamber. "Take whatever you need from my wardrobe. We are about the same size and build. Horace will help you."

"The ladies are not going to be happy. They want you."

"I never made Jasmine or Chloe any promises. They'll get the message and move on."

Bonham seemed surprised. "You are not ever going to consort with them again, are you? Has Lady Berry already got you so wrapped up?"

"No one controls me, as you well know."

"That's right, barricades always up. Weapons always at the ready." Bonham rose to march to his bedchamber. "But have a care. The lass can be quite disarming."

As it turned out, Lady Berry and Lord Berwick were both available on such short notice. Gideon was grateful for it, for they were both popular among their elite circles and probably received two or three invitations in a single afternoon.

As for him, none of their ilk would ever give him the time of day.

Not that he cared. He did not require their friendship, but gladly took a cut of their gambling winnings.

That evening, he left Joss in charge of the Musket Club, and ordered his carriage to be brought around to the club's front door.

He had extended his invitation to Lady Berwick as well as her husband, but Lord Berwick immediately responded by conveying his regrets that it would only be him dining. No doubt his wife understood this was to be a business meeting and did not wish to interfere.

He picked up Lord Berwick and then had his driver take them to Duchess Square to pick up Berry. He gave his neighboring property only a quick perusal as they reached the pretty square of homes. He would return early tomorrow morning to supervise the installation of the glass doors to his ballroom.

Perhaps it was a foolish expense, for no one in the Upper Crust would ever attend if he held a ball. But none of them could ever say his ballroom was inadequate, even if they refused to set foot in it.

He climbed down from his carriage, noting the graceful arch of wisteria over the doorway as he strode up Berry's front walk. The blooms ought to have faded by now, for everyone knew they were at their best in May, but they looked bright as ever by June's early evening light.

Her trusted butler opened the door to him. "Welcome, Mr. Knight."

"Good evening, Melton. Is Lady Berry ready?"

"I shall see." The man stepped aside to allow him in.

Berry had been in the parlor and now walked out with a big, welcoming smile on her face. She wore a silk gown the color of apricots, the fabric seeming to hug her body and worship it. He'd never seen fabric drape on a woman with such perfection.

Of course, when he looked at a woman it was usually to undress her with his gaze. But still, perfection was perfection.

And Berry was perfect.

"Are you ready?" He held out his arm to escort her to his carriage.

"I have been longing to try the duck cassoulet at the Denby Arms. I hear it is their specialty."

"Yes, and it is very good," Gideon remarked, for he often ate out and the Denby Arms was one of his favorite haunts. Indeed, it was one of the finest and most popular establishments in all of

London catering to the elite.

He liked the place so much, he had acquired a controlling interest in it about a year ago.

Of course, this was not public knowledge, and he preferred to keep it that way.

Berry scampered into his carriage and took a seat beside Lord Berwick.

Gideon had the opposing seat bench to himself, a necessity because he was a big man and his shoulders were broad.

It did not take them long to arrive at their destination, even though the London streets were bustling at this hour.

The dining establishment was already filling up, as it often did no matter the time of day, but was particularly busy in the evening hours. The maître d' came running over to him. "Good evening, Mr. Knight. Your table is ready, sir. Right this way."

He led them to a private alcove that afforded them some separation from the other tables. This particular spot was always reserved for him and would only be given out to others if the staff knew he would not be in attendance.

Gideon especially liked this table because it allowed him to see the entire room. Several large chandeliers spread ample candlelight and provided him with an excellent view of all that was going on. However, no one could see into the alcove without actually poking their head in. Nor could the diners occupying the nearby tables hear their conversation.

"It is a pleasure to see you again," the man said, sounding quite obsequious. Well, he probably suspected Gideon was an important personage, since the manager treated him like a king whenever he dined there.

It would not be a large leap for him to figure out Gideon was a silent partner. However, Gideon had been adamant about the truth of his ownership being kept confidential.

The maître d' eyed Berry. She was not the usual sort of lady seen on his arm.

Gideon had taken Jasmine and Chloe here last week, and

those beauties were quite memorable. Tall, lithe, and unabashed-ly mercenary. They were every man's fantasy, and yet he had never felt a tug to his heart for either of them. Not even a glimmer or a twinge.

But Berry put his heart in spasms.

Not that he would ever admit it to her.

No, he could never. They were from different worlds and could very well destroy each other if ever they got too close. Worlds colliding. Would not end well.

It would crush him if he ever hurt Berry.

Besides, why change anything? Why upend his comfortable existence? He was better off with meaningless dalliances, escorting ladies like Jasmine or Chloe who looked out for themselves first and only.

And he was no good boy, either. He liked to provoke those Upper Crust wastrels like Hawthorne.

This was why just last week, he had walked in here with those two stunning ladies on his arms, ordering the best champagne, and tossing coins to the help so that they clustered around him and ignored their other well-heeled patrons.

He had done it purely for the joy of shoving his wealth and power in the faces of so-called gentlemen like Hawthorne.

It was completely foolish, childish, and unbecoming of him.

He did it anyway.

Berry had never been here before, and her eyes were wide with curiosity. "They gave us the best table in the place," she remarked as he held out a seat for her. "Is the owner a friend of yours? I noticed the maître d' turned away several diners, but he led us right in."

"Yes, the owner and I are the best of friends."

She cast him another of her disarming smiles. "Well, he ought to be very proud. This is a lovely establishment. I cannot wait to try the duck cassoulet."

Lord Berwick eyed him speculatively, no doubt suspecting he was more than a mere patron here.

Gideon ignored the man's stare and ordered wine for them. He then made suggestions about the fare, for he knew which dishes were the most popular besides the cassoulet.

Once they had ordered, he began the business discussions. "Lord Berwick, will you tell me your thoughts on what ought to be done with the funds raised at Lady Berry's charity affair?"

He then turned to Berry. "I'd like your opinion, too, Lady Berry. I'll listen for now. I would like to learn your process, watch how the two of you make your decisions on how those funds are disbursed, what reserves to hold back, and what the priorities for your spending are, since it has obviously worked out well for many years."

"The children are always the priority," Lord Berwick explained. "We budget for their needs first. Food, shelter, clothing, education. We estimate our spending for the month, the quarter, and the entire year. We also allocate for supplies and building maintenance. Unexpected repairs are always a concern."

"There's also wages for the teachers and staff," Berry added.

Gideon added the numbers in his head, and then frowned. "Seventy mouths to feed daily, the upkeep on clothes, wages for five teachers, would you say? And an equal number of clerical staff?"

Berry nodded.

"But there must be a shortfall."

"Yes," Lord Berwick said. "Lady Berry makes it up from her personal investments every year."

"My needs are fairly modest," she explained. "My largest expenditures are my own staff, my horses, and my gowns, and those are easily covered by my income, which always exceeds my expenses due to Lord Berwick's wise management. But what we have not been able to do is expand the size of the orphanage. No matter how we look at it, we cannot support more than seventy orphans a year."

"But that is seventy lives that you have saved, Lady Berry," Gideon said with sincere gratitude, for he had been one of those orphans. "It is very generous of you."

She blushed. "Thank you, Mr. Knight. I am pleased, of course. But I would love to increase that number to one hundred children, if possible. I have an idea for how to do it, but neither Lord Berwick nor I have the expertise necessary to bring it about."

"What is the idea? I am fairly well connected in business circles. Perhaps I can help."

Their food was served, so their discussion was set aside for the moment while they ate.

Gideon took pleasure in watching Berry sample her dish.

"Oh, this duck is delicious!" She smiled at him as though he had delivered a miracle. "No wonder everyone wishes to dine here. I have never tasted anything so good. Which gives me an idea for next year's charity event. Do you think the owner would allow me to hold it here? Or is it a foolish idea? I suppose the cost would be too high. But it might be worth comparing budgets, the cost of setting it at my home versus the costs of having it held here."

"We can price it out," Gideon said. "I think the owner would be amenable and might even reduce his prices to accommodate you. Write out a list of what you'll require and I will evaluate the costs for you."

Lord Berwick liked the possibility. "A change of venue, the best food in London. We could get more donors than ever."

"And they might be more generous on a full and sated stomach," Berry added.

"The Denby Arms is a draw in itself. You might charge a small fee for attendance."

Berry appeared shocked by the suggestion. "How can I charge my friends? No, that is impossible."

"This is not a dinner party, but a charity event to be held at London's most exclusive dining establishment. They know they are being invited to help raise funds for the orphanage. If they refuse to pay over a few pounds to have the finest meal they will ever experience in their lifetimes, then you do not need them attending. Wastrels like Viscount Hawthorne are never going to give you so much as a shilling toward those orphans. But he will order the most expensive champagne and guzzle it down like there's no tomorrow."

Perhaps he had been a little too honest with Berry. She appeared distressed. "You really dislike Lord Hawthorne, don't you?"

"Yes, and men like him. They are given every privilege and show not a smidgeon of gratitude. In fact, they… Never mind. And do not fret about the suggestion of an attendance charge. I would never press you to do it. But if you are amenable to considering it, we could meet with the directors of other major charities and get their opinion on its effectiveness. I know of a few that have done this with success. Let's gather the facts and then you and Lord Berwick can decide what to do."

"Fair enough," Berry said.

Gideon chose to divert the topic to something less confrontational. "What was your special idea for the orphanage's expansion? You mentioned that you haven't the expertise to bring it about. Why don't you give me a try at it?"

"It is something I would have to show you," Berry said. "I understand from Bonham that you will be on Duchess Square tomorrow morning."

"Yes, the ballroom doors are to be installed. The next step is furnishing the house and decorating it. That is woefully outside my area of expertise," he said with a pained laugh.

"I can help," Berry eagerly volunteered. "Let me know once your doors are in and I'll walk over. Did Bonham tell you I had some ideas that might be helpful to you?"

Gideon grinned. "Yes, he said I would be a fool not to take your advice."

Berry laughed. "He's quite a character. How did he lose his hearing?"

He choked on his wine and had to cough to clear his throat.

"About that…"

"Do you think there is something that might be done? Perhaps if I had my physician look at him."

Gideon coughed again. "No, not necessary."

"Why?" She frowned. "Is it hopeless? Have you already sent him to doctors and they could do nothing for him?"

Gideon smothered the urge to laugh. "He is quite a lost cause, I assure you."

He felt some remorse for perpetuating the misunderstanding. He really ought to tell her that Bonham was his business partner and best friend, not his butler. Nor was Bonham deaf. But she was enjoying her cassoulet and the evening was going pleasantly. He did not want to end it on a sour note. He would tell her the truth tomorrow.

Lord Berwick cast him another speculative look, then shook his head and grinned.

Ah, he'd figured it out. Was he going to tell Berry?

No, Lord Berwick was not going to stick his oar in this harmless jest. He smiled at Gideon, and then asked the wine steward to pour him another glass. Perhaps he understood that Gideon was serious about protecting Berry and would never truly hurt her in any way.

Gideon hoped that much was clear.

When they finished their excellent repast, they stepped out of the Denby Arms into the warm night air to await his carriage. Loitering just outside was Viscount Hawthorne and a group of his drunken friends who had just been turned away.

"They let you in here, Knight?" the wastrel remarked, tossing him an imperious sneer that rankled Gideon. "They've certainly lowered their standards."

"No, they're still quite high. They tossed you out, didn't they?" Gideon shot back, knowing he ought to have kept his mouth shut and not goaded the sot, especially while Berry and Lord Berwick were looking on.

But the man got under his skin. He had run up debts all over

London. He drank to excess and lost at the gaming tables because he violated every commonsense rule when playing cards. First rule, stay sober.

Nor did Gideon like that the man was obviously lusting for Berry's fortune. Not Berry herself. Hawthorne wanted to dig his claws into that big pile of money Lord Berwick had built up for her over the years.

Hawthorne cared for no one but his wastrel self.

"You filthy guttersnipe!" Hawthorne growled, and took a swing at Gideon.

Gideon saw the punch coming, easily blocked it, and twisted Hawthorne's arm just hard enough to make him fall to his knees with a yelp of pain. Hawthorne's three friends thought to attack him, but Gideon's lethal glower froze them in their places.

He lifted Hawthorne up by his collar and shoved him at the friends. "Take him home and sober him up."

They tossed daggers at him with their gazes, but were too afraid to actually challenge him. Wordlessly, they dragged a howling Hawthorne away.

Berry stared at him, wide-eyed. Lord Berwick was frowning.

Gideon had no intention of apologizing. "He started it."

Gad, had he just said that? He sounded like a schoolboy being taken by the ears to the headmistress for fighting in the class-room.

"You could have ignored him," Berry remarked.

"No, I could not. The man is a monumental...idiot." Gideon had been going to call him something far more insulting, but Berry was already peeved. He was not going to give her more reasons to be angry with *him*. "He threw a punch at me, or did you miss that friendly gesture?"

She sighed. "I saw it."

"He thinks his courtesy title gives him the right to stomp on people. I was merely reminding him that it does not. He's fortunate I taught him a gentle lesson. I could have broken his arm or laid him out flat with a counterpunch."

"Gentle?" Berry rolled her eyes. "You think twisting his arm almost to the point of breaking was gentle?"

"Yes. In my world, you do not show mercy when someone attempts to assault you. He's fortunate I chose to play by *your* rules."

His carriage arrived and he helped both of his companions into their seats, and then settled in the one opposite theirs.

Blast. The evening had gone smoothly until that cur had shown up and interfered.

Would Berry agree to see him tomorrow? Or was she going to remain angry and refuse to have anything more to do with him? Was Lord Berwick regretting his choice in successor trustee?

Gideon sighed. "I have no intention of apologizing to that oaf, but I do apologize to both of you. I am not a gentleman, as you may have guessed. If someone insults me, I defend myself. If anyone were to insult *you*, Lady Berry, I would defend you."

"And if I were the one to insult you, Mr. Knight?" she asked.

He cast her a wry smile. "I would apologize to you without hesitation."

His response obviously surprised her. "You would? Why?"

"Because you are the sweetest, kindest lady I have ever met, and no one has more compassion than you. If you were ever to insult me, I would immediately know that I was at fault and had somehow hurt your feelings. I would feel awful about that and seek to atone."

"Oh." She laughed softly. "I see."

His response obviously met with Lord Berwick's approval as well, for he chuckled. "Well said, Knight. You dug yourself out of that hole."

Gideon leaned back against the fine leather squabs, relieved they were no longer angry with him, especially Berry.

Her impression of him mattered. He wanted her to like him, to admire and respect him.

Which was odd, because he generally did not care what others thought of him. And yet he yearned for Berry's approval.

He hoped she would see him tomorrow.

Well, he would repair the damage if she remained angry. He knew how to charm a lady. He had mastered the tricks of seduction by the age of fifteen.

Not that he meant to seduce her, only charm her. If that did not work, then he would have to do a bit of groveling.

Bollocks.

He was never good at bending the knee and apologizing. In fact, he had never done it before. Not even as a child. This simply was not in his nature.

But he would do it for Berry.

She was studying him. For once, he could not read her expression.

Was he forgiven? Or was he still stuck in that hole?

CHAPTER FIVE

B ERRY STARED OUT the window of her upper-floor parlor the following morning and watched Gideon Knight's men putting in the massive glass doors at the rear of Fiona's old townhouse that now belonged to him. He was there with them, his shoulders straining as he worked alongside them, hefting a door into its fitted frame.

She was not certain what to make of him. He was like no man she had ever met before. His thin veneer of polish masked a raw masculinity. She ought to have realized he was polite to her only because he held himself on a tight leash.

She had never heard of dragons ever being restrained by a leash. No, dragons broke free and burned everything in sight when they were angry.

Even when restrained, Gideon Knight lived by a simple rule: *Hurt me and I will hurt you harder.*

Perhaps this was a code of the streets. She had very little experience with men outside of her social circle, and likely never would while sheltered within the confines of Duchess Square. Here she was shielded from so much of life's harsh realities.

But he was a product of a harsher upbringing. The orphanage protected the children they took in, but it wasn't the same as having loving parents or guardians. The children had to leave by their fifteenth birthday for boys and sixteenth birthday for girls. If the orphanage could not place them in apprenticeships or other positions, they were left to fend on their own. Of course, the orphanage staff did their very best to have every child placed somewhere safe when it came time for them to leave.

Gideon was older than her by five or six years, she estimated. Older by a thousand years when it came to experience. She did not know if he had been one of the boys unable to be placed, for he did not strike her as the sort to take orders from anyone, not even when he was a lad.

Good morning, she mouthed when he looked up after securing the first door in its place.

He smiled and waved back at her. *Good morning,* he mouthed back, and then returned his attention to the work of putting the second glass door in its frame.

After a full month of hammering and smashing old glass, repairing slate, and replacing massive beams, the silence was disquieting. Funny how one so quickly forgot how silent this square of homes usually was. Their street was not a thorough-fare, so no one entered unless they were visiting one of the six homes comprising Duchess Square.

There was a small park in the center that held a few shade trees, several lilac trees, some benches, and an abundance of flowers that her gardener maintained. Most of the flowers were rose cuttings from her garden, but other flowers had been planted as well, starting with daffodils and irises in the late spring and ending with hollyhocks and sunflowers in autumn. In between were poppies, lilies, and Italian alkanet that was hardy enough to bloom throughout the summer and was a stunningly vibrant shade of blue.

Mr. Knight finished placing and securing the second door, and then glanced up at her again.

She beckoned him to come over.

Perhaps it wasn't proper, but who would notice or care? Certainly not her friends, Miranda and Gwendolyn, each of whom occupied a house in the square. As for the owners of the remaining two townhouses, they were not in London at present.

"Mrs. Bolton," she called, "would you bring a pitcher of lemonade and two glasses onto the terrace? And have Melton take several more pitchers and a dozen glasses next door to Mr. Knight's workers."

"Is that wise?" her housekeeper remarked, casting Berry a wry smile. "And I am not speaking of the neighborly act of bringing over something to those workers to quench their thirst. I am speaking of the man you have just invited over here. Be careful, m'lady. He is wickedly handsome and appears polite enough, but…you ought not encourage him. He isn't quality."

"He does not hold a *title*, nor is he descended from nobility. But this is all he lacks. Were I forced to choose between him and Viscount Hawthorne, I would not hesitate to choose him," Berry said with finality.

"Then let's hope you never have to make such a choice, because neither one is suitable for you. But at least with Viscount Hawthorne, you would maintain your good reputation and popularity among your *ton* friends."

"While he gambles away my fortune? No, thank you." She glanced out the window again, hoping Mr. Knight would make his way over to her soon. "Mr. Knight will be assisting Lord Berwick in managing my financial affairs and I have offered to assist him in furnishing his home. He is woefully inept when it comes to matters of décor. And we don't want a garish house ruining our lovely square, do we?"

Mrs. Bolton did not appear convinced. "It is not his violating that beautiful house that worries me, but what he might do to *you*."

Honestly!

It was a good thing her housekeeper had bustled away after tossing out the remark. Any other mistress might have discharged her housekeeper for impertinence. But Mrs. Bolton had been there since before Berry was orphaned. Her position was secure. In truth, Berry dreaded losing any more people around her that she trusted and loved.

She went downstairs and walked into her garden to await Mr. Knight.

Melton soon set out the pitcher of lemonade and glasses. "Will that be all you need?"

Berry nodded. "Yes. This is perfect."

"Then I'll run next door and deliver the other pitchers."

He had no sooner walked away than Mr. Knight climbed over the stone wall between their properties, easily scaling it. "Are you going to tell me how rude I am for presuming to hop over and not come to your front door?"

"No, but try not to make a habit of it," she said with a light laugh. "My servants are already commenting about you."

"What are they saying? Bad things, I suppose. Servants can sometimes be more scathing than their masters about who is quality and who is not. They are not wrong about me, I suppose."

She frowned at him. "I shall tell you the same thing I just told my housekeeper. You are not *titled*. But that is not the same as *quality*. If I were forced to choose between marrying you or Lord Hawthorne, is there any doubt which of you I would choose? The man intent on stealing my funds and gambling them away, or the one who will invest them wisely and protect me?"

He grunted. "Let's hope you are not required to choose either of us. Your wealth would be protected, but you would lose all your *ton* friends if you were to marry me."

"That's what my housekeeper said."

"Well, now you've heard it twice. Let that sink in."

They sat and had their lemonade.

He was in a sweat because of the physical labor he'd just completed, but he still smelled awfully nice, that undertone of citrus and sandalwood.

The weather was also cooperating. Still warm, but not quite as hot as it had been last week. There was a gentle, cooling breeze that rustled through the trees and lightly ruffled Mr. Knight's hair.

She itched to reach out and brush her fingers through his slightly-too-long, dark hair.

But that was a ridiculous impulse.

"Shall we talk about your house?" Berry asked, setting down her glass after taking a sip.

Mr. Knight gulped his down, for the poor man had been working very hard in the morning heat and must have been intolerably thirsty. "Yes," he said, setting down his glass, too. "I need so much help. I have all the workers I need, since so many of my businesses require constant upkeep. Painters, for example. They are ready to go, but I don't know what paint colors to tell them to use. Or should some rooms have wallpaper? What about the stain for the floors? Or should I rip up the wood floors and put in marble?"

She took pity on him because he appeared so genuinely confused. "Let me give you a tour of my home," she suggested, "and then we shall walk over to yours."

He shrugged, but then nodded and smiled at her in obvious gratitude. "All right."

"Would you mind if I brought along my sketchbook and drew some ideas while we walked through your house?"

"I would be grateful." He cast her another smile, this one boyishly endearing. "So, you can draw?"

"Yes, it is one of the many useless talents ladies of good breeding are encouraged to acquire. Singing and playing the pianoforte are also musts."

"How are you at those?

She playfully winced. "Not good at all."

Berry could not recall ever spending a more pleasant morning, she decided as she led Mr. Knight through the principal rooms of her home. On the ground floor were the formal parlor where she held her soirées, the dining room, the music room, and the kitchen areas. One flight up were her library, her study, the ladies' salon where she held her tea society meetings, a sewing room, and two guest bedchambers. Another flight of stairs up were the family bedrooms and dressing areas. Above that were the servants' quarters.

She only showed Mr. Knight through the first two floors of the house, since these main rooms were the only ones most visitors to his home would see. Besides, she dared not show him her own bedchamber because that was simply too intimate. "Is there anything you particularly liked? Paint color? Wood? Drapes?"

He laughed and shook his head. "All of it is impressive. You are talking to a boy who grew up sleeping in a cot along with twenty other boys in a room painted gray and sparsely windowed. We were given uniforms and shoes, mint with which to brush our teeth, and a comb for our hair. Everything else we shared. I am not complaining. The orphanage was our salvation."

Berry sighed. "Then you are the perfect one to advise me and Lord Berwick on what we are doing wrong."

He tucked a finger under her chin and nudged her gaze upward to meet his. "Other than perhaps a more cheerful paint color for the place, you have done nothing wrong for these children."

"I'm sure there is plenty more we could do."

"There is always something more that can be done, but you cannot take it all upon yourself. I have some ideas. Would it be possible to meet at the orphanage tomorrow? I can give you my suggestions."

She nodded. "I would love it, but Lord Berwick ought to accompany us. I'll send word to him and see if he's available. You see, my chaperone has been feeling very poorly lately and I dare not ask her to accompany me."

"Mrs. Garland?"

"Yes, and I cannot be seen going about London without her or another suitable chaperone."

"Especially with the likes of me," Mr. Knight muttered.

"With the likes of any man under the age of fifty," she countered. "Although I shall soon be of an age where no one will care. Most ladies are considered on the shelf by my age, but I am still sought after because I am an heiress in my own right. The fortune hunters salivate when they see me."

"The men of quality would also salivate because you are beautiful." He dropped his hand from her chin and rubbed his neck as he took a step away from her.

She liked his touch, for he had rough, workman's hands, and yet was gentle.

Well, better that she not pursue that thought.

"I am nowhere near as beautiful as the ladies I saw you with at the theater the other night."

He grunted. "No, Lady Berry. They cannot hold a candle to you. They are vain creatures, while you are kind and considerate. They are haughty, while you are intelligent and have a gentle sense of humor. Your smile is warm and welcoming. Theirs are calculating and mercenary."

She arched an eyebrow, surprised by his assessment. "But they are still beautiful. Is this not what men value above all else?"

"Some do. Not I."

She laughed in disbelief. "Are you suggesting you would choose me over those ladies?"

"In a heartbeat. Never a doubt. I knew you were someone rare and special the moment I set eyes on you."

"Oh."

He rubbed his hand across the back of his neck again. "I shouldn't have said that. Perhaps I had better leave."

"No, Mr. Knight. Please don't go. Now that you have had a tour of my home, let us attend to yours. I want to help make it perfect for you, and it has nothing to do with my desire to do good."

"You do not view this as a good deed?"

"No, I do this for reasons you will think quite wicked. You see, I was unsettled by your confrontation with Lord Hawthorne last night."

He nodded. "I am truly sorry for upsetting you."

"Oh, do not apologize. Lord Hawthorne was completely rude and boorish. This is why I wish to help you. I would love nothing better than to have you show up those pompous wastrels like the viscount. Give them a kick in the teeth to show them you are not only as good as they are, but far superior in every way." She cast him a dimpled smile. "Is that not wicked of me?"

He laughed, a deep, rich peal that had her tingling. "Bravo, Lady Berry. I feared you were too softhearted, but I'm glad to see you are not spineless. However, you are still a lamb and they are wolves."

"And I now have a dragon to protect me," she said, lightly touching his upper arm where his dragon lay beneath his shirt.

He gave her cheek a light caress. "Yes, you do."

Berry tried to suppress the tingles that coursed through her. His touch, his laughter, his nearness—everything about him had her in a flutter.

And the scent of him. *Dear heaven.* Sandalwood and the heat of his skin were a perfect blend.

She was utterly lost when he smiled. She had no idea what she would do if he kissed her again. Probably kiss him back with ridiculous ardor.

Well, that was dangerous.

"Let's have a look at your home," she said, and hurried out ahead of him.

Berry was just about to walk out the front door when she glanced out an entry hall window and spotted Lord Hawthorne's carriage drawing up in front of her home.

She stopped suddenly. "Oh dear. Melton, please advise Lord Hawthorne that I am out for the day. The *entire* day, and he is not to hang about Duchess Square for my return because you have no idea when I will be back."

"As you wish," the butler said. "I'll make certain he is chased away."

She turned back to Mr. Knight. "What shall we do? I cannot march out of here or he will see me."

He took her hand. "Come with me. How are you at climbing walls?"

He thought to have them leave the same way he arrived? "Not good at all, Mr. Knight. I have never done any such thing before."

"No worries, I'll help you." He led her out onto the garden where they had been sipping lemonade not half an hour ago. He took the sketchbook from her hands and tossed it over onto his side of the wall. Then he lifted her as though she weighed no more than a feather and plunked her atop the wall. "Stay right there."

He hauled himself up beside her, and then dropped onto his lawn with the grace of a cat. He turned to her and raised his hands. "Just lean toward me. I'll lift you down."

She tried to keep her gown from riding up her legs, but he grew impatient as she wriggled about, and simply grabbed her by the waist with strong, sure hands. In the next moment, she was in the air as he carried her down and set her gently on the grass beside him. "There, that wasn't so hard. Was it?"

She shook her head and took hold of his upper arms to steady herself.

It was like clinging to rock.

"You are a very bad influence on me, Mr. Knight." But she laughed. "Of course, it wasn't hard for me. Need I point out that you did all the work?"

"I didn't mind." He still had his hands around her waist, then realized that and released her to pick up her sketchbook.

Her hands slid off his arms.

It had felt nice to touch him. Every lady must think so, she mused. It was no coincidence that she and her friends had been ogling him all month long.

"Come along," he said, his voice husky. "I'll show you the current shambles that is my home."

She walked alongside him, eager to get indoors on the chance Lord Hawthorne happened to peer into Mr. Knight's home and spot her outside.

His workmen had cleaned up the debris created when putting

in the doors and were nowhere to be seen. But she smiled when she saw Bonham standing in what was the new ballroom.

He smiled back, tossed Mr. Knight an odd look, and then darted away.

Berry thought it strange, but said nothing about it, since they would probably run into him while touring the house. "I'm surprised he is still so bashful around me."

Mr. Knight appeared to smother a laugh. "He's been busy chasing mice. Probably was eager to get back to the task."

"Oh."

"Do they scare you?"

"A little. I would jump onto a chair if I saw one, but you don't seem to have a stick of furniture in here."

"You can leap into my arms if we see one."

Berry was suddenly never more eager to encounter a mouse.

She cleared her throat. "Um, shall I give you my thoughts on the paint colors for this room?"

CHAPTER SIX

GIDEON BEGAN TO wonder whether Bonham was right about Berry, because she was disarming.

And charming.

And graceful.

And achingly sweet.

His heart skipped beats whenever she smiled at him, which she did often because it was in her nature to be warm and sunny.

Bollocks. What a time to find out that his heart was not permanently frozen and he might fall in love.

What a disaster this would be. A cataclysm of incompatible worlds colliding. As much as he ached for Berry, she was not for him. He would never have her, even though she was the pinnacle, the dream woman he had wished for but never expected to find.

Berry was the one who would be hurt the most in attaching herself to him. The *ton* would be cruel and unforgiving because she was a shining star in the firmament and he was entrenched in the gutter.

Well, he came from the rookery streets and had been found wandering there as a child. That much was true. He had done everything he could to lift himself up from the dregs, but it would never be enough for those like Hawthorne whose views represented most of the *ton*.

For the past several years, Gideon and Bonham had been

working to shed their gaming hell investments and build respectable enterprises. But the transition would take several years because they were not going to give their clubs away for nothing. Only a sale for fair value would be acceptable.

Also, these gaming hells were profit centers for them and provided employment for many of the lads coming out of the orphanage. He supposed any new businesses acquired could take in most of them, and perhaps even a few of the girls.

"Eggshell white for the walls and antique ivory for the trim," Berry said, regaining his attention.

"What?"

"Your new ballroom. These are the colors you must have. And three chandeliers, because the room is so large. Shall I help you select those?"

He smiled. "Yes, Lady Berry. That would be very much appreciated."

"As for floors, I think oak, hickory, or maple woods are best. But my preference is for a dark oak."

"Then oak it is. Next?"

She laughed. "Aren't you going to question me as to why?"

"No, I trust your judgment."

"Oh. Well, thank you. Mr. Knight, I—"

"Do you mind if we set aside formality? I prefer that you call me Gideon. May I refer to you simply as Berry? Of course, in public I realize we must maintain decorum."

She nodded. "I suppose it is all right. You have a fine name. Gideon. I like it."

He cast her a wry look. "So do I. It is all made up, of course. Gideon Knight. I spent the first fifteen years of my life as Gideon No-Name. I think the director of St. Brigid's gave me the name Gideon, just pulled it out of thin air because I had no idea what my mother had called me. I don't even know if the woman who abandoned me on a London street was my mother. No idea who my father was or whether he ever saw my mother again after I was conceived. Who knows if they were acquainted at all? It is highly possible I sprang from a five-minute encounter between strangers."

He gave a dismissive snort and continued. "Sorry, Berry. I did not mean to be so crude."

"No, it is all right. Please go on," she said gently, and gave him an encouraging look.

"Bonham and I are about the same age. We grew up at the orphanage together and left together. His name really is John Bonham, by the way. He even has a birth record to prove it. But as for me, I could have been dropped to earth from a cloud for all I know."

"How did you end up with the surname of Knight?"

"Bonham and I happened to be watching a parade shortly after we left the orphanage and were scraping by on our own. There was a man dressed in shining armor upon a massive steed. His armor was the brightest silver and blinding in its brilliance. I had never seen anything so impressive. Someone mentioned the rider was supposed to be a Knight of the Round Table out of the legends of King Arthur."

"Goodness, and this is how you came up with your family name of Knight?"

"Knights lived by a code of honor. Their code of chivalry. Do no harm to ladies. Be loyal to the Crown. Be merciful. I thought it was a good code to live by. So I became a knight. Gideon Knight." He cast her a pained smile. "Pathetic, isn't it?"

"No, it is a testament to your honor and courage. This is why Lord Berwick knew you were meant to be his successor...my very own knight in shining armor."

He noticed a tear spill onto her cheek and gently stroked his thumb along her soft skin to brush it away. "Berry, you are far too sentimental. Do not cry because of what I've just told you about me."

"But it is a beautiful story, Gideon. A tale of courage and perseverance. Of triumph against all odds. Yours is a story that ought to be told to others."

He shrugged. "To the orphans, perhaps. A way to inspire them and tell them to not believe those who might put them down and insist they will never amount to anything. But I'm not sure it is a story to be told to your *ton* friends. They would not see it as a victory for a young boy who started out with nothing."

"I see. They would believe you are a threat to a societal hierarchy that has placed them at the top."

"Quite so, and they do not want an upstart pushing them off their precious pedestals." He took her gently by the elbow and led her to his study. "What about this room? How should it be decorated?"

She perked up right away and began tossing out ideas. "Mahogany desk and bookshelves. Although a cherry wood would also work nicely. Do you have a preference?"

"No, Berry. Whichever you think best."

"They are both beautiful. I lean toward the cherry."

He nodded. "So be it."

"Warm, dark colors are most appropriate here, for it should be a masculine room. Do you prefer maroon or green?"

He shrugged. "No preference."

She sighed. "Green. A deep, pine-forest green. Maroon leather wing chairs for your guests. A manly carpet. Paintings of horses."

He laughed. "What is a manly carpet?"

"I'm not sure, but I'll know it when I see it." She cast him an impertinent smile. "Dining room next?"

"Yes, Your Highness," he said lovingly. "I am but your humble servant."

She scribbled notes to herself as they moved on from his study. "Fiona had wallpaper here, as you can plainly see. Isn't it lovely?"

"Pure heaven," he remarked, not meaning to let his sarcasm slip in. But how could he not? She did not need his input when she clearly had a more refined palate than he had or ever would have. All she needed him to do was bob his head as they went from room to room and she spouted ideas, all of them brilliant as far as he was concerned. "Yes, it is lovely."

"The wallpaper certainly took a beating during her move. It has to be replaced, but I think we ought to stay close to this oriental flower design and its color scheme, don't you?"

"Berry, if you think we must, then so be it. I have complete faith in you."

We.

If *we* must?

Yes, somehow this was no longer just about him, but *them.* He could see her in his home. Indeed, he could think of nothing nicer than coming home each night to be greeted by Berry's smiling face.

But who was he fooling? He was slipping into his dreams again.

"Kitchen next?" she asked as they finished with the rooms on the main floor.

"Sure."

"Go on ahead. I'll meet you in a moment. I just want to check on a measurement in the library."

"I can wait for you. Do you need my help?"

She shook her head. "No, I'll be right there."

"All right." He strode ahead to the kitchen to see how Bonham was faring with the new water pump he'd decided to tackle this morning.

Bonham looked up as Gideon walked in. "Where's Lady Berry?"

"She went to check on something in the library. What's wrong? You don't look happy."

"Because I'm not. I'm trying to prevent a flood in here," he grumbled.

Gideon frowned as he approached. "That doesn't sound good. What happened?"

"Oh, no. Don't get too close or you might get soaked. I think I am missing a part."

"How is it possible? I saw for myself what was delivered, and everything was there."

Bonham was on his back, but now sat up with a grunt. "Blast, it's that new lad, then. I thought he looked shifty—did I not warn you about him? This is the third time Henry's done this to us."

"Fourth, actually," Gideon muttered. "I'll need to have a talk with him. He may be stealing parts and selling them elsewhere."

Bonham looked angry. "I'll tan his hide if that's what he is doing. We've given the little wretch every opportunity, and what does he do? Steals from us."

Berry suddenly emerged from the doorway. "Wait…you heard Mr. Knight?"

Bonham's eyes widened. "What?"

She gasped. "You heard me, too."

Gideon's heart shot into his throat.

Oh, hell. How much of their conversation had she heard? And why did his friend have to look so guilty?

"Gideon, tell her," Bonham said, releasing a deflated breath.

"We might have been teasing you just the littlest bit," Gideon said, inwardly groaning because he had meant to tell her, and should have told her much sooner, about their little prank. "Bonham's hearing is perfectly fine."

"Well, it was perfect before you spent hours shouting in my ear," Bonham said, thinking to make a jest of it.

But Gideon knew Berry did not find it funny and had taken it to heart. "Gad. Shut up, you dolt."

Her expression went from shocked to angry to utterly wounded in the span of three seconds. "You were both mocking me all the while? Letting me make a fool of myself and saying nothing? Why would you do this to me?"

"Never that," Gideon said emphatically, his stomach now twisting into knots because he had never had to deal with someone as gentle and trusting as Berry before.

She was a little angel, so achingly good and sweet. She looked so hurt.

"No, Berry." He raked a hand through his hair. "This was my mistake, and never something planned. You are the last person on earth I would ever purposely insult or demean. Bonham was rude that first day when you stormed over and almost got hit on the head by that falling board. He should have answered the front door when you knocked, but he didn't, and I did not want you to think we were rude boors."

"Which we were," Bonham interjected.

"I readily admit it," Gideon affirmed. "I did not know what to say…or what to think. I just blurted the stupidest thing that came to mind. And Bonham is not my butler but my best friend and business partner, which you might have guessed now, too."

"Then why do you call him Bonham? Isn't that his family name?"

"Yes, but there were several boys named John at the orphanage. It was just easier to call him Bonham instead of having seven heads turn whenever I called out to him."

"Oh, perfect. So your butler is not really a butler but your good friend. And since he had no trouble hearing a single word you said, he was never deaf. Really? And *you* are the man Lord Berwick chose to protect me. The smartest man in London, he said. And you do this?"

"Well, when you put it that way…" His hand shot through his hair again.

"And later you never bothered to correct it, even after I befriended you."

Bonham stepped forward. "Blame it on me, Lady Berry. I should have said something when you came by that next time. Please believe me when I say that we never meant to be cruel. But you were so lovely and innocent. And, well, Gideon and I have never encountered anyone as sweet as you before."

Gideon nodded. "Or anyone so trusting. We thought it was harmless fun, at first. A jest shared between me and Bonham. But then we realized how much our idiotic prank would hurt you, and we didn't know how to undo it."

"So we remained complete cowards and let you go on believing I was deaf." Bonham groaned. "I am truly and ardently sorry."

"Same goes for me," Gideon said. "You have shown me nothing but acceptance and kindness. I have never spent a more enjoyable time than when I am with you. At your charity affair. At the Denby Arms. Now here, walking through the rooms of my house with you. I've never told anyone the things I told you earlier."

"You haven't?" she asked.

"Well, only Bonham knows because he was there with me when we saw the parade. I'm sorry, Berry. It was *never* my intention to hurt you. But this is what comes of my arrogance and pride. I never apologize to anyone, but I am apologizing to you now. Humbly and sincerely. From the bottom of my heart." He waited for her to say something, but she simply stood there struggling to hold back tears. "I am so sorry."

"I have to go."

"Please don't," Gideon said, reaching out to her.

"I have to think about this." She turned and fled the kitchen.

Bonham stared at him. "Aren't you going after her?"

"I don't dare."

"Gad, I've made a mess of this for you. I'm so sorry, Gideon. I wasn't thinking."

"No, it's my fault. That prank was not harmless and I ought to have confessed it right away. But she looked at me with such faith. Such trust. And that beautiful, dimpled smile… I could not break that magical spell."

"Seriously?"

"She is magical, don't you think?"

Bonham grinned. "She's pretty, I will grant you that. Are you falling in love with her?"

"I don't know," Gideon said with a groan. "Possible. This assumes I even know what love means."

"Well, neither of us has had much experience with that."

Gideon had to acknowledge that the breathless feeling whenever she was near, the yearning to see her and be close to her, had to mean something. "As we walked from room to room, all I could think about was that…" He paused and took a deep breath. "That if nothing ever came of us, of our ever being together, I would have this house to remind me of her. Every wall. Every carpet. Every bookshelf. They would have Berry's touch. They would be a reflection of her. That I could close my eyes and feel *her* around me."

Bonham's mouth dropped open. "Hell's bells. You've got it bad."

"I know. Perhaps this is for the best. How could it ever work out? She's a lady. I am…" Gideon gave a mirthless laugh. "I don't even know what I am or who I am. Berwick trusts me to protect her finances and keep an eye out for bounders getting too close. I ought to leave it at that. A professional arrangement. Let her find love with one of her own. Just not with that cur, Hawthorne."

His friend slapped him on the back. "You'll get over her in time. There are plenty of ladies eager to help you forget her. Even if Jasmine or Chloe find benefactors, they will always—"

"No, that wouldn't be helpful." Gideon let out a breath. "Just leave it alone, Bonham. I'll work through this on my own."

But he wasn't sure he could ever forget Berry. Even if he never saw her again.

She was already burned into his heart, wasn't she?

How did others manage the pain of it? Perhaps if he had a fickle heart. But that was not him.

Apparently, even nameless guttersnipes could fall in love.

Assuming this was the real thing and not some passing infatuation.

He walked out of the kitchen and into the new ballroom that he and his workers had just finished building. Berry was in there, turned away as she struggled to stop her tears.

He strode to her and took her in his arms. "I thought you had gone home," he said in a ragged whisper, relieved when she did not attempt to push away.

Instead, she rested her head against his chest. "I meant to, but Hawthorne is still out there. I cannot walk out your front door, and I am not tall enough to make it over the garden wall without assistance. I want to get away from you both."

But she did not appear eager to move out of his arms.

He was not going to point this out to her.

"Don't leave. I will humbly get down on bended knee and apologize to you as many times as it takes. Seeing how bad I have made you feel just destroys me."

"You needn't get down on one knee," she said with a sniffle. "I think I need to learn how to be tougher."

"No, you are perfect as you are."

She laughed. "I doubt that."

"The world is filled with boors and selfish oafs. Petty, narrow-minded fools. Thieves and cheats. For every thousand of them, there is one treasure…you. You are the ray of sunlight on a grim day. The one who smiles when all others are frowning. Don't change a thing about yourself, Berry. There is no one finer than you."

The tension appeared to flow out of her as she peered up at him and cast him the smile that he would give a king's ransom to see every day for the rest of his life. "My friends insisted on holding our tea society meetings at my home every Thursday this month."

"I noticed."

"We could have switched to someone else's home. I could have insisted on it, but I did not. We were all watching you. We could not wait to see you climbing up the ladder or standing on the roof. That was not very nice of us, the way we ogled you."

"You didn't do it in front of me."

"No, we did it behind your back. And I let them do it. And I did it myself."

"Berry, is this your way of forgiving me for the prank Bonham and I pulled on you?"

She nodded.

He gave her a chaste kiss on the forehead. "Thank you."

She stared up at him with her gorgeous, soft eyes. "Will you forgive me?"

He laughed. "I was never angry with you. Those seven faces pasted to your window every Thursday pretty much gave you away. I would have said something if I were peeved."

"But it was not nice of us. Weren't you the littlest bit perturbed?"

He held her gently by her shoulders now. "Berry, if I told you more about my life after leaving the orphanage, I would have you crying again. What you did was not proper by *ton* standards, but harmless to me. I have encountered far worse. Can we leave it at that?"

She gave a reluctant nod.

"Will you help me make my home elegant?"

She nodded again.

Will you marry me?

CHAPTER SEVEN

BEFORE BERRY LEFT his home an hour later, she wrote out a detailed list of paint colors for each room in his house. "Have your painter bring samples tomorrow. Just the samples of each."

"Why not a full supply? Then his crew can start right away."

"Because the colors must be perfect before I give him the nod. I'd like to see how they look on the walls in daylight and in the evening, especially the ballroom. I need to imagine how the chandeliers will reflect the candlelight."

Gideon smiled. "All right. You're in charge."

"No, it is up to you to decide. This is *your* house. You need to like what's being done." She handed the list to him. "Then we will select the right stain for the oak floors. And I have an idea for the entry hall."

"Sounds perfect."

She laughed incredulously. "But you haven't heard my idea yet."

"I have no need. I trust you."

"I think you have reached the limit of your endurance on decorating choices in a day. May we resume tomorrow? What time will the painters arrive with their samples?"

Gideon shrugged. "What time would you like them here?"

"Well, you would need to be here, too. I don't mind making my recommendations, but you must approve them. This is your house and you will be the one living in it," she repeated.

But he wanted this to be her house, too.

He shook out of the thought, annoyed with himself that it kept slipping through his barricades.

Berry was not for him. It was that two-worlds problem again.

He could not live like a saint. She could not live like a sinner. She could never be his.

Should never be his.

Since Hawthorne's carriage was still on the street, Gideon returned Berry to her home by way of the stone wall between their houses. He waited for her to scamper inside before he scaled the wall and returned to his kitchen, where Bonham was still struggling with the pump. "Cap it for now and work on something else. I'll deal with young Henry. That lad is going to get himself hanged before he reaches his next birthday if he doesn't mend his ways."

"I'll go with you. I can deal with Henry."

Gideon shook his head. "No, I need you to stay here. That arse, Hawthorne, is still lurking on Duchess Square. Keep an eye on him, especially if you notice Berry stepping out of her home. I don't know what he is scheming to do, but I certainly don't trust him."

"Is he plotting something mad, do you think? Is he fool enough to abduct her?"

"I did not think he had the bollocks to try, but he might if he's grown that desperate. Perhaps I ought to have a word with him."

"I'll come with you," Bonham said with a nod. "The cur might think to draw a weapon on you, but he won't try it if he has two of us to take down."

"All right." Gideon did not mind having his trusted companion to back him up. As Bonham had said, Hawthorne might reach for his pistol if facing him alone. That snake was just the sort to shoot a man in the back once he'd turned away.

But to take him *and* Bonham on? The man was too cowardly to try it.

Hawthorne's driver eyed them warily as they approached but did nothing more than study them.

Up close, the carriage appeared to have seen better days. There were scratches and gouges on the door. The leather on the driver's seat was torn.

Gideon threw open the door and caught Hawthorne by surprise. He reached in and dragged the cur out, catching a strong whiff of scotch on the man's breath as he cried out in alarm. "Hodgkins! Hodgkins! Shoot the man!"

But Bonham already had his pistol out and aimed at the driver, who did not seem inclined to forfeit his life on behalf of his wastrel employer. Instead of reaching for his weapon, he raised his hands in the air. "I ain't making a move, sirs. No need to point that pistol at me."

"A wise choice," Bonham said, "but keep your hands raised."

"Aye, sir. As ye wish."

Gideon concentrated on Hawthorne, removing a pistol out of the lip of his boot and another on his person. "Now you and I shall have our little talk."

"I have nothing to say to you! You are nothing but a low, wretched creature. How dare you think you are better than us? My friends and I shall show you. We'll have you on your knees and licking our boots." Each angry word came out slurred, for Hawthorne was deep in his cups, and it was not even noon yet.

"Are you through? My turn now." Gideon grabbed Hawthorne by the lapels. "Keep away from Lady Berry."

Hawthorne cursed at him and then snorted. "Who are you to tell me what to do?"

"I am the man who is going kill you if you dare harm Lady Berry. Forget her, Hawthorne. Neither Lord Berwick nor I will ever let you marry her. If you attempt anything improper with her, I will kill you. If you enlist your friends to help, I will kill *them* and then I will kill *you*. Care to deliver that message to your circle of toadies? Or shall I do it next time I see them at my club?"

"You'll pay for this!"

"No, you shall be the one to pay. You do not want to hear what I will do to you if you ever lay a finger on her." Gideon shoved him back into his carriage, tossed a few coins to his driver, and said, "You did not hear this conversation."

"No, sir. All ye did was bid 'im good day. Amiable as could be, ye were."

He nodded and told the driver to take Hawthorne home.

"My weapons!"

"Forfeited," Gideon said with a growl. "Be thankful it was not your life I chose to take."

He and Bonham stood on Duchess Square watching Hawthorne's carriage depart.

Lady Miranda and her niece, Gwenys, came running out of their house toward him. Another neighbor he had met at Berry's charity affair the other day, Lady Gwendolyn Carstairs, also ran out of her home across the square and stopped beside them. She had another lady with her that she introduced as her cousin, Suzanna Carstairs, visiting for the summer from Devon.

Berry must have been watching from the entry hall window, for she now tore out of her home and ran to him.

She seemed about to ask what he'd said to Hawthorne when she noticed Lady Gwendolyn's cousin and forgot him for the moment. "Suzanna! When did you arrive?"

"Late last night," the pretty brunette replied as they embraced each other. "I'm so sorry I missed your charity tea. How did it go?"

"Very well. Come over for tea and ginger cakes later, and I'll tell you all about it."

"And will you tell me the rest of what's been going on?" She turned toward Gideon and Bonham. "Who was it that you gentlemen chased off the square?"

Berry rolled her eyes. "Ugh, that wastrel. Lord Hawthorne."

"Is he still after you?" Suzanna asked.

"Yes, he simply won't give up. It isn't me he wants, of course. What a horrid man! He sat there for hours this morning watching my house. He thinks if he clings to me like a barnacle to the keel of a ship that I will eventually agree to marry him." She turned to Gideon. "What did you say to him to make him go away?"

He wasn't about to confess that he had threatened to kill the man. "I explained to him that neither Lord Berwick nor I would ever allow you to marry him, so he ought to look elsewhere for his pot of gold."

Berry gave a small shudder. "Good, I hope he does."

"I am sure you were the soul of politeness." Miranda tossed Gideon a knowing look. "It is a good thing you have moved onto Duchess Square. I think Berry is in need of this added protection. Hawthorne presently is the most persistent, but he isn't the only one after her."

"You mean, after my pot of gold," Berry muttered with a snort. She then properly introduced the ladies to Bonham, since none of them had met him yet.

"You must excuse the mess I am," Bonham said as he bowed to all of them and then motioned to his clothes. "I have been dealing with a wayward water pump this morning."

"He thinks pieces are missing," Gideon explained.

"A Cowpers & Lynton silver model pump?" Suzanna asked.

Bonham turned to her in surprise and nodded. "Yes, the very devil."

"My father had one installed in our kitchen only two weeks ago. He cursed like a demon. I can show you the trick to putting in this pump, if you do not mind taking instruction from a lady?"

"I do not mind at all," Bonham said, looking ready to sink to his knees and shout hallelujah in gratitude.

All five ladies walked over with Bonham.

Gideon joined them but only for a few minutes. He was curious to know whether all the pieces to the pump were there before he had his talk with young Henry. He was not about to accuse the lad of stealing those pieces if he was innocent. Although Henry had probably done something else to merit having his ears boxed. The boy was not quite on the straight and narrow path yet, and needed supervision. Gideon would alert Pudge and Joss to keep an eye on him.

He breathed a sigh of relief when Suzanna advised them nothing was missing. "It is that the bolts and screws go in from the underside of the pump and there are only four instead of the usual six. Of course, the company does not include an instruction for this, which would be helpful and save hours of frustration."

He left Suzanna kneeling beside his friend and pointing out where a bolt should be tightened or a screw slipped in. The other ladies watched in fascination, and he sensed Bonham was enjoying his lovely audience immensely.

"I had better get back to work," Gideon said quietly to Berry, for he needed to return to the Musket Club before it opened to patrons. "I'll see you here tomorrow at nine. Better yet, I'll come to your door and escort you over. Do not walk over on your own. In fact, do not go anywhere alone for these next few days, not even to cross the square to visit Lady Miranda or Lady Gwendolyn. Have Melton or one of your footmen escort you wherever you need to go."

"Are you that concerned about Lord Hawthorne?"

Gideon nodded. "He sat in his carriage for hours waiting for you even after Melton had instructed him you were not at home. Who in his right mind would sit there drinking and no doubt stewing in anger when he had clearly been sent away? I cannot trust him or his motives. Will you promise me to be careful, especially when around him or his friends?"

She nodded. "All right."

He strode away before he gave in to the urge to kiss her, an urge that struck every time she looked up at him with her big green eyes.

Berry also had the sweetest lips, sweet as cherries. They beckoned him, but were they not as dangerous as a siren's call to lure a man onto the rocky straits and drown him?

He returned to his club, eager to drown himself in work and stop thinking about Berry.

Henry was nowhere in sight when he arrived, so Gideon sent Pudge off to look for him. "He's probably hiding in the larder or the wine cellar. Bring him up to my office when you do find him."

"Right away," Pudge said, and hurried off.

Pudge was another orphan Gideon had taken in about ten years ago when this club was newly established, a shy boy who was heavyset and a little clumsy on his feet. But he was honest and hardworking. As he shot up in height, growing as big as an oak tree and maintaining his heft as well as developing muscles, he became a daunting figure on the gaming floor. No one was going to challenge Pudge.

Jasmine approached Gideon as he started upstairs. He frowned, for he had work to do and did not look forward to dealing with her petulance.

"Gideon, I need a moment of your time."

Joss was nowhere in sight, so Gideon could not pretend he had an urgent problem at the club to address with him. He sighed, knowing there was no way out of talking to Jasmine.

"Come into my office."

She ran her hand lightly along his arm. "We could be more private in your bedchamber."

"No, that is over and done."

"Are you certain?" She cast him a seductive look, then took his hand and placed it on her breast. "Isn't this better?"

"No," he repeated sternly, drawing away from her. "If this is all you want, Jasmine, then go use your charms on someone else."

She slapped him. "Beast!"

He caught her hand when she attempted to slap him again. "Try that again and I'll ban you from the club permanently. What are you doing here? Did you not just find yourself a new benefactor? The Marquess of Haverstock is a decent fellow. He honors his debts and is a gentleman. Did he buy you that necklace?"

"Yes." She tossed him a petulant look. "But he isn't you."

"Be grateful for it. I would never be as nice to you as he will be."

"Who's your new partridge?"

"I don't have one. But what I do have is a lot of work. If you will excuse me."

He started up the stairs and had gotten halfway up when she blurted out Berry's name. "Lord Hawthorne saw you with her the other night at the Denby Arms."

He paused and turned back to her. "Keep away from that fellow. He's trouble."

She tipped her chin up in defiance. "He's a viscount."

"Jasmine, do not embroil yourself with him. He is deeply in debt and getting desperate now that his family has refused to step forward and help him out. Guard those jewels you've worked so hard to acquire, because he won't hesitate to steal them from you."

She followed him into his office. "Haverstock will never marry me."

"I know," he said gently, for he resented these barriers imposed by the *ton*. "But he will be generous with you and leave you well protected for the future."

Since she was still in a snit, she cast him a cruel smile. "Nor will the lofty Lady Berengaria ever have you."

He knew this only too well. "What is your point?"

"You and I make a good team. We could make a go of it. And if you wanted Chloe to join us in bed, I would not mind. Nor would I mind your seducing the proud Berengaria. In fact, I would find it quite amusing. Do you think she would join us? Or mind my watching the two of you?"

Bloody blazes, was this what she thought he wanted out of life? To defile Berry, the most worthwhile lady he had ever met?

"We could never make a go of it, Jasmine. As for Lady Berengaria, just look around you. Every one of us is here and making a living, given a chance at a decent life because of her and her family. And you think I would repay her by ruining her?"

He shook his head and grunted. "I don't care that you or Chloe chose to lead the life of courtesans when a more respectable path was offered to you. What I do care about is your lack of character. You are loyal only to yourself. You have no appreciation for those who go out of their way to help you. You think they are fools to be used and manipulated. Do you want a man to love and respect you? Then try loving and respecting *him*. Just don't waste that effort on me."

"Here's my respect for you!" She picked up a vase and tossed it at his head.

He stepped aside and it smashed against the wall. "Go away, Jasmine. Leave me alone and let me work."

She stormed off.

Gideon sighed. Just what he needed.

More trouble.

CHAPTER EIGHT

BERRY HAD TAKEN Gideon's warning to heart and stepped out yesterday with two armed footmen to escort her wherever she went. She now paced in her formal parlor, staring at the ornate clock on the mantel as the morning hour approached nine o'clock.

She looked forward to seeing Gideon and helping him put his house in shape. Of course, her friend Fiona's home had always been lovely. But it was Gideon's now, and he needed to make it comfortable for him and be a representation of *his* tastes.

She heard voices at the front door, recognized Gideon's, and rushed into the entry hall. "You are right on time."

She tried to tamp down the sudden pitter-patter of her heart. Gideon Knight was too handsome by far.

"So are you." He smiled and held out his arm for her. "Ready to take on the exciting task of watching paint dry?"

She laughed and wrapped her arm around his as they walked outside. "I am breathless with anticipation. But I cannot stay long. I am due at the orphanage later this morning."

"Would you mind my company?"

She looked up at him, surprised.

But she should not have been, for he had expressed interest in touring the orphanage. "That would be lovely. I would not mind your company at all. In fact, it would put me at ease. I did as you suggested and went everywhere with two footmen as escorts yesterday."

"Did you encounter Hawthorne again?"

"No." But she frowned. "However, I could not shake the feeling that I was being followed. Did you by any chance have someone watch over me?"

"No, although I should have considered it."

"Perhaps we are making too much of Lord Hawthorne's behavior lately. It is disturbing, and I intend to relate my concerns to Lord Berwick when I see him Saturday evening. We have been invited to a soirée at the British Museum to launch one of their new exhibits featuring the Lyme Regis cave drawings."

Gideon smiled. "So have I."

Her eyes rounded in surprise. "Truly? I mean…no offense, but how did you manage to secure an invitation?"

"No offense taken. One of the directors is a regular patron at the Musket Club, but he's a steady fellow. He doesn't ever bet above his means. Nor does he drink to excess. We got to chatting last night about the hazards of organizing these charity events. He's sending an invite for me to the club."

"Oh, that is kind of him. And very helpful."

"Yes, I thought so."

"Well, it does make sense," she said with a nod. "You are wealthier than most of the elite who will be in attendance. And this event is really about raising funds for the museum's purposes. I would not be surprised to see a smattering of wealthy merchants rubbing elbows with dukes, earls, and others of rank."

"I'm wondering if this might not be worth imitating for your next event," he mused as they walked through his front gate.

"Certain aspects of their charity affair, for certain. The museum's board is very good at raising funds. I think it is because they do a marvelous job of raising awareness and excitement. This is what I feel has been missing from my charity events lately," she said, letting out a soft breath. "I am afraid my annual tea is getting too predictable and boring."

"We'll figure it out."

"We? Oh, I'm so glad you don't mind taking on an active role."

"But I still need to stay in the background."

"Remain invisible? Oh, because of your wicked reputation?"

"Yes. It could do you more harm than good."

She gave a dismissive shake of her head. "Sorry, but isn't it a bit outrageous? Everyone struggles to go up in standing while you are wishing to encourage a bad name for yourself."

He grinned. "I know. I cherish that bad reputation. But I've given much thought to my involvement in good causes. I am not going to shy away from them. With a little push in the right direction, people can be convinced I am extending my power and influence, and would become more dangerous, not less."

"Oh, Gideon. Is that not awful?"

He shrugged. "Yes, I suppose. But I prefer to see it as the best possible outcome, to give to those in need and also maintain my wicked reputation. However, now that I am named as Berwick's successor trustee, I'll need to walk a very fine line. I cannot risk a judge removing me because he's declared me unfit."

Berry regarded him in dismay. "We ought to discuss this with Lord Berwick. Can he designate a string of successors? So that if you are removed, then someone else of his choosing is placed in charge. I am quite the heiress, and I fear a judge could be bribed to appoint one of his friends in your place. Is your removal a possibility, Gideon? I would never seek it. Who would have standing to plead to the court if I were not the one to bring suit?"

"There shouldn't be anyone other than you with that ability, but a man determined to gain control of your trust funds might find a way. Bribe doctors to have you declared incompetent or mad. Have himself appointed as your guardian."

"A man such as Hawthorne?" She frowned again.

"I am not saying it would be easy or even possible, but I cannot see any other way such a thing could happen."

"I would marry you before it ever came to pass. Then you would be my husband and no one could challenge you."

Dear heaven.

Had she just said that?

She glanced up at him and swallowed hard. "I mean, it is one possible solution."

He placed a hand over hers. "Berry, I will do anything needed to protect you. Marriage to you would be an honor. It is you who would be hurt, mocked by the *ton* for marrying a nobody. But between us, if ever it were to come to that, I would do all in my power to be a good husband to you and make you happy."

He was going to make her cry. Weren't those the loveliest words she had ever heard?

This was why Lord Berwick trusted him. Gideon may have come from nothing, but *he* was not nothing.

He was her knight in shining armor.

They had walked to the rear of the house to enter through the newly built ballroom, but he stopped her and tipped her chin up so that she had to gaze at him. "Are you sniffling again?"

She nodded. "What you said was beautiful."

"Gad, you are such a kitten," he said with a wry, slightly bemused chuckle. "No tears, Berry. You shall always be safe with me. All right?"

"Yes."

"Good. We are going to choose paint samples now. The painters will think I have been cruel to you if you walk in crying."

She took out her handkerchief and quickly dried her tears.

Only a few drops had fallen. "There. Better?"

He cast her a smile that made her legs turn weak. "Much better."

They spent the next hour deciding on paint colors, a chore she had expected him to find excruciatingly dull. Then she realized he was looking at it as the fulfillment of a dream, the home he had always craved and never had until now. He did not know who he was or where he came from, so this was his chance to create a place for himself.

By the time they had finished walking from room to room with the painters, they had gathered a following.

Bonham was there, guarding the house and escaping boredom by trying to fix things around the house. He set aside his latest project, yet another that vexed him to no end, and joined Gwendolyn and Suzanna Carstairs, along with Miranda and Gwenys Lawson, in following them from room to room.

It really was completely improper that Berry's friends should saunter over uninvited. But Gideon was not one for formality and did not take offense that his neighbors were snoops and could not resist stopping by.

Bonham did not seem to mind either. In fact, he was delighted. Was she imagining it, or had his eyes lit up upon seeing Suzanna march up the walk?

Everyone had an opinion and a comment as the painters brushed various samples on the walls of each room. They all stood there and watched the paint dry.

Berry was surprised when Gideon went with her choice of color each time.

Toward the end, their followers and the painters were snickering each time she gave her answer.

Berry was not proficient in many things, but no one could ever fault her refined tastes or her sense of fashion. Had she been born a man, she might have worked alongside prominent architects and designers such as Henry Holland or John Nash.

She was pleased to put her knowledge to good use. Her learning extended beyond mere paint colors. She was well versed in neoclassical architecture and art, too.

Odd that Gideon seemed to appreciate her talents and accept her advice when no one among her elite circle would give her the time of day on such matters.

They met again at nightfall, all of them walking around with candles and torches to confirm that the paint colors Berry had chosen were the right ones for each room, especially the ballroom.

"Are we done? All good?" Gideon asked. "Then I had better get back to the club. See you bright and early tomorrow morning."

With the colors now agreed upon, they all parted ways.

Berry hardly slept because she was so excited that Gideon's home was starting to take form.

The painters arrived early the following morning, and Berry was there to watch them set about mixing the color shadings to her precise formulations.

She looked on, hardly breathing as they began their task.

Her snooping friends soon joined her, as did Bonham and Gideon. They spent a full hour discussing the colors.

"As much fun as this is," Miranda said, "Gwenys and I really must take our leave."

"Thank you for stopping by," Berry said, although this was not her home but Gideon's.

Still, she felt very much like the lady of the house. Gideon had made her feel that way by respecting all her decisions.

Miranda and Gwenys returned to their home because they had planned a day of shopping in preparation for Gwenys's formal come-out that was still months away. But one had to get an early start, since so many gowns would be required.

Gwendolyn and Suzanna mentioned that they were at leisure. When Suzanna happened to ask Bonham what he had been working on that vexed him today, he responded with a grumble about the service shaft that was used to lift food or other items from a lower story to an upper story without need for the servants to climb up and down the stairs. "The pulley ropes are frayed and need to be replaced."

"Ah," Suzanna said. "Curiously, we had the same problem in our home last winter. Will you permit me to have a look at your shaft?"

Bonham and Gideon both coughed suddenly.

Since neither seemed able to speak for the moment, Suzanna continued. "Hargreaves and Sons sells an excellent pulley system that is easy to install. But I shall have to measure the width of your shaft. Precise measurements are necessary, obviously. Do you mind?"

The pair were coughing again.

"Because the platform must fit snugly within the opening. However, it cannot be too tight or you shall hear such squealing noises whenever the shaft is in use. And I expect you will be using your shaft often."

"Oh, Lord," Bonham said, sounding quite pained as he turned away and appeared to double over.

Suzanna frowned. "Are you all right, Mr. Bonham?"

He nodded. "I will be in a moment."

"Well, all I mean to say is that the pulley will need constant oiling if the fit is not exact, and then the ropes will fray too quickly. I watched as the workmen replaced ours in our home, so I am quite sure I can guide you through the installation with my steady hand."

Bonham's grin was wide as he straightened to his full height once again and expressed his enthusiasm for Suzanna's idea. "Miss Carstairs, you are priceless."

She cast him an enchanting smile. "Thank you, Mr. Bonham."

Berry thought Bonham was going to lift her friend up in his arms and twirl her around, for he was that enthused.

After a moment, he turned to Gideon. "The painters are here all day, so the place will be well enough guarded while I dash to Hargreaves. Any objections?"

"None."

Bonham then turned to Gwendolyn and Suzanna. "Could I... Might I impose... Well, no. I don't suppose..."

"We'd love to come with you, Mr. Bonham," Suzanna replied. "I can show you exactly which pulley system will work best. Would you mind showing me what is presently in this house?"

He cast Suzanna a look of relief. "Come right this way."

Berry was pleased the residents of Duchess Square would remain as friendly and helpful to each other as they had been when Fiona resided here.

With the Carstairs cousins now gone off with Bonham, the

painters already off to the ballroom to start painting, and Miranda and her niece fled to go shopping, Berry was left alone in the entry hall with Gideon.

He was smiling from ear to ear.

Berry could not help but grin back. "Suzanna is a wonder, isn't she?"

"Yes," he said with a tender laugh. "You are quite wonderful, too. Do you mind that we will be spending a large portion of the day together?"

"No, I expect to enjoy it immensely."

"So do I." He regarded her thoughtfully. "You and your friends have been remarkably kind to me and Bonham. I feel even more of a wretch for the prank we pulled on you."

"About Bonham's hearing? You've apologized several times already and I've forgiven you each time. I understand now that you meant no harm by it. Truly. What hurt me is that I thought you did not like me."

"Not at all. I thought you were charming from the first moment I met you."

"I feel we have developed an excellent rapport, haven't we?"

"We have," Gideon insisted.

"I believe you look upon me favorably now. So, either you are very good at faking sincerity, or we are on the way to becoming good friends."

He grunted. "Berry, my problem is that I am in danger of liking you too much. You are quite extraordinary."

Her eyes widened. "Oh."

"But you needn't worry. Our relation shall always remain professional and never a step beyond. I shall always look out for you, just as Lord Berwick has done over the years. I hope ours will be as good a friendship as you have had with him."

"I see. Um, thank you." She was not surprised he wanted to keep his distance, for they were from vastly different backgrounds. His was a much rougher upbringing.

She was not so naïve as to think he had merely given Hawthorne a polite warning. Gideon had a very tough, primal core beneath his veneer of polish.

In truth, this was probably his nature. A kill-or-be-killed attitude that one might find among animals in the wild. That he was always on his best behavior around her probably took conscious effort.

She glanced around. "Is there anything more you must do here?"

"No, that's all I planned to accomplish at the house today."

"Then let's go to the orphanage. But we must take separate carriages. Mrs. Garland is still feeling too poorly to leave her bed, and I cannot be seen riding alone with you."

"Understood. Take your two footmen with you. They ought to be guarding you no matter where you go or who you intend to meet."

"All right. Give me but a moment to collect my gloves and reticule. I'll meet you at St. Brigid's shortly."

She meant to dart off, but Gideon held her back. "I'll walk you home."

"But it is only a few steps away."

"I know," he said as they walked out of his house. "But you must never let down your guard, Berry. Anything can happen, and within the blink of an eye."

This was the primal animal within him speaking, she knew.

And he was not wrong. There was a hired carriage standing just off Duchess Square that she had noticed earlier this morning when walking over *to* his home. Well over an hour had passed since then and the carriage was still there.

She would have thought nothing of it but for the fact it was a hired hackney. Why would it still be sitting there and not taking on new customers?

"Gideon, did you see that carriage over—"

"Yes, I noticed," he said, taking her by the elbow and propelling her forward. "Don't look back and don't point to it. As soon as we leave the orphanage, I am going to engage a Bow Street

Runner to follow Hawthorne around. I've had dealings with one of the best."

"Oh, who?"

"An investigator by the name of Homer Barrow. The men he has working for him are also quite clever and reliable. I helped him out on an important investigation last year, placed his men as dealers at one of my copper hells."

"*Your* copper hell?"

"Yes. Well, mine and Bonham's." He turned to her and groaned. "Those seedy gambling houses are a part of our business. It is how we built our wealth. Nor am I ashamed of it, so do not give me any moral lectures. I have never cheated anyone, and I do not allow anything beyond gambling to take place there."

"You seem to think I disapprove."

"Don't you? Shouldn't you?"

"Those in the *ton* think I should, but this is because they wish to maintain class differences to protect their privileges. Morality and righteousness have nothing to do with it. Selfishness and entitlement are their reasons. The ones fighting hardest to protect the benefits of their rank are those who are least deserving, men such as Hawthorne. They offer nothing helpful or productive and yet demand the most."

"That's remarkably forward thinking of you."

"You seem surprised."

"In truth, I am. Perhaps because I am coming to think of you as a *ton* diamond. You do have a lovely brilliance about you. If one were to put forward an example of why the nobility is better than us, they would point to you."

"You are full of compliments for me today," she said, feeling the heat of a blush sweep upward from her neck to her cheeks.

"May I ask you a personal question, Berry?"

She nodded.

"You are a diamond in every respect, and I mean that sincerely. You are one of those rare ladies who are lovely inside and out.

Why have you never married? You must have had a line of suitors out the door."

"I did," she said with a frown. "But my heart never sang for any of them. I do not think I will ever make a love match, not among the *ton* elite."

His eyebrow shot up. "Why is that?"

"Too many scoundrels like Hawthorne, men who are only interested in me for my trust fund."

"But there are good men out there, too. I've met several."

"I know they are not all fortune hunters. However, too many of them still think of marriage in terms of a business alliance. They will be kind and respectful of their wives, support them properly, and sire offspring to continue their line. But they also see nothing wrong in setting up a mistress and visiting her regularly. This is viewed as acceptable conduct for married men, but it is not an arrangement that would ever work for me."

"You would want your husband to honor his wedding vows and be faithful to you."

She nodded. "Since I will only marry for love, I would be devastated if my husband sought affection elsewhere."

"What surprises me most," he said as they reached her door, "is that you never found such a man. There must have been a dozen or more suitors in love with you and who would never stray from their marriage vows."

She cast him a wry smile. "If there had been, they hid their feelings well. It doesn't matter. I am not complaining about my situation. Nor am I worried about what's to become of me now that I know you are to be Lord Berwick's successor."

Her remark seemed to please him. He smiled. "Run inside and fetch your gloves and reticule. I'll wait until your carriage is brought around and see you into it before I wave down a hackney carriage for myself. In fact, I may walk over to that carriage standing next to Duchess Square."

"Be careful, Gideon. What if Hawthorne is inside and has a weapon aimed at you?"

"I'll be careful," he said, a little too confidently for her liking.

She did not belabor the point. Gideon had risen above his poor beginnings through intelligence and being quick on his feet. He must have dealt with the dregs of society along the way, especially when establishing his gaming houses. He knew when to be cautious and when to spring into action.

She hurried inside and fetched her things. Her driver had already been instructed to bring the carriage around. She saw him enter Duchess Square and pull up in front of her home as she walked out with her two footmen.

Gideon nodded his approval and walked her to her carriage.

A tingle ran up her arm the moment he took her hand to assist her into her seat. She thought he might have felt the jolt, too. His eyes had widened just the littlest bit before his expression turned unreadable again.

While his touch was pleasant, Berry was not pleased by her attraction to him. This would complicate their professional arrangement.

"I'll see you at the orphanage, Berry."

She nodded. "Be careful about that hired carriage."

"I will." He cast her a feral look, one that revealed he had escaped far more dangerous situations.

It hurt her heart to think of what he had endured in those early years. She had been raised to the manor born, indulged and pampered like a princess. He had been abandoned on the London streets at the age of three.

It was a miracle he had survived.

But this began to raise more questions in her mind. Who had delivered him to the orphanage? A child that young could not have known to walk to St. Brigid's on his own.

Was it possible the headmistress had a record of it in Gideon's file?

Her grandfather had established a strict procedure of keeping detailed records on each child. She was suddenly curious to learn what a young Gideon had been like. Was he quiet and withdrawn? Rebellious and a troublemaker? A good student? The files were confidential, but she would have access to them all.

Had Gideon ever read his file? Surely he had to be curious.

Even if he were not, should she not be curious on his behalf?

CHAPTER NINE

GIDEON'S HEART SHOT into his throat the moment he arrived at St. Brigid's Orphanage. The mere sight of the well-maintained gray-stone building stirred up a wealth of feelings, some he would like to forget. Perhaps this was the reason he had not been back in almost twenty years, or why he could not find the courage to step out of the hackney carriage just yet.

Most of his employees or tradesmen he hired were orphans out of St. Brigid's. But it was Bonham who had established the connection and always Bonham who attended meetings or conducted interviews with those orphans about to be sent out into the world.

Indeed, *he* never seemed troubled by returning here.

The reason could be that Gideon's friend knew who his parents were and knew they had loved him. He had arrived here because they had died and there was no family left to take him in. While they had both been raised in the orphanage, Bonham had not grown up with a gaping lack of knowledge regarding his existence.

Different circumstances and different perspectives.

Gideon shook out of his morose thoughts.

The building looked smaller than he remembered. But he had lived here as a child. Everything must have looked big and daunting back then. He had left this place at the age of fifteen along with the other boys his age.

Along with his best mate, John Bonham. The two of them had been best friends from their earliest days here and vowed to conquer London together.

Well, they had done all right for themselves.

Berry was standing on the front steps looking like a shimmering angel amid a circle of sunlight that brought out the vibrant gold of her hair and tinges of strawberry mingled within.

Gad, she was beautiful.

She had waited for him, perhaps wanting them to enter together. Not for her sake but for his. She must have thought her holding on to his arm would reassure him as he reentered a world he had longed to escape.

He laughed inwardly. This was such a Berry thing to do.

Her smile as he finally stepped out of his hackney and strode toward her was like a stunning burst of sunshine. "I just arrived here myself. You got here fast, Gideon. What happened with the hackney carriage lurking near Duchess Square?"

"The driver took off the moment I started toward him."

She nibbled her fleshy lower lip. "Then we were right to be suspicious."

"Yes, and my next stop will be to Mr. Barrow's office on Bow Street to engage his services. At a minimum, I'll request one investigator to follow Hawthorne and another to keep an eye on whoever comes in and out of Duchess Square."

"I'll let Lord Berwick know what you are doing when I see him tonight. This is a valid expense of the trust and you ought to be recompensed."

"I'll be at the museum soirée, too. And no, Berry, he is not to reimburse me. I do this for myself."

She arched an eyebrow. "It sounds an awful lot like you are doing it for me."

"I'm doing it for *me* because I want to protect *you*," he said with a grin. "Come on, let's go inside."

She held him back a moment. "Gideon, there is something more."

"What is it, Berry?"

She let out a soft breath. "There is something I wish to do for *me* because I want to protect *you*."

Bollocks.

She was going to do a tender Berry thing for him, and with it steal his heart.

Well, she had no need to steal it. He had already lost it to her, hadn't he? His feelings for her were becoming impossible to deny to himself, much as he wished he could.

"Would you let me look at your file?" she asked.

"Here? At the orphanage?" What was she trying to do? Grab his soul, too? "Forget it. Do not look at it."

"Why not? I would keep whatever I learned in strictest confidence. Upon my honor. And there may be something in there, a clue as to—"

"You'll find nothing about my origins. Do you think I have not looked? I was desperate to find someone, anyone who could tell me who I am or where I came from. It is too late now. I no longer wish to know. More important, whoever abandoned me does not *deserve* to know anything about me. I do not need them coming around and leeching off me once they learn I have made good."

"I see your point. I'm sorry I raised it, especially since it is so hurtful to you."

"It's fine. I don't begrudge you because everything you do is out of kindness. Let's meet the headmistress and then you can take me on a tour. I suppose you engage with the children whenever you are here. What exactly do you do with them?"

"I read stories to the little ones," she said with a smile, obviously liking her role here. "I chat with the older ones. However, I doubt the older children will pay any attention to me now that you are here. They will be excited to meet you, St. Brigid's greatest success story."

He did not know why he was dreading this moment. Perhaps because he did not want to disappoint Berry or those children.

Since coming out of the orphanage, Gideon had faced street gangs and some vicious thieves straight out of the Seven Dials. He'd taken beatings, usually giving as good as he got. He'd even been stabbed a time or two and had the scars to show it, one on his arm and one on his leg. He'd endured freezing nights, and days when he had gone without a meal. Not even a crumb to fill his belly.

But none of what he had faced felt as bad as his feelings upon returning here.

It wasn't the orphanage to blame. He had been safe here.

It was this rage he felt toward those who had abandoned him.

These feelings of anger and resentment had always simmered within him and now rose up like a fire-breathing dragon bent on destroying whatever got in his way.

Berry placed her hand on his arm. Just a light, reassuring touch. "Gideon?"

He nodded.

Her touch and the sweet sound of her voice was enough to get him back in control.

It was not well done of him. He could not walk in angry or he would scare the children, and most of them were scared enough as it was.

Like him, they had been abandoned.

Well, most had arrived here for reasons similar to Bonham's and knew who their families were. But there were others like him, forced to make up their own identity because they were just tossed away and given no clue as to their lineage.

He had survived and succeeded against all odds.

So why was he wallowing in rage and pitying himself?

"I'm good," he said quietly.

She cast him an indulgent and encouraging smile. "Not just good—you are the best."

Gad. Kitten.

He walked through the halls that had remained unchanged for decades, and spoke to the older children who immediately crowded around him. He asked them questions about their plans as they prepared to leave the orphanage. Most of them were scared, although some tried to hide it with obviously false bravery.

Some showed academic aptitude, and he made a note to discuss the possibility of setting up scholarships for those children who should be helped in continuing their education.

He was pleased to hear that almost all of those who were about to leave the orphanage because they had come of age did have a place to go. There were ten boys and five girls in this situation. Some would go into service as maids or footmen, others as apprentices to tradesmen. Five of them were to start in his employ.

"Unfortunately, we are always left with one or two who are hard to place," the headmistress, a kindly woman of middle age with graying hair by the name of Miss Prescott, confided. "It breaks my heart, but we cannot save them all, no matter how hard we try."

Gideon did not remember seeing the headmistress during his time here. She must have been hired not long after he had left. Perhaps starting first as a teacher. "By your comment, I presume you have a couple of misfits here," he said.

"Yes, just one this year. A very difficult child by the name of William Dexter. He is always angry, always the troublemaker."

If out of a group of fifteen children, all but one had been safely placed and given the chance to make a future for themselves, then this was not a bad result, Gideon thought.

But why not try for a perfect fifteen?

"Would it help if I spoke to him?" he asked. "Not today, for I must leave soon. But I could come back another day this week or next."

Miss Prescott was delighted with the idea. "Yes, please do. If anyone can inspire him, break through in any way, it will most likely be you."

"I'll do my best."

"That is all we can ask for, Mr. Knight." The headmistress bustled off to attend to other matters concerning the orphanage.

"She is a gem," Berry said. "She sincerely cares about the fate of each child."

"So do you."

She shook her head. "Yes, but Miss Prescott is here every day, working from sunup to sundown. I toss money at her and come by once a week to read to the little ones. It isn't quite the same."

"Both are necessary. Do not make light of your importance."

Gideon stayed on a little while longer to listen to Berry read to the youngest children. He felt a viselike grip to his heart as he realized her mother had done the same thing when she was alive, and Gideon had been one of those children sitting enthralled at her feet while she read to him, Bonham, and their mates about knights and magic, dragons and princesses.

He tried to recall her mother's face.

Sadly, he could not. What he remembered was her kindness, and how he and his mates always felt good whenever she visited them.

And here was Berry, another sweet angel carrying on her mother's tradition.

He saw the looks on the faces of these young ones. Yes, they were feeling the enchantment.

When she was done, Gideon took her aside. "I had better leave now. I dare not put off hiring Mr. Barrow, and it is already getting late."

"All right. I have a few more things to do here before I go," she said, suddenly fidgeting with a string of her reticule.

She was going to read his file. He saw it on her face. This was why she could not look him in the eye.

Well, where was the harm? There was nothing in there anyway. He had scrutinized his file, desperate to find the slightest speck of a clue, and would have known if there had been anything to discover. "Stay alert when you walk out of here. Make certain your footmen are aware when you step out."

"Yes, I'll make sure of it."

"Tell me if you find anything in my file."

Her face immediately turned a hot red and then her shoulders sagged. "I…I… You knew."

He nodded. "Your eyes reveal everything. Read it as many times as you like, Berry. There's nothing there. I have to go. See you at the museum tonight."

He strode out of the building and into the sunshine.

Since Bow Street was not far and the day was pleasant enough, he decided to walk to Homer Barrow's office. He was not certain he would find the man there, because Barrow was so often in demand and constantly called out on urgent investigations. But Gideon would leave word for him and ask him to stop by the Musket Club.

He was in luck, however. Homer Barrow was seated at his desk, finishing up a report for a client before heading out on another investigation. He was a big, portly man with jowly cheeks and a bulbous nose, but he had one of the keenest minds Gideon had ever met. "Do have a seat, Mr. Knight. What can I do for you?"

Gideon quickly told him the situation.

"I'll put Mick to following Lord Hawthorne. He's part bloodhound, and no one can shake him off the tail," Barrow said with a jovial smile. "George will keep watch on Duchess Square. Would Lady Berry be averse to taking him into her home in some capacity?"

"I am certain she would be amenable. If I am wrong, then my home can be used. It is not yet furnished or staffed, but my friend Bonham has been staying overnight to make certain no one breaks in. George can conduct this surveillance from there, too. It is well positioned on the square. We also have two very inquisitive neighbors who can be trusted to cooperate," he added, thinking of Berry's friends, Miranda and Gwendolyn.

"Sounds like we won't have a problem getting set up. However, it will take me a few days to put this in place. You see, we have other commitments these next few days, and I am already short of qualified Runners to handle them. I am stretched a bit thin right now. Can you afford to wait a few days? I would understand if you needed to seek elsewhere for these services."

"No, I'll wait for you."

"That is much appreciated. I'll do my best to get to you as quickly as possible. You did me a good turn last year, and I owe you the favor. If you feel the danger is imminent, I—"

"No, Mr. Barrow. We can wait another two or three days." Gideon raked a hand through his hair. "I'll advise Lady Berry to stay close to home in the meanwhile. On my recommendation, she has been taking two armed footmen with her whenever she goes out."

"That is good."

"She is attending a soirée at the British Museum tonight and will not cancel. But Lord Berwick will be picking her up in his carriage to escort her there, and I will be meeting them, so she should be all right. Lord Berwick will escort her home afterward and I'll ride with them for an added measure of protection."

Barrow frowned. "You're quite concerned about her."

"I am probably fretting too much. No doubt it is needless. But Hawthorne is refusing to move on after she has rebuffed him, instead becoming more persistent. Desperate men do foolish things, and I cannot shake the feeling that he is planning something nefarious."

"To abduct her?"

Gideon nodded. "But I don't see how that will help him, since Lady Berry will never agree to marry him. And he must know that neither Lord Berwick nor I will ever release a farthing of her trust fund to him. Well, it all may be nothing and I am worrying too much. I'll be with her this evening and tomorrow, as well. I've also put one of my lads to following Lord Hawthorne in the meanwhile. But the lad is a little questionable himself."

"Give me two or three days," he said, then smiled wryly. "I do not think you will mind staying close to Lady Berry until then."

Gideon laughed. "I don't suppose I will."

"You shall have my complete attention and my best men on the task within a few days' time."

Gideon thanked the Bow Street Runner and headed to the Musket Club. Since the streets were crowded and the carriages did not appear to be moving along these bustling thoroughfares with any speed, he chose to walk again. The club was not all that far away.

In truth, Gideon needed to walk off the turmoil of this day, most of all trying to ignore his growing feelings for Berry. He had listened to her as she explained to his painters how antique white differed from ivory white and why one color was perfect for the parlor and the other was perfect for the ballroom. Or maybe she'd said eggshell white for the ballroom. Who remembered?

Not that it mattered to him. What mattered was Berry turning his house into a home.

Watching her walk from room to room made him yearn to have her in his life, to make her his wife and build the loving memories he had always craved.

Well, it was all fantasy.

Wasn't it?

They hardly knew each other. He had to be certain of both their feelings before he ever dared say anything to her.

Assuming he would ever do such a thing. Because once words were spoken, they could not be unspoken.

There was a lot to think about, so many reasons why his dreams of making a life with Berry were purely wishful thinking and had to remain as nothing more.

Most of all, he would not do anything to jeopardize his position as her trustee. Lord Berwick was relying on him to protect her when he was no longer able to perform his fiduciary duties, and he could not fail this good and decent man.

Gideon entered the Musket Club through the back entrance and climbed the stairs to his bedchamber, hoping to avoid encountering anyone, not even Pudge or Joss.

His thoughts were still in a roil, not only because of Berry. Walking through the orphanage had hit him hard.

Staring at that gray stone building was a bit of bitter reality, a hard slap in the face to wake him up and remind him of all the reasons why Berry was a foolish dream that would never come to pass. He *was* those children, those abandoned souls who had nothing and came from nothing.

More important, the *ton* would view him as nothing despite all his accomplishments. He would never be accepted because nobodies did not marry princesses, and Berry was a princess if ever there was one.

"Mr. Knight, you look as though you want to punch a hole through the wall," Horace said, scurrying into Gideon's bedchamber with his freshly pressed evening attire. It was to be black tie and tails.

"I'm fine. Are you certain the museum event is formal attire?" Gideon should have thought to ask Berry, but his mind was on a thousand more important things.

Horace rolled his eyes. "Yes, I am certain. It said so right on the invitation, which you would have seen had you bothered to read it. Even if it hadn't, these events are always formal, whether held in a ballroom or a museum. Your tub will be brought up directly. Use this soap when you wash."

Gideon took it from Horace's outstretched hand and inhaled. "What is it? Not my usual sandalwood."

"No, this has a hint of musk. The women will claw you to shreds." Horace formed his fingers into claws and gave a purring growl that sounded like no animal Gideon had ever heard.

"Dear heaven." He tossed it back at Horace. "You use it. I'll have my usual soap."

The only woman he wanted clawing him was Berry. He wanted her nails digging into his back and her legs wrapped around his hips while in the throes of passion.

That was what he wanted.

That was the worst thing that could ever happen.

And it would *never* happen.

"Oh my. You look like you want to punch that wall again."

"Go away, Horace."

His valet ignored him and continued to fuss over his attire. Then the tub was rolled in and the new hires on his staff carried in the steaming water.

Once that was done, he turned once again to Horace. "Out. Come back in fifteen minutes."

"All right, sir."

Gideon sank into the hot water and closed his eyes for a moment. He allowed the heat to soak into his bones. He then hurriedly washed his hair and body, grabbed the towel Horace had left on a nearby stool for him, and climbed out of the tub.

After drying off, he wrapped the towel around his waist and then rolled the tub into the corner where Bonham had installed a drain so that the water could be poured out, sparing the need to lug buckets up and down.

He could have left it to his staff to do, but he was still on edge and needed to occupy himself with something.

He was about to reach for his comb when the door opened once more. "Horace, you're five minutes early."

"Good, then you and I will have five minutes to ourselves," Jasmine replied, slipping into his bedchamber.

"For pity's sake, what are you doing here? Out."

Her gaze was avid as she studied him. "Horace said you were out of sorts. I thought I would come up and soothe you."

"I do not need your *soothing*. Where's your benefactor?"

"Haverstock is in the cards room. He'll be occupied all night and I am already bored."

"Too bad. I'm busy."

"I can give you a quick—"

He held Jasmine by her wrists when she attempted to remove his towel. "That isn't going to happen."

"Are you spurning me? Who do you think you are?" She had

pretended to be hot for him, but that mask of adoration quickly fell aside to reveal her true character, which was petty and vengeful. "Let go of me or I shall scream."

"Go right ahead, and I will toss you out of here so fast your head will spin."

"I could cause trouble for you, Gideon."

"You would do this after everything I have done for you?"

She spat at him.

He hauled her to the door and called for Pudge.

"Yes, Mr. Knight," the reliable young man said, immediately lumbering up the stairs.

"The lady seems to have lost her way. Escort her downstairs. If she gives you any trouble, throw her out and never allow her in the club again."

"You'll regret this," she hissed, and stormed downstairs, clawing Pudge's hand when he attempted to escort her out.

"Angry cat," Pudge muttered, putting a handkerchief to the scratch that was beginning to bleed. "I think her benefactor is already regretting their arrangement. He rarely plays cards when he comes here, but he's settled in for the entire night, and I can see by the look in his eyes that he dreads going home with her."

"Watch her closely, Pudge. She's acting oddly and may do something foolish. Alert Joss, too. And put some brandy on that cut to cleanse it thoroughly."

He nodded and marched downstairs to catch up with Jasmine.

Gideon picked up his soap and washed the spit off his face.

Horace returned to assist him in dressing, as usual fussing over every detail, including the length of cuff showing beneath his jacket sleeve. But Gideon let Horace go about his business without snapping at him. After all, the lad was doing a good job in dressing him like a gentleman and took pride in his work.

In truth, he liked Horace. He was honest and loyal, not to mention meticulous.

"There is an art to being a gentleman," Horace always said.

"One must look perfect without appearing as though one spent hours achieving that perfection."

Horace was another of those good souls who would have been eaten alive if left to manage on his own on the streets.

In a way, Horace, Joss, and Pudge had become family to Gideon. Bonham, of course, was his best friend and the brother he had never had.

Jasmine could have become a part of their misfit family, not as his mistress or love interest, although he would be lying if he claimed never to have taken her into his bed. But that was long over, and she knew he would always protect her as a sister.

He had even offered her a respectable job. But she had chosen the life of a courtesan, servicing gentlemen who lavished her with expensive gifts until they got tired of her and moved on. She was exclusive to one man at a time, but none stayed long. She would then find herself another gentleman and negotiate her arrangement with him. In between, and sometimes during, she would offer herself to *him*.

He used to take her up on those offers in the early days.

Never now. Jasmine had a petulant nature and would often throw tantrums, but tonight's behavior was the worst he had ever seen of her. Tonight's incident felt different.

She worried him. Not for her threats against him, but for her own well-being. She could have confided in him and asked for his help instead of leveling her threats. Why this sudden leap from petulant to destructive?

If she was still here when he returned, he would have a talk with her. But he could not do it now, for he was already late for the museum benefit.

He had his carriage brought around. And indulged Horace while the lad fussed over his attire once more. "Enough. No one will care," he said finally.

Horace rolled his eyes. "*Everyone* will care. You are the outsider and they will all be looking at you, hoping to find fault. It shall not be with the way I have dressed you."

Gideon laughed. "All right. Point made."

His carriage drew up in front of the club. It was time to head to the museum.

Would Hawthorne be there and already bothering Berry?

CHAPTER TEN

GIDEON WAS RELIEVED to find Berry and Lord Berwick as quickly as he did amid the crush of guests attending this elegant soirée held in the grand entrance hall of the British Museum. The place had been decorated to appear as though they were standing atop the Acropolis under a night sky. If one looked up, one could see gods and goddesses in Greek mythology portrayed amid the stars.

But none of those goddesses were as beautiful as Berry. She was dressed in shimmering gold silk and had a smile for him that sparkled in her captivating eyes.

"Good evening," he said, bowing over her gloved hand and forcing himself to appear more cheerful than he felt.

But her smile went a long way toward easing the strains of the day.

He bowed over Lady Berwick's hand next, and then greeted her husband. "Has Lady Berry told you all about our fascinating day?"

Berry laughed. "I would hardly call selecting paint colors fascinating."

Lord Berwick politely disagreed. "It is the most exciting thing to Mr. Knight because it is the realization of a dream he once thought impossible to achieve. Is that not so, Mr. Knight?"

Gideon nodded. "I could not have said it better myself."

After a polite exchange of conversation, Gideon raised the

matter of scholarships for those orphans who showed academic promise. "We needn't discuss it now, but I wanted to mention the possibility. Something to consider the next time we meet." He then turned to Berry. "Nor have I forgotten that you had an idea for increasing the number of orphans St. Brigid's could take in."

"We'll put all of it on the agenda for next time," she said, obviously pleased he had remembered. "There is no rush, since this idea of mine has been simmering in my brain for years already. And there has been a lot going on lately that is more important."

"I'm sure the idea has great merit," Gideon said. "I am eager to hear more about it."

"But tonight is for us to enjoy this affair, drink lots and lots of champagne, and speak only of trivial matters," Lady Berwick declared, no doubt having had her fill of business conversations. Her husband and Berry must have spoken of nothing but the orphanage and trust finances while riding over here tonight.

Berry locked her arm with Lady Berwick's and laughed lightly. "Oh, you and I shall walk about the room and make snide comments on what the other ladies are wearing. Gentlemen, do you mind if we leave you for a few minutes?"

Gideon did mind, for he did not like Berry to be out of his sight for long.

Lord Berwick must have sensed his concern. "Berry, stay within this hall and come back to us immediately if you spot Lord Hawthorne in attendance. I am aware of what has been going on and am quite concerned."

She nodded. "I understand."

"I'm sure we will be permitted to tour the exhibits shortly, and I want you to remain with me and Lady Berwick during that time. Mr. Knight, would you mind accompanying us?"

"Not at all. It was my intention." Gideon turned to Berry. "You mentioned that you are a scholar of Greek and Roman art. Would you guide me through those exhibits and point out whatever might be of interest?"

Her eyes once again sparkled. "It would be my pleasure."

She and Lady Berwick strolled off.

Lord Berwick gave him a friendly pat on the back to regain his attention, for he had been staring at Berry. "You and she seem to have hit it off well. Perhaps a little too well?"

"She's charming. Doesn't everyone think so? You needn't worry that I will ever step out of line with her. I take my responsibility toward her very seriously. I won't disappoint you."

"I didn't think you would."

Gideon arched an eyebrow. "But you're just making certain?"

Lord Berwick laughed. "Honestly, I'm not sure what to think at this moment."

"What do you mean?"

"Come talk to me if ever your feelings for Berry become ardent."

If ever?

He was there already. He hardly knew her and yet he felt as though he had known her forever.

It was their orphanage connection. And a month of exchanging glances from a distance as he worked on his new home.

Even if they'd had none of that, five minutes in her company would have been enough to seal his fate. His heart had felt their connection at once.

"Oh, hell. Hawthorne's arrived," Gideon said, his view to the museum's entry unimpeded because of his height. "He's with those same three wastrel friends. If you don't mind, I would like to fetch the ladies and bring them back to our side."

"Go to it, Knight."

Berry and Lady Berwick were chatting with some of their Society friends, but Berry looked up at once when she saw him approach.

Her smile faded. "Is he here?"

Gideon nodded. "With friends."

"Oh."

"Lady Berwick, your husband has asked me to retrieve you and Lady Berry."

The ladies begged their friends to excuse them and returned to Lord Berwick's side.

Berry immediately went on her tiptoes and craned her neck to look for Hawthorne. "Where is he? Do you see him, Mr. Knight?"

"Yes, he's off beside the potted ferns drinking with his friends."

"Has he seen us yet?" she asked.

"No, but he's now scanning the hall and I'm sure it is you he is looking for."

"Drat." She edged closer to him. "Are we permitted to tour the exhibits yet?"

Lord Berwick nodded. "I see the guards have just let some of the guests through to the Greek statuary."

Berry smiled. "Perfect. Let's go."

Gideon was ashamed to admit he had never been inside a museum before. To say he was awestruck was an understatement. This was the history of the entire world brought to one place. He could wander through here for hours and never get bored. "Have you ever considered bringing the orphans here?" he asked Berry.

"No, but it is something to add to our list of things to organize. Perhaps take the children in groups of ten at a time. We can ask the museum's head curator, although I do not think tonight is the right time to approach him."

"Perhaps reach out to him in a couple of days," Gideon said. "He is too distracted right now by tonight's charity affair."

She nodded. "I would need trusted people to assist me in supervising the children, assuming he will agree to having a group of orphans here. A few of the wayward boys might wander off, and I cannot have them getting lost."

"Or breaking something priceless," Lady Berwick added.

They moved through the hall of statuary, Gideon enjoying

Berry's explanations. Each statue held significance. Some were connected to a myth that was usually bloody and had a bad ending for one or both star-crossed lovers. Others were simply a celebration of the human body, each featuring the male or female anatomy in accurate detail.

Since every statue had a story associated with it, they quickly fell behind everyone else while Berry related this wealth of information to him. She was gracious about it, indulging all his questions and not seeming to mind their slow pace.

Most of the statues depicting men had either a fig leaf or strip of cloth carved into the marble, but there was a row of three statues they now came upon that revealed every detail of the male anatomy.

Nothing hidden.

He smothered a grin upon noticing Berry discreetly peering at one of the naked male statues and then glancing at him.

He leaned in and whispered in her ear, "Yes, Berry. It is accurate."

Her eyes widened as she gaped at him. Then her cheeks turned quite a bright shade of pink. "I have no idea what you mean."

Berry may not have seen the male anatomy in the flesh, but she would recognize it and hopefully not be shocked by it when she finally did have her moment with a man.

Of course, he wanted to be that man.

Was their situation not a modern myth in the making? He was the mortal who loved the goddess he could not have, the mortal who ached to take her in his arms but knew that a night spent with her might lead to her downfall, and his.

As he contemplated their situation, Berry suddenly turned toward the entrance of the statuary hall and inhaled sharply. "Gideon, he's found us."

He followed her gaze and saw the lone guard trying to keep Hawthorne and his friends out. "We are only allowing one party through at a time," the man insisted.

This was not true, for others had been in here along with Gideon's party only a moment ago before walking into the next hall of exhibits. But Gideon understood the guard was simply trying to keep these drunken sots away from the valuable works of art.

He left Berry's side and stepped forward to assist the guard. "Hawthorne, go back to the main hall. You cannot stumble around drunk in here."

"Who are you to tell me what to do, you guttersnipe?" Hawthorne lunged at Gideon and attempted to shove him against one of the statues, but Gideon easily stepped aside and the viscount landed in a sprawl on the floor.

His friends then attempted to grab Gideon's arms to hold him down while they shoved him and beat him, but his years of street fighting served him well. He took a few punches that they never would have landed otherwise. But it was more important for him to push them away from the works of art. Once they were safely out of reach of the statues, he had little difficulty dropping them to the floor with a well-placed knee to the groin for one, tripping another, and a quick twist of the arm behind the third man's back to drop him to his knees in surrender.

Several museum guards arrived along with the head curator and a man that Lord Berwick quickly introduced to Gideon as one of the directors. "These men are drunk and belligerent," Lord Berwick reported. "They have no place here and need to be thrown out." He then pinned his gaze on Hawthorne and his friends as they staggered to their feet. "All of you are a disgrace. Rest assured, I shall be reporting this incident to your fathers. Have you no respect for anything? Or are you all so wasted as not to realize where you are or what you might have damaged with your reckless actions?"

Hawthorne cursed at Lord Berwick. "You'll regret this, you old goat!"

Gideon wanted to punch him, but Lord Berwick held him back. "You are the better man, Knight. He's merely goading you in the hope you will sink to his level."

The museum's curator and director thanked Gideon and Lord Berwick profusely. "I'll be more careful in the invitations sent out next year," the director said, shaking his head. "This night could have been a disaster because of those curs. We are so grateful to both of you for stepping in to assist when you did."

Gideon smiled and responded with something polite, but this night was turning out to be as unsettling as the day had been. First Jasmine turning into a banshee, and now Hawthorne being led out cursing and threatening him and Lord Berwick.

He did not care about the threats Hawthorne leveled against him. But a solid, respectable man like Lord Berwick?

There were certainly gremlins about tonight doing their best to cause mischief.

Berry and Lady Berwick stepped out from behind the statue of a naked man killing a lion. Lady Berwick ran to her husband. Berry ran to Gideon.

"What a scene. I'm so glad you were with us," she said with a tremor to her voice, and perhaps feeling the need to touch him to make certain he was unharmed. She took out her handkerchief and dabbed it at the corner of his lip. "Oh, those fiends. They cut your lip."

He took the handkerchief from her hand and glanced at the spot of blood on it. Hardly anything.

"I'll be fine," he assured her as she smoothed the lapels of his jacket and then fussed with his cravat before letting out a breath and taking a step back.

"Would you mind staying close to us for the rest of the evening, Mr. Knight? And riding home with us? Or did you bring your own carriage?"

"I brought my own, intending to follow you home. But I'll dismiss my driver now and ride with you, if you don't mind," he said, turning to Lord Berwick.

The shaken lord nodded enthusiastically. "That would be most welcome."

"However, I have not moved into my house on Duchess Square yet. Would you mind dropping me off at my club once we have Lady Berry safely delivered home?"

"Not at all, Knight. Glad to have you with us. You came to my notice because of your brains, but I am glad you also have the brawn to protect Berry."

"And to protect *you*," Gideon said with a frown. "Hawthorne threatened you, as well."

"Bah! He's a drunken fool and won't even remember what he said or did tonight."

Gideon hoped that was true.

"Berry," he said quietly, "do not forget that Bonham is right next door should you need assistance. Send Melton to alert him if you have the slightest concern."

"I will, but you needn't worry. Those oafs will go off to some disreputable haunt and not wake up until tomorrow afternoon."

He expected she was right.

Although he had come out of the fight with little more than a harmless spot of blood to his lip, it took him a while to calm down, because they might have hurt Berry. But he finally did manage to relax, and the rest of the night went smoothly.

Gideon made a donation to the museum's charity efforts, earning more gratitude from the director. "My wife and I are hosting a ball next month," the man, who happened to be the Earl of Stanhope, mentioned. "Expect an invitation."

"Thank you, my lord. I look forward to it," Gideon said, doing his best to mask his surprise.

Berry lit up like a little beacon. She looked up at him, her expression one of jubilant pride.

"He is now my neighbor on Duchess Square," she said to Lord Stanhope, gracing the man with one of her luminous smiles. "Send his invitation there…along with mine. That is, I hope I am invited."

Stanhope laughed. "It would not be a party without you, my dear Lady Berry."

Berry cast Gideon an impish grin when it was once again just the four of them standing together. "Hawthorne will be livid when he finds out it was his boorish actions that brought you to the notice of Lord Stanhope. And now you shall be invited to his ball while Hawthorne will be cut from the guest list, no doubt. Is it awful of me to cheer? But isn't this the perfect comeuppance for him?"

Gideon smiled. "Yes, the best revenge."

But this was also a watershed moment for him.

An earl had just invited him to a ball. No doubt the ladies on Duchess Square would all be invited, too. And Lord Berwick and his wife. He would have friends there to support him. He may even have a lord or two brave enough to acknowledge him, perhaps walk over and chat with him, or invite him to play cards.

Berry gave a light tug on his arm, her eyes big and shining as she grinned at him again. "A ball, Gideon. Your first. I shall have to teach you how to dance."

He had been taking lessons from Miss Feswick, a tall, thin woman who was all about discipline and never smiled. But she knew everything there was to know about these ballroom dances and had taught him well.

But to have Berry in his arms?

Let her think he was an ignorant clot. He was never going to let on that he was proficient and could probably teach *her* a thing or two about the seductive power of a dance.

"That's right," he said, frowning thoughtfully. "I shall require a lot of instruction. When can we start?"

CHAPTER ELEVEN

"YOU ARE AN utter cad," Bonham accused Gideon the next morning when he walked into his home on Duchess Square, which reeked of paint fumes. Not that Gideon minded the pungent scent, for it meant the painters were diligently turning this house into Berry's vision of his sanctuary. "Why did you not tell her that you already knew how to dance?"

Gideon rubbed a hand across the back of his neck. "Because I've only ever danced with Miss Feswick, and that cannot count at all. Why should I not practice with someone I might actually partner at a ball?"

"You could have told her you'd taken lessons."

"It did not seem relevant at the time."

Bonham shook his head and laughed. "You hound. You want her melting in your arms."

"So what if I do? And you are not to tell her."

"Me? Tell her?" Bonham laughed again. "I want in on this action, too. It will take less than ten minutes before Gwendolyn and Suzanna scurry over to watch you learn how to dance. I'm going to be there, looking my pathetic best and wishing someone would teach me, too."

"So, you are going to pretend you have never taken lessons, either?"

Bonham winked at him. "You catch on quick for a dumb orphan. Do you think Suzanna will mind teaching me?"

Gideon arched an eyebrow and grinned. "Have you gone soft for Suzanna?"

To his surprise, his usually irreverent, smart-mouthed friend turned serious. "What are we doing, Gideon? I mean, what good does it do us to fall in love with ladies who are so far above our station, we are more likely to catch a star in the heavens than ever catch them?"

"I know."

"These ladies are not the sort one claims for a quick tumble on a warm summer night. They are for marriage. Do you think you could be faithful forever?"

"With Berry?" Gideon groaned. "Yes, because she makes it so easy to love her and want to be with her. But how could it ever work between us? I would gain everything, and she would lose everything married to an oaf like me. Her friends. Her social standing. Her respectability. All of her hard work for the orphanage would crumble as her donors abandoned her one by one."

"I suppose it would be much the same for Suzanna," Bonham said. "I would not like to see her cast out of her social circle because of me. But it is nice to dream that all might work out, isn't it?"

"So long as we remember it is just a dream."

Bonham nodded. "These ladies on Duchess Square are gems, aren't they? Not *our* gems, however. Even if Berry and Suzanna felt about us the way we are coming to feel about them, how long before they realize their mistake and grow to resent us?"

"Enough of this maudlin conversation, Bonham. It is just a dance lesson. Let's not make anything more of it." Gideon had strolled in with good cheer and now felt quite upended, but he shook out of it because there were more important things to think about than love or marriage. "We can still enjoy these moments, so long as we remember to walk away afterward. If we view this dance instruction as nothing, then so will they."

Bonham slapped him on the back. "Right. We can do this.

How can two virgins possibly best us?"

But this was the danger, Gideon knew. Berry's innocence. Same for Suzanna with regard to Bonham.

It was so obvious neither of them had ever had a romantic encounter with a man.

And he and Bonham were two idiot males exhibiting every possessive, arrogant, primal behavior known to man. They may act like gentlemen on the outside, but inwardly they were caged apes desperate to break free.

And mate with their chosen female.

All Berry had to do was smile and the caged ape inside of him went wild.

Mine.

I want her.

I want to create little wild apes with her.

Well, wanting her and having her were not the same thing.

"Oh, hell."

"What's wrong, Gideon?" Bonham let out a groaning laugh as he peered toward the front door.

The sound of giggles could be heard in the entry hall. "Brace yourself," Gideon said with mirth. "We are about to come under siege."

In the next moment, five feminine heads poked through the open door to the ballroom.

Bonham waved them in. "Come in, ladies. What do you think?"

Berry was the first to stroll in, her smile one of sheer delight. "The paint color is perfect. What do you think, Mr. Knight?"

Gideon thought she was the perfect one, for he really did not care about the color of the paint. If Berry chose it, then he was going to like it. "Exactly what I had in mind."

"I see the floors are covered in cloths," she said, delicately lifting one of the coverings. "Perhaps we ought to leave the matter of flooring for another day."

He nodded. "Whatever you think best."

She laughed and shook her head. "Are you always this agreeable in the mornings? It is quite irritating, you know."

He grinned. "No worries, I am usually a growling bear. But it is very hard to growl at someone as kind and helpful as you."

"Ah, yes. As to that… We need to teach you how to dance. That is most urgent," Berry said. "All eyes will be on you at Lord Stanhope's ball. Most will be cruel, just waiting for you to fail. You must prove them all wrong."

"May I join you?" Bonham asked. "I know I will never be invited to a ball, but Gideon is not the only one who wishes to improve himself."

Suzanna stepped forward, or perhaps her cousin had pushed her forward. "Um, I can teach you. That is…if you don't mind my tutoring you, Mr. Bonham."

He smiled at her. "I would be honored. Thank you, Miss Carstairs."

Gideon let out a breath. Gad, what were they getting themselves into?

He had never seen such a look on Bonham's face. It was all there. His hopes and dreams, his yearning for Suzanna.

Gideon felt the same about Berry, but he knew this could only lead to trouble. Hadn't they just spent the last ten minutes cautioning each other?

It's just a dance lesson. Make no more of it.

Yet they were ignoring every warning.

And now he, Bonham, and the five ladies walked over to Berry's house for a morning of dancing.

Miranda sat at the pianoforte. "What shall I play for you, Berry?"

"Since the ball will likely open with a quadrille, that is the first dance we ought to teach the gentlemen."

It turned out Miranda was quite proficient and played beautifully. But this was what made these ladies stand apart from commoners. They were well versed in the genteel arts.

Gwenys and Gwendolyn joined in as the third pair, since it

was decided that Miranda's niece needed some practice for her debut, too.

"We ought to have a fourth couple, but we can pretend they are here for now," Berry said as they moved into position. But before nodding to Miranda to play a tune, she placed her hands on Gideon's shoulders and then ran them down his arms. "First impressions are important, so before you ever take a step, everyone will be looking at your stance."

"What is wrong with my stance?" The question was sincere, since Miss Feswick had gone over that lesson often enough and given his elbows a sharp rap with her baton if he did not have them pointed outward just the way she wanted.

Berry stared up at him with her big, beautiful eyes. "Your elbows are too far forward. Appearances are everything to the *ton*. One must work hard at looking casual, as though one had been born with grace and self-possession. Arms loose. Elbows only slightly forward. Back straight, but not stiff." She glanced at Bonham and nodded to Suzanna to get him in a proper stance, then continued. "Now present your right shoulder to the opposite dancer and *glissade*."

Berry and Suzanna showed them how it was done.

Then Berry started tossing out more French words that he had learned from Miss Feswick, but they sounded so much sweeter on Berry's tongue. *Chasse, jete, assemble.* Advance. Cross back.

"I may have to sit this one out," Gideon muttered, for Berry's figures were more complex than those he had been taught, and how could a man not look foolish while hopping about like a rabbit?

"No," she said sternly, "you are not a coward. The first comments Lord Stanhope's guests will make about you is that you are too common to master the quadrille. They will dismiss you immediately as unworthy. So you must get out there with swaggering confidence, look straight in their faces, and shove your gracefulness down their throats."

Gideon laughed. His little kitten was sounding like a tigress.

She tipped her chin up proudly. "You must show them all up. Oh, was that too bloodthirsty of me?"

He laughed again. "Perhaps the littlest bit."

She shook her head and sighed. "I do not want them to beat you down. I hate cruelty, and they will be so cruel to you if given the slightest opening. Shall we continue?"

He nodded.

If Berry wanted him to be a bloody hopping rabbit, then so be it.

He almost fell to his knees in relief when she declared success and moved on to the waltz. "This dance is perhaps the most important because it is just you and your partner, and any mistakes cannot be hidden or blamed on anyone else. Since the man leads, any false steps from you or your partner will be attributed to you."

"Got it," Gideon said, knowing this was his battlefield and he held all the advantage. Berry might have danced the waltz before, but never with him.

He knew just how to hold her and touch her. Knew how to make her follow wherever he led. The waltz was a dance of seduction, and he knew how to seduce a woman.

Berry did not stand a chance.

A blush stained her cheeks the moment he took her into his arms.

He knew he was affecting her because she began to babble, first with instructions and then with compliments. "It took me forever to learn these steps and complete the proper turns and twirls, but you caught on so quickly. Obviously, you have a natural aptitude for dancing. I fear I have two left feet."

No, he had an aptitude for seduction.

Berry was too innocent to realize what she was experiencing was passion. It had her completely out of sorts.

Miranda arched an eyebrow as she played the waltz on the pianoforte, obviously warning him to stick his prowess back in his breeches and just dance.

She was right. What he was doing to Berry was not fair. She was a kitten. He was a big, bad dragon.

But he was not unaffected, either. Bolts of lightning shot through him as he held Berry in his arms.

He never wanted to let her go.

His heart was pounding and fire tore through him.

She was talking to him, but he hardly heard a thing for the hot roar of blood rushing through his veins and clogging his ears.

Blessed saints.

He would ride through the jaws of death to hold Berry in his arms like this every night of his life.

"Are you listening to me?" she asked, frowning when he did not immediately respond.

He nodded. "We move in a circle."

"And?"

"Step forward with the left foot. Then a step to the side with the right foot. Then bring the left foot even with the right. Isn't this what I was doing?"

"Yes," she admitted. "I did not think you were listening. You seemed a thousand miles away just now."

"I am right here." Beside her, where he ached to belong. "What's next?"

"Then we step backward with the right foot. Then to the side with left foot. And bring the right foot to the left. This completes the box and we start over again."

Perhaps he and Bonham should not have mastered the steps so quickly, for Berry soon declared success and wanted to move on to teach them something she called the *Boulangere*. It sounded like another of those dances that would entail more hopping about like a rabbit.

Bonham suggested that he and Gideon ought to waltz with Gwendolyn and Gwenys, because wasn't it rude to leave them out? And did Gwenys not need to practice the art of the waltz, too?

Berry gasped. "Yes, of course. How neglectful of me! Never mind about the Boulangere. We shall leave it for another day."

Gideon and Bonham shared a waltz with Gwendolyn and Gwenys, and then Berry played the pianoforte while Miranda danced with Gideon.

"You are a cad, you know that," Miranda whispered in his ear. "She was melting in your arms."

He nodded. "I know, but I will never hurt Berry. I give you my oath."

This seemed to mollify her.

However, Gideon took her warning to heart. There was a very strong attraction between him and Berry, one he would have acted upon were he anyone of rank.

But he wasn't. He could not encourage these feelings beyond this harmless dance.

As the clock struck noon, he and Bonham bade the ladies farewell.

"Shall we resume the lessons tomorrow?" Berry asked, her gaze hopeful.

"I don't know if I shall have the time," he said. "Haven't I learned enough?"

She bit her fleshy lower lip, once again sending flames shooting through his veins. "You've only learned the two basic dances. You really ought to learn the Boulangere and the Sir Roger de Coverly, too. These four dances at a minimum."

Against his better judgment, he agreed. "Bonham and I will meet you here at ten o'clock tomorrow morning. All right?"

She nodded. "Yes, that's perfect."

He and Bonham strode back to his house.

"Gideon…"

"Don't say it. No, it cannot be real. This can only be a dream for us."

"But the Earl of Stanhope invited you to his ball."

"And will likely suffer for his kindness. You'll see."

"I hate those people," Bonham said with a growl.

Gideon laughed. "You are falling in love with one of *those* people. What you hate is that you are as good as they are but *they* will never believe it or accept you. I exclude the ladies on Duchess Square, of course. They are the kindest people I have ever met. But their acceptance is actually worse. It makes us believe that happiness is within our grasp. Do not be fooled. It is not."

Bonham raked a hand through his hair. "I think Suzanna might reciprocate my feelings."

"And what do you think her parents will say when she brings you home? You grew up in an orphanage and made your fortune owning gaming hells. Do you think they will allow this for their daughter?"

"No," he said morosely. "I suppose it is even worse for you because Berry's standing in Society is so high."

Gideon nodded. "And my circumstances are so low. Same orphanage and same gaming hells as you."

"Right, and you are the majority owner in all of them."

"I am only fifty-one percent to your forty-nine percent share. We could have been fifty-fifty partners. We *should* be."

"No, you have the better instincts. I don't ever want to be in a position to block your decisions. I know they will always be made with the best intent for both of us. More important, if I am gone, then I do not want any of my heirs able to interfere with your decisions. End of discussion, Gideon. You will not change my mind about this."

"All right." Although Gideon still did not agree with his friend's point of view. They were both dumb orphans, were they not? They had both put their hearts and souls into building something for themselves, had they not?

They walked back into his house and inspected what the painters had done. Then Bonham walked Gideon to his carriage. "So, what now? Are you going to go back to escorting Chloe and Jasmine? Accepting advances from the highborn ladies gambling at the Musket Club?"

Gideon shook his head. "None of that. I'll probably turn into a monk for a while. Maybe forever."

Bonham grunted. "Feeling the same way myself. Your house is coming along nicely, though."

Gideon laughed. "See you later. Try not to wreck the plumbing."

Upon returning to his club, Gideon completed tabulating the accounts, and then rode with Joss to the other gaming hells to do the same and check the inventory. He spent the evening also doing spot checks on the various clubs, something Bonham usually took care of, but he had been busy guarding Gideon's house.

It was well into the wee hours of the morning by the time he returned to the Musket Club and slipped up the back stairs to his bedchamber. All he needed was a solid three or four hours of sleep and he would be refreshed for the morning and his next dance lesson with Berry.

His decision to remain a monk, to have no one but her ever share his bed, had significant drawbacks. The first was that Berry was unlikely *to* ever share his bed. The second was that his knowing he would likely never touch her in any intimate way made him think of nothing *but* touching her intimately.

Indeed, he was trying hard not to think about her.

But there was just something about her body that shot heat through him at the mere sight of her, at every time he touched her. His dreams these past few nights had been filled with fantasies of putting his mouth to her soft skin and tasting her on his tongue.

She would banish him for life if she knew what ran through his mind.

"Bah," he muttered, needing to fall asleep and not dwell on her, nor dream about the glorious shape of her bosom or her long, slender legs.

He was serious about reforming his ways, for he meant to be true to Berry, and stay true to her until every last glimmer of hope she might one day be his was extinguished.

Why would he want anyone else when she was perfection?

Especially her breasts, which were ripe and round, although one could not tell by looking at her from the back. Her shoulders were not at all broad. He could easily span the width of her back with one hand. But when she turned to face him, there were those splendid mounds that were delightfully prominent compared to the slenderness of her hips and legs.

Perfection.

He awoke aroused, fortunately before Horace bustled in to ready him for the morning. He took care of his necessaries...*all* his necessaries, and had finished addressing his urges and washing up by the time there came a knock at his door.

He wrapped a towel around his naked torso. "Come in."

Horace marched in with bundles in hand. Polished boots. A cleaned and pressed jacket.

"Let me shave you. You look like a mountain troll with that dark stubble of beard," Horace remarked. "You'll scratch Lady Berry's cheek if you get too close with those bristles. And here's a crisp lawn shirt for you to wear. Now, for the cravat. This teal green with the light-gray swirls for today, I think. And this dark-green jacket. Buff breeches. Lady Berry will not be able to resist you."

"No, that's bad. I am not trying to seduce her."

Horace rolled his eyes. "If she responds to you the way you respond to her, then it is too late for both of you. Just get naked and enjoy the inevitable."

"Go away, Horace. Seriously, I'll shave myself. Nobody's clothes are coming off."

"If you say so. I give it a week before your resolve breaks. Do not forget that I am not long out of the orphanage myself. I've seen Lady Berry in action, walking the halls, reading to the little ones, and chatting with the older orphans. Her smile is a ray of sunshine upon that gray place, and she is cute as a button, isn't she? She even rouses my manly urges, and you know how improbable that is."

Gideon tried not to laugh because he did not want to encourage his wayward valet. "Horace, go away."

"I'll shave you first. As I said, mountain troll." Horace bustled out and returned with more clothes in a bundle. "These are for Mr. Bonham. If he's to be taking dance lessons, too, then he needs to look the part of a proper gentleman. I packed soap and fresh shaving gear for him."

"He'll appreciate that."

Gideon headed over to Duchess Square early, since Bonham would need time to get himself ready. Also, Gideon wanted to check on the progress of the painting and scout out the square to make certain Hawthorne or one of his lackeys was not lurking there.

To his dismay, that same hired hackney he had seen the other day was sitting in wait just outside of Duchess Square. Was Hawthorne in there?

"Brent, stop the carriage! I'm getting out here."

"Aye, Mr. Knight. Is something wrong?"

"Not sure yet. Keep your weapon at hand." He stepped down with his own pistol drawn and strode toward the hired carriage.

The driver let out a shrill whistle and then took off as soon as he noticed Gideon approaching. There did not appear to be anyone inside.

An empty carriage? A warning whistle?

Berry.

"Brent, summon Mr. Bonham and have him meet me at Lady Berry's!"

"Yes, Mr. Knight."

Gideon was about to pound on Berry's front door, but Melton must have been watching, and the door opened quickly. "Mr. Knight?"

Gideon strode into the entry hall. "I won't stay, but I need to make certain Lady Berry is all right. I saw that carriage lurking just outside the square again."

Melton nodded and hurriedly fetched Mrs. Bolton, but Gideon dared not wait politely when Berry might be in trouble. "Berry! Berry!" he cried out, rushing up the stairs.

He realized then that he did not know which door was hers.

One to his right suddenly opened and Berry hurried through it, her golden hair tumbling over her shoulders and down her back in a magnificently wild cascade. She was clutching her robe closed, since she hadn't the time to properly button it up. "What's wrong? Has something happened to your house?"

He breathed a sigh of relief. "No, I was afraid something had happened to *you*." He quickly explained about the hired carriage at the entrance to Duchess Square. "The driver whistled as a warning to someone and then raced away."

"Oh, I see."

"Are you all right?"

She nodded.

He marched into her bedchamber and strode to the window to peer down into the garden below.

She followed his movements. "Do you think someone was trying to break in here?"

"Yes, it is quite possible. I'm going to check outside your window. That driver was definitely acting as lookout for someone. And when I say someone, I mean Hawthorne. There's a trellis along the back wall of your house, and it leads straight up to your room. I'm going to climb it. Do not be alarmed if I peer into your bedchamber."

Mrs. Bolton rushed in and her eyes widened upon her catching sight of him. "Mr. Knight! You cannot be in here!"

"It is all right, Mrs. Bolton," Berry said. "He is not trying to peep at me, but he was worried Lord Hawthorne might have been attempting something improper."

"Such as breaking into your bedchamber? Or abducting you?" Mrs. Bolton asked, noticing Gideon's attention on the window frame.

"Have you found something?" Berry asked.

"No...maybe. I just want to make certain the latch isn't damaged."

Berry drew her robe a little tighter around her body. "Which would indicate someone was trying to break in?"

He nodded. "I'll have a closer look outside."

Bonham ran over just as Gideon came out of the house. "What happened?"

"I think Hawthorne was here. Did you notice anyone hopping over the wall or darting toward the mews?"

"No, sorry. I was talking to the painters as they set up for the day."

"Check out Lady Miranda's rear garden, and Lady Gwendolyn's, too. It cannot hurt to be thorough, although I'm sure Hawthorne has run off already. He must have had a prearranged pick-up location in the event he or his carriage were spotted here."

"Got it."

While Bonham ran off to check the other houses, Gideon strode into Berry's garden and looked for fresh footprints in the soil. It worried him when he found several. But they were smudged, so he could not tell if they were made by one man or two.

Hawthorne and an accomplice?

He slowly climbed the trellis and found a bit of cloth caught on an edge at one of the spots where the trellis connected to the masonry. It was only a tiny shred, so he could not tell if the color was a dark blue or a black.

Berry was good with colors and might be able to tell him.

When he reached her window, he rapped lightly against the pane to alert her that he was there.

Not that he expected her to forget and begin to disrobe. Ah, his eyeballs would never recover from the sight of her shedding her nightclothes.

Well, she wasn't undressing. He ought to have known better than to allow his thoughts to drift in that direction. But to his concern, he could not see her in the bedchamber.

Had she stepped out?

He returned his attention to the possible intruder and saw scratches and chipped wood along the window latch.

Dear heaven.

That toad really had tried to abduct Berry. Or perhaps he merely thought to break into her bedchamber and impose himself on her.

Gideon cursed himself for a fool. While he had been off having unmentionable dreams about Berry, Hawthorne had actually been trying to grab and defile her.

He glanced up at the heavens, thankful that Hawthorne had failed. What would he try next?

The Bow Street Runners would soon be on the trail of that wastrel lord, perhaps starting tomorrow. In the meanwhile, Gideon was not going to leave her side.

A sharp rap on the window startled him out of his thoughts and almost had him tumbling off the trellis.

Berry's lovely face stared back at him.

Big eyes. Big smile.

She opened the window. "What have you found?"

"Someone tried to break your window latch."

"Oh dear. Did you find anything more?"

He nodded.

She reached out to take him by the arms. "Climb inside and tell me."

He laughed. "That's going to raise eyebrows. A man seen climbing into your bedchamber?"

"I did not mean it that way. Isn't it safer than climbing down that flimsy trellis?"

"No," he said with a groaning laugh, for he was going to kiss her if she did not move her face away from his. "Get dressed and come downstairs. I'll meet you in your parlor."

"All right. Watch your fingers. I'm going to lower the window."

She did not bother to dress, and instead came scurrying down the stairs just as Melton let him back in. Her robe was held in place by a belt hastily tied around her trim waist, and none of the buttons were done up. Her hair remained long and loose, a bit of a wild mess that he thought looked exquisite on her.

"Well? What have you to report?" she asked.

"Melton, summon Mrs. Bolton and join us. You both need to hear this."

"At once, Mr. Knight."

Gideon found himself momentarily alone with Berry as he led her into the parlor. She took a seat on the delicate silk settee and looked up at him in that typically beautiful way she had of opening his heart. He found it hard to tear his gaze away from her.

Why could he not have been born respectable? He would kiss the ground before him and count his blessings hourly if ever he were allowed to wake up to the sight of her each morning. Big, sleepy eyes. Full, blushing lips. Bosom unbound by a corset. Strawberry-tinged golden hair.

He tried to remain outwardly calm. Inside, he was a screaming ape.

Her housekeeper and head butler rushed in.

"There were footprints made recently at the base of the trellis," Gideon began to explain. "Perhaps made less than an hour ago, because those impressions were left in the grass after the dew had formed. I also found this trace of cloth, like a scrap of a jacket or cape."

He showed it to Berry.

"Oh, dark blue," she said, holding it up to the sunlight. "I suppose it is a common enough color for a man's attire. I know Lord Hawthorne was wearing a jacket in this exact shade of blue the other day."

"There are also scratches along the windowsill and glass panes, and the latch on your window is broken and will need to be replaced." He frowned. "I'll send over one of my carpenters to repair it today. Did you hear anything last night? Or early this morning?"

Berry shook her head. "I had a headache, so I took a sleeping powder, which is why I am still drowsy this morning. It was such a stupid thing to do, I realize now. I rarely ever take anything to put me to sleep, but my mind has been racing and my head hurt. I did not expect Lord Hawthorne to try anything so soon after the incident at the museum."

"He knows his time is running out, and he hasn't a moment to lose. Mr. Barrow will soon be on the task and foil his efforts. Until then, you must all keep alert."

Mrs. Bolton and Melton assured him they would.

Gideon turned back to Berry. "I'm going to stay close to you for the rest of the day. All right?"

She nodded.

"I'll relieve Bonham tonight, let him handle our business affairs while I remain here to guard my house overnight. Of course, I'll mostly be keeping an eye on yours."

Berry put a hand to her throat. "It is a bit unsettling to know he was watching me and trying to break in. Even more unsettling that I did not realize it."

Gideon nodded to acknowledge her concern. "Do you want to spend the night elsewhere? Perhaps at Lady Miranda's or with Lord and Lady Berwick?"

She shook her head. "No, I do not wish to cause any of them trouble. I may have Harriet or Cora sleep in my room tonight. That ought to be enough to dissuade him and any of his friends who are foolish enough to go along with his schemes."

"I'll have the footmen armed and on watch tonight for any intruders," Melton added.

"Just make sure they do not shoot me or Mr. Bonham," Gideon said.

Melton nodded. "I'll instruct them to be careful."

"Well, I'll leave you to ready yourself," Gideon said to Berry. "I'll be just next door if you need me. Otherwise, I'll return at the appointed hour for our dance lesson. Or do you wish to postpone it?"

"Please, let us continue with the morning as planned. I rather enjoyed yesterday's tutorial. You and Mr. Bonham are quite able students. It took me weeks to memorize the steps to the quadrille, but you picked them up with impressive speed."

Mrs. Bolton eyed him suspiciously.

He cleared his throat. "Bonham and I might have had a few lessons from time to time, at the orphanage and at other times. And we've certainly seen people dancing. But you are also a very able teacher."

"I hope so, because I would like you to stay close to me at Lord Stanhope's ball. Will you claim me for two dances? A waltz and the supper dance?"

Gideon was pleased but surprised. "If you wish it."

She shook her head. "I do wish it, especially if Lord Stanhope has invited Lord Hawthorne to his ball. I'll have to make certain all my dances are claimed before he approaches me."

"I doubt Stanhope will invite him. You'll be safe enough once you are in his ballroom. And I'll keep watch over you whenever we are not dancing together. So will Lord Berwick. And I expect Stanhope will leave strict instructions for Hawthorne to be tossed out on his ear should he be so brazen as to show up there. In the meanwhile, you'll have me and Lord Berwick looking out for you. Soon, the Bow Street Runners, too."

"I do wish Mrs. Garland was feeling better. I've had to rely heavily on Lord and Lady Berwick to act as my chaperones lately. It is not fair to them."

"I doubt they mind at all," Gideon assured her. "Well, I think that is everything. Just make certain the entire staff is put on alert. I'll return shortly."

He left Berry's home and met Bonham coming out of Lady Miranda's garden. "No one's been back here or at Lady Gwendolyn's. You?"

Gideon told him what he'd found.

"The little toad," Bonham said with disdain. "Glad you showed up when you did and chased him off."

"It troubles me that he was here at all."

"I know, but you are on to him now. His efforts will come to naught. Do you still have Henry following him?"

Gideon nodded. "But I have no idea what that lad is up to. I did not see him by that hired carriage or skulking around Berry's home."

Bonham sighed. "Nor did I. Henry will turn up again eventually, I suppose. I'll ask the grooms in the mews if they noticed him this morning. And he does have weasel instincts. He knows how to squirm out of danger."

They strode to Gideon's home, which was a hive of activity. Men were working in almost every room, a jarring contrast to the serenity of Berry's house.

Not only were the painters working their way through the dozens of rooms, but the old service shaft had been removed and the new one was taking up most of the hallway while waiting to be installed. Two boys from the orphanage had become carpenters' apprentices, and were now here with their masters trying to assemble the pulley system. "Perhaps I ought to call on Suzanna and ask for her assistance," Bonham grumbled as one of the pulley pieces fell to the floor with a startling *clang*.

Gideon eyed the scene with concern. "I won't stop you. None of these men seem to know what they're doing."

"It isn't them. I think the instructions are wrong." Bonham rubbed a hand across the back of his neck. "Suzanna will know for certain. I might also ask her to help me with the pipe joints in the kitchen."

Gideon winced. "Don't tell me you've botched the plumbing again."

"I haven't botched anything," Bonham insisted. "I have been working on some plumbing innovations and had to tear up part of the kitchen floor because of it."

"And now you've reached an impasse? By all means, summon

Suzanna."

Dear heaven. Gideon hoped his precious sanctuary would not come tumbling down about his ears.

However, as important as his house was to him, Berry was far more important. It troubled him greatly that he had not seen Henry on the trail of Lord Hawthorne. True, the lad was not the most reliable. But nor was he unreliable. And as Bonham had remarked, the lad was a little weasel.

Still, he was worried.

Had Hawthorne and his friends harmed Henry? Was the poor lad lying in a ditch somewhere?

No, Henry was resourceful. He knew better than to be caught by some drunken lords.

But then, why hadn't Gideon seen him outside of Berry's home this morning?

CHAPTER TWELVE

BERRY'S HANDS SHOOK as she readied herself for the day, although she tried her best to appear composed while her maid fussed over her and styled her hair. "Stop squirming, m'lady," Harriet said, sticking a butterfly clip above her ear to secure the upswept curls.

She added a matching clip above her other ear and then stepped back to admire her work. "His eyes will pop wide when he sees you."

"Oh, for certain if I walk down like this," Berry remarked with a soft laugh as she stared down at herself clad only in her chemise.

Harriet set out two gowns on her bed, a dusky rose and a robin's-egg blue. Both were muslin with silk trimming. "Which one?"

"The rose," Berry said, reaching for it.

"I think the blue," Harriet countered. "It makes your eyes shine like moonlight, and he will be staring into them while he dances with you."

"But my eyes are green. What difference does it make if I wear the rose or the blue? Oh, all right. The blue." Berry always took Harriet's advice on what to wear because she had an even better eye for fashion than Berry had, which was saying a lot, because Berry was known to set fashion style among the ladies of the *ton*.

She looked forward to giving Gideon his next dance lesson and hoped Harriet was right about the shimmer in her eyes.

Her neighbors were already gathered in the parlor and fluttering around Gideon by the time she walked downstairs. Only Suzanna and Bonham were missing, and Gideon explained they were trying to untangle the mess made of the pulley system at Gideon's new house.

"If anyone can fix the tangle, it is Suzanna," Berry said with sincere conviction.

"We ought to practice the waltz again," Gwenys blurted, casting a moon-eyed gaze at Gideon as he took off his jacket and flexed his gorgeous muscles while rolling up the carpet in Berry's music room to create a dance floor. "It is ever so important."

Gideon turned toward Berry and arched an eyebrow, as though awaiting her instructions. She liked the way he sought her opinion and often took her advice.

He made her feel important. Valued.

Perhaps this was why she was so drawn to him. He did not regard her as a bit of fluff to be patted on the head and dismissed.

"Yes, it is a good idea. Gwenys, you dance first with Mr. Knight. This way, I can see where you each might need improvement. And it is good practice for him to dance with someone who is not as proficient as he is. My apologies, Gwenys. I do not mean to imply that you are not a proficient dancer."

"Oh, no offense taken. I know I am not very good at this yet." Gwenys smiled up at Gideon. "But you are a dream, Mr. Knight. You waltz divinely."

He turned to Berry and winked. "I have an excellent teacher."

This was why she had never fallen in love before, she realized.

The men she had met over the years, whether honorable or fortune hunters, viewed her as a means to a goal. They did not see her as a person with hopes, dreams, or talents. And they never considered asking for her opinions. To a man, they saw her as a wealthy heiress and salivated over the prospect of gaining access to her trust fund. The honorable ones might have felt a sense of duty to be a proper husband to her, but what did that mean?

Their idea of *proper* meant not running up large gaming debts and being discreet when setting up a mistress in a townhouse just outside of Mayfair. It had nothing to do with actually valuing her.

But Gideon?

She thought he might be in love with *her*.

Or perhaps it was merely wishful thinking on her part. She had always wished for a husband like him. One who was strong when he needed to be. Fierce. Protective. Thoughtful. Intelligent. Indulgent but never dismissive.

She knew he admired her.

He also made her feel safe, especially after yet another unsettling incident regarding Lord Hawthorne.

"So, is it to be a waltz?" Gwenys asked. "Now? Can we start now?"

"All right. Miranda, play a waltz," Berry said in order to stop Gwenys from bouncing up and down and whispering, *"Please, please, please."*

Gideon, as expected, took masterful control while he and Gwenys made their way in a graceful circle around the room.

Berry studied them closely. *Dear heaven.* The man moved with the grace of a jungle cat on the prowl. His every step and twirl powerful. Intensely focused. Irresistible.

He was completely gorgeous and charming. She could not blame Gwenys for being infatuated with him. Everything about this man was seductive.

She helped Gwenys by correcting a few mistakes in her posture.

"And mine?" Gideon asked.

She shook her head and smiled up at him. "Flawless."

He laughed. "No, seriously."

"I am being serious. The waltz was made for you. No wonder the patronesses at Almack's consider it so scandalous. Every young lady will swoon when dancing in your arms."

He shook his head and cast her a surprisingly endearing smile, all the more surprising because Gideon Knight was not at all soft. "It works both ways. A man might also lose his heart when holding a charming lady in his arms."

Although Gwenys was in his arms, Gideon was staring straight at *her*.

Tingles shot through Berry's body.

Did he mean it? Had he lost his heart to her?

Gwenys giggled, drawing her out of her thoughts. "It is transporting. I cannot wait until I am out in Society. I think I shall fall in love after every dance."

Miranda pounded a discordant chord on the pianoforte. "My girl, you had better stay clear-eyed and clearheaded or you will end up married to a scoundrel who will steal your wealth and your happiness. Is this what you want?"

Gwenys sighed. "No, Aunt Miranda."

"Then do not give in to silly infatuation. Marriage is a serious business. There is no easy fix to a mistake in marriage."

"How am I to know when it is right?" Gwenys asked, sounding quite petulant.

"First, it must *feel* right," Berry said, clasping her hands as she spoke, and trying not to look at Gideon because he had felt so right to her from the very first moment of their meeting. He was still looking at her in that soft way that was making her tingle.

Well, it wasn't really soft. More like hungry.

Devouring.

She cleared her throat. "It is important that you simply enjoy being in his company. But that is just a beginning."

"That's right," Gwendolyn said, now offering her opinion. "Does he listen to you when you converse? Or does he simply dismiss you? Does he take the time to get to know the things you like? Appreciate the things you know how to do? Will he be faithful to you and honor your wedding vows? Trusting in each other is most important. A man who keeps a mistress while he is courting you is unlikely to be faithful."

Gwenys appeared confused. "But so many men do this. Mr. Knight, is Gwendolyn right? Would you keep a mistress?"

"No," he said emphatically, and fixed his gaze on Berry again as though he were speaking directly to her. "If I were in love, she would be the only one for me. I would make her that promise and hold to it until my dying breath."

Berry's heart stood still.

Was he promising this to *her*?

"But not everyone marries for love," Gwenys argued. "Some must marry to bring wealth into their family."

He nodded. "But that is *not* you, Gwenys. Nor am I saying that you must dismiss anyone who is poor. It is all too common for a good man to inherit the burdens of a wastrel ancestor. What matters is finding a man of valor, one who will care for you, keep to his promises, and do all in his power to make you happy. All the better if he holds a title, I suppose. The *ton* has strict rules on who is deemed worthy and who is not."

"Those rules are antiquated," Berry said, indignant on his behalf because there was no way on this good earth that Lord Hawthorne was worthier than Gideon Knight.

"But those in power still follow those rules and punish those who do not," he pointed out.

Oh, he was still looking straight at her as he leveled the warning.

"Being cast out of Society would not be much of a punishment for me." She tipped her chin into the air. "My close circle of friends will not abandon me. So what if I am no longer invited to balls and musicales or al fresco picnics?"

"What about your annual charity event on behalf of the orphans?" Gideon reminded her. "It is not only you who will be punished if you stray from *ton* rules."

The air went out of Berry. "That is true."

He studied her for a long moment. "You mentioned that you had an idea to increase profits. Why don't we take a break from dancing and I'll listen to what you have to say over lemonade and cakes?"

Gwenys clapped her hands with glee. "Yes, an excellent idea. My throat is parched. Do you mind if we listen in, Berry?"

"Not at all. It is no secret." Berry rang for Melton to deliver refreshments on the terrace.

Bonham and Suzanna joined them, for they had just finished putting the lift and pulley together.

"It is all working perfectly," Bonham said with much satisfaction. "Lady Suzanna is brilliant and realized the mistake in the instructions at once. We could not have completed the installation without her."

Suzanna blushed.

"Nor could I have figured out the plumbing on my own," he added, casting her a sincerely warm smile.

"I enjoyed helping out," Suzanna remarked.

"Fortunate for me," Bonham muttered. "But we interrupted your discussion. What were you talking about?"

"We hadn't started," Berry said. "I was about to tell our friends about my idea for a doll to sell, the proceeds going to the orphanage fund. My hope is that the toy will appeal to all little girls no matter their family wealth or bloodlines, whether daughters of noblemen and gentry, or merchants and tradesmen. I hope it will appeal to all classes who might be able to afford these dolls for their daughters. I'd like them to be soft, something a little girl can wrap in her arms as she falls asleep. Not too fancy but not raggedy, either. However, I do not know anything about how to make them in quantity."

Gideon and Bonham exchanged glances.

Then Gideon leaned forward. "We can do this for you."

Berry's eyes widened and she smiled. "Truly? You have the facilities?"

"Yes. Well…we will have the capability once we convert one of our old gaming clubs. It won't be hard to do. The club is already shut down and we were considering selling the building."

"Or finding another use for it," Bonham interjected.

Gideon nodded. "The building itself is set up to accommodate rows of tables where seamstresses can work, and the light is good. If you are not too selective about your material, we can get some of it quite cheap. Cotton purchased in bulk. Remnants from upholstery shops. Linen. Lace. Chintz. Damask. Silks will be most expensive, naturally."

"Can you price it out for me?" Berry asked, excited that her doll project might actually come about. "Detailing the costs for each part of the process. The materials, the lease of your old gaming club space. The wages we must pay the workers. The shipping costs. Another concern is that these dolls must be distinctive, but I'm not sure in which direction to go for that."

"What do you mean?" Suzanna asked.

"Do we settle on one design and have all the dolls look alike? Or should we offer various choices?"

"More designs will increase the cost," Bonham said. "And shouldn't the excitement be around the one doll that *everyone* must have?"

"But how would Berry keep these dolls exclusive enough for the Upper Crust to desire but still affordable for the common man?" Suzanna asked.

"That is a good point," Berry said, liking the opinions that were being tossed around. "I would love every little girl to have one of her own, but it must also make business sense. The wealthy will not purchase something that a milkman can afford to purchase for his daughter. Or do we sell a variety of dolls, some exclusively for the Upper Crust? That would be a reason to make different dolls."

"But then it would not be something *everyone* wanted," Gwenys pointed out, reinforcing Bonham's point.

Berry sighed. "I had another idea about that, although it is something not commonly done."

"Go on," Gideon said.

"When I was younger, I used to make clothes for my dolls because I liked them to dress according to what we were pretending to do. Tea gowns for tea parties. Nightgowns for bedtime. Fancier gowns, even silk gowns, for the balls or theater or dinner parties I would pretend to hold. At Christmas, I would write out invitations to my Snowball Ball."

"Your Snowball Ball?" Gideon repeated with a gentle laugh.

"Yes, not the brightest name for it. I suppose I could have named it the Snowflake Ball," Berry admitted, wondering whether he thought the idea about different clothes for the dolls silly, too, "but I did not think of it at the time."

Gideon obviously thought her girlhood play amusing, but he seemed to be listening quite carefully to her ideas and business goals without a hint of dismissal.

"This is something I thought the girls might like," she added.

"Because you enjoyed playing in this manner?" he asked.

"Yes. It wouldn't be just about the dolls, but about making clothes for them, too. So, a wealthier merchant might buy everything for his daughter, an entire wardrobe for the doll. Gowns, shoes, gloves, hats. But a poorer family might be able to afford just the doll and the pretty gown she comes with. Our profits would go straight to the orphanage fund, assuming any of this undertaking is feasible."

She paused a moment to allow for Gideon's response, but he seemed to be lost in his thoughts. Perhaps he was calculating the costs of producing a wardrobe for the doll.

"This is the idea I had planned to raise with Lord Berwick," she said. "In fact, he and I have touched upon it a time or two, but his knowledge lies in investments. He does not know enough about actually running a business. Nor do I. For this reason, we never moved ahead."

"But this is so clever," Gwenys said with enthusiasm, "especially your idea about making clothes for the dolls. I would have adored dressing my dolls and pretending we are off to a tea party or a Covent Garden theater."

Berry smiled at Gwenys, pleased with her response.

"Was it lonely for you?" Gideon asked.

"Having to play by myself? Sometimes," Berry admitted.

"This is why I enjoyed my dolls so much. There were no other children on Duchess Square at the time, so my toys became my friends. Being young, I was rarely taken to public events. Nor did I go to boarding school with other girls my age. I had private tutors for everything."

"And no friends," Gwendolyn said with a shake of her head.

Berry shrugged. "Going to the park was the worst, for my governesses were so worried about being rebuked or losing their position if I came home with stains on my clothes or a scraped knee that I was forbidden to play with the other children. They would sometimes relent if the children were deemed to be of my family's stature—you know, sons or daughters of an earl, marquess, or duke—but few of them ever were."

"Oh, that is awful," Miranda said. "I never realized how locked away you were."

"Well, it is in the past now. It wasn't intentional and I was always treated with kindness. But this is why I looked forward to the times my mother would take me to the orphanage. There were so many children around my age there. Unfortunately, even then I was not permitted to play with anyone. That was such a frustration. But how could I ever complain when I was given so much and the orphans had so little?"

She cast Gideon a thoughtful look as she continued. "I believe that, in this small way, you were quite fortunate. You always had friends around you. Not that I am dismissing the importance of a family life, for I am not. And I expect the utter lack of privacy frustrated you to no end. But being treated as a princess also had its drawbacks. At times, excruciating boredom. Adults do not play with children the same way children play together. Mrs. Garland was no substitute for a dear friend."

Gideon raked a hand through his hair. "I'll price all of it out for you. Let me give some thought to the question of a single doll versus a variety of dolls. But I think Bonham is right. The more variety, the higher the cost and also the less special it might be viewed."

"So, this is your inclination?" Berry asked. "To start with one doll design?"

He nodded. "It might make sense, assuming the costs are not prohibitive and kill this project before it can ever get started. I like the idea about clothing for these dolls very much. This is what will set apart the wealthy buyer from the poor. They would all get the doll, but the emphasis will be on the extensive wardrobe that only the rich will be able to afford. This might be enough to create the necessary distinction between the classes. But who knows?"

"Oh, I think you have very good instincts. I trust your judgment," Berry said, relieved he would give her ideas serious consideration.

"May I add another thought about the doll?" Gideon asked.

"Yes, of course."

"Start with one doll. Call it the Berry doll."

"Named after me?"

"Yes," he said, grinning. "Big eyes. Wide smile. Flaunt the connection to you and your involvement with the orphanage."

Miranda frowned. "Oh, I don't know. Putting Berry's face on a doll could be viewed as scandalous among the *ton*, her stooping to common trade."

"Even though it is clearly designated for charitable purposes?" Gwenys asked.

Gwendolyn nodded. "They will blame Mr. Knight for lowering her standards and leading her astray. I love the idea, and Berry has just the sort of face that everyone adores, doesn't she? Don't we all just want to hug her? But perhaps name it something other than the Berry doll."

"It pains me to agree," Suzanna said. "There is nothing fair or right about it, for I love the idea of a Berry doll, too. But there are too many powerful people ready to tear her down merely because they are jealous of her. We must be practical and think of the orphanage's needs. What will best accomplish your goal of housing one hundred orphans? I don't think stirring up controversy will do it."

Gwenys let out a breath. "I would buy a Berry doll and all her wardrobe. I adore the idea. What little girl would not aspire to be you, Berry?"

"Oh, thank you," Berry said, blushing at the compliment.

"No need to make any decisions today," Gideon said, slapping his hands to his thighs as he rose from his chair. "Bonham and I will work on the pricing and costs. Lord Berwick will surely have an opinion regarding the Berry doll. He can decide about the risks and benefits once we present him with the numbers."

"A doll with my name isn't important," Berry said, although she was flattered that he had raised the idea.

Gideon grunted. "I'll let you and Lord Berwick decide this matter. You can give it whatever name you want, but I firmly believe the doll needs to look like you and have your smile."

She laughed.

"See," he said, casting her a surprisingly affectionate look. "Your smile is pure sunshine. No one can resist it. Mention that to Lord Berwick."

After another brief dance lesson, Gwenys and Miranda went off to run errands while Suzanna and Gwendolyn agreed to return to Gideon's shambles of a townhouse with Bonham to work on yet another plumbing innovation.

Gideon frowned at his friend. "I thought you took care of all the plumbing issues."

"I did," Bonham said. "But Suzanna has a brilliant idea about a piping system to bring running water directly up to your private quarters. She says the Romans had these types of water conduits in place a thousand years ago. One can see just this example in the Roman baths that still exist in the town of Bath, she claims."

"Those old Roman baths? Are you talking about a communal bathing system? In my own dressing room? Am I supposed to throw a party every time I bathe?"

Bonham chuckled. "No, you arse. Although you can take whomever you wish into your bath. But would it not be convenient to shorten the time and effort in getting water to you? As much as you need within reach of your hand."

Gideon sighed. "All right. Just show me the plan, but do not rip up any floors or walls until I give the nod."

"Got it," Bonham said, and walked off with Suzanna and Gwendolyn.

Berry was now left alone with Gideon. "Will you return to your club now?" she asked.

"No. I meant it when I said we would spend the entire day together. I am not letting you out of my sight."

"Because of Hawthorne? He's probably drunk by now," she said, not bothering to mask her disdain. "It troubles me that he got so close to me. In truth, it scares the wits out of me. What if I had slept with my bedroom window open? He could have climbed in, and I would have been stupidly unaware because I took that sleeping powder. What a foolish thing to do."

"It wasn't foolish. Just don't take anything tonight."

"You can count on that. I doubt I will sleep a wink this entire month. I pray he loses interest in me and moves on. But what am I to do if he refuses? How am I ever to be rid of him while my fortune remains a temptation to him?"

"Hopefully, his creditors will run him out of England soon."

"Even so, what's to stop another greedy fool like Hawthorne from attempting the same? I am a target for every cad and bounder so long as I remain unmarried."

Gideon frowned. "Are you contemplating marriage? Do you have someone in mind?"

"Yes and no. Yes, I need to think seriously about marriage. I never expected to remain a spinster. But here I am, approaching thirty and no prospects in sight. And no to your second question, I do not have anyone in mind."

"No one at all? Berry, rushing into marriage with the wrong man will only lead to a different set of problems. You cannot accept just anyone who asks you to be his wife."

"Then what is the solution? Am I to stay awake with a shotgun in hand every night?"

"Of course not. I'll be guarding you. No one will get into your rear garden tonight, or any other night. I have a clear view of your home from mine, as you well know."

Yes, a clear view.

And it worked both ways.

She and her friends had been ogling him all month long while he toiled on his renovations.

"How can you possibly work all day and stay up all night guarding me? And you run your clubs at night, so don't you need to be there?"

"I'll hire permanent guards for you. *My* expense."

"That is foolish."

"No more foolish than your choosing to marry in haste or out of fear."

She sighed. "I won't. But marriage is a sensible solution that I ought to pursue more seriously. That's all I mean by it. Since we are to spend the day together, we can think on it and come up with a workable plan to solve this problem. In the meanwhile, would you like to shop for furniture?"

He let out a breath and laughed. "Sure, why not?"

"Or we could select floorboards and stains for the floors of your house. But it must be marble tile for your entry hall, and I have an idea about that tile flooring. How tight is your budget?"

He shrugged. "Spend whatever you like."

Her eyes rounded. "No, really. Tell me what your limit is for the entry hall decoration."

"No limit. The moon's the limit. I am entirely in your hands. Spend whatever you think necessary. But if it will make you feel better, give me an estimate of the cost."

"I have to price the malachite. It is the most beautiful green stone you will ever see. I heard there was a Russian czar who had an entire staircase made of it. He believed it had protective powers to ward off evil spirits. I'm sure he made a lot of enemies who wished evil on him. The stone is also known to promote health, wealth, and *fertility*. So be careful if you bring a young lady to your bed," she teased.

"Berry, there will be no ladies brought here."

"Oh, I see. Yes, of course. You would take them to your club. Like the beautiful ladies I saw you with at the theater the other night."

"This is not a proper topic of conversation," he cautioned her. "Tell me more about the malachite stone."

"Well, I have no intention of using it on an entire staircase. It will be used sparingly on the design of the entry hall floor as an accent piece. Even that small piece will be expensive. But extremely tasteful."

"Everything you do is tasteful. I know I am in the best hands with you. Is there a shop we can go to that will have this precious green stone?"

"Yes, there's a warehouse near the docks. We'll find the malachite and wood samples, and whatever else we might need for the other rooms in the house."

"All right, let's go," he said. "But we'll use my carriage. Brent is my driver and he is most reliable in a fight. Still, bring along your two armed footmen."

"Do you think there will be a fight? It isn't a good part of town, but ought to be safe enough at this hour when the docks are so busy. The thieves and cutpurses generally come out later in the evening."

"It is Hawthorne I am concerned about. He might be following us. Well, it is you he would be following."

She looked up at him and cast him a fragile smile. "I'm not afraid when I'm with you, Gideon. You make me feel safe."

"Gad, the way you look at me," he muttered, casting her a wry smile in return as he caressed her cheek. "Oh, Berry. I am not safe at all. Careful, or I might be tempted to take *you* into my bed."

"I hope so," she whispered, and then gasped. "I mean… Oh my. I…" She clutched her stomach. "That came out wrong."

But she did mean it.

And now he knew how she felt about him.

"I…" She let out a breath that ended in a pained groan.

She avoided his stare by gazing directly into his chest, his broad and hard-as-rocks chest.

He tucked a finger under her chin and tipped her head upward. "Berry…"

She *eeped* and immediately closed her eyes because she was too ashamed to look at him.

"Berry, open your eyes."

"No. How can I when you now know how I feel about you? Although you must be used to ladies swooning over you. I've never swooned over anyone before. Not even an errant tingle. But I turn feverish whenever I look at you. It is awful. Tell me this is nothing serious and will quickly pass."

He gave her cheek another light caress. "Nothing serious? Are you talking about love?"

"Oh, you must not mention that word."

"Love?"

She groaned. "I don't know what this is. My heart races and I can never catch my breath when I am with you. I do not like this helpless feeling at all. I'm so sorry. This must be so awkward for you. It certainly is for me. I do not understand what is going on with my heart."

"It is no different than how I feel about you," he said, his voice husky. "Why do you think I said that I would never bring another woman into my house?"

"Because it is your sanctuary," she replied, her eyes still firmly shut.

"No." He ran his thumb lightly across her lower lip. "It is because of you, Berry. I have been in agony ever since meeting you. Here is my truth, and I can assure you I am not happy about it, either. I have spent a lifetime guarding my heart and ensuring no one would ever take possession of it. Five minutes with you, and all my defenses crumbled. You've had my heart since our first encounter. You are the only woman I ever want sharing my bed."

Her eyes flew open.

He cast her a wry smile. "I had resolved never to tell you, but it would have required me to lie to you. And I want only the truth between us, especially about something as important as this. I am in love with you. There, it's all out now. But we are going to do *nothing* about our feelings for each other."

"Nothing at all?"

"No, not a thing."

"Not even a kiss?"

Chapter Thirteen

A KISS?

Gideon knew this would be the most reckless thing he could ever do. There would be no taking back that kiss.

And where would they go from there? Into his bed?

He was aching to do this, but he refused to take Berry outside of the bonds of marriage.

And marriage for them was out of the question, at least for now.

He drew away. "There are a thousand reasons why a kiss between us is a bad idea."

"But you already kissed me that day I stormed over to your house to complain about the noise."

"And almost had a beam fall atop your head," he said with a grumble. "That kiss did not count."

"Why wouldn't it count?"

"Because I only kissed you on behalf of the orphans at St. Brigid's, and not for myself."

"It was still your lips."

"But not my heart, not at that precise moment. It took several days before my brain understood what my heart acknowledged at first glance."

Yes, this had been quite a shock for him. He'd never expected love to work so fast. Wasn't it supposed to start slowly and build over time? Instead, it had struck him in an instant, like a well-aimed cannonball to the chest.

He raked a hand through his hair. "Here's another truth...I wasn't completely honest about the dancing."

She shook her head in obvious confusion. "What do you mean?"

"Bonham and I have been taking lessons from a dance instructor by the name of Miss Feswick."

Berry let out a trill of laughter. "Old Feswick? She was my dance instructor in the year before I made my debut. I knew it! Isn't she awful? I thought the set of your arms was suspicious. Elbows pointed outward. Hands curled inward. But I will admit you had me fooled for a while. But the way you mastered that last series of hops, skips, and glissades was just too much. It took me weeks to get those figure formations just right, and you had the moves perfected within minutes."

"Why did you not call me out on the deception?"

"I thought you might be embarrassed if I did. After all, you have a bad reputation to uphold. How would it look if others knew that a big, strapping man like you who runs gaming hells and is not afraid to plunge into a bare-knuckle fight against multiple opponents was taking dance lessons?"

"You were protecting my reputation?"

She nodded. "I would never do anything to shame or hurt you."

This girl.

Did she have to be so sweet? He fell deeper in love with her every time they met.

"It is the same way I feel about your reputation, Berry. Your *good* reputation. I will never do anything to destroy it. Perhaps in time those in the *ton* will come to accept me, but they will not do so now. Lord Berwick played a dangerous game in appointing me his successor trustee, but I suppose he was right in guessing that having a business relation with you is something the *ton* will accept. But as to matters of the heart? They would sooner accept your having an affair with me than marrying me. It is the marriage that would destroy your good standing."

"You would marry me?"

He nodded. "If it were possible, I would already have the license in hand. But right now, we both know it is impossible. You would lose all hope of maintaining your respectability, and the orphanage would suffer for it. So, how can I ask you to choose me over the *ton*? This might change in time, but it would be too much of a scandal for you to survive right now."

He took her gently by the arm. "Gather your things and let's head to that warehouse on the docks. Is Miss Garland well enough to chaperone you?"

"No, I'll have my maid join us. Harriet will have to do for now because Miss Garland isn't getting any better. But I do not have the heart to pension her off just yet. She still thinks she is able to look after me."

"You are very kind, Berry."

"So are you." She smiled at him. "Look at all the orphans you've hired, and helped get their footing in this harsh world. I've never met anyone more loyal or considerate. But I will not reveal that secret to anyone."

"Do not make a saint out of me. I am not softhearted. I protect the people that matter to me, and treat people the way they treat me. If that makes you think I am kind, then so be it. But I am not a kind person. Come along, let's go to that warehouse. Do you have plans for this evening?"

"Yes, but it is just a dinner party with some close friends of Lord and Lady Berwick," she replied. "You needn't concern yourself about that. I know for certain Lord Hawthorne is not invited. The Berwicks will pick me up in their carriage around seven o'clock and drop me off at home again, probably around midnight. Since Lord Berwick can be as apishly protective as you, he will walk me to my door and make certain I am safely inside before he walks away."

"All right," he said with some reluctance.

He could not imprison Berry just to assuage his own concerns. And wasn't an intimate supper at some lord's house safe enough? He could even get in a few hours of work at the Musket Club while she was at her party.

"Berry, I'm not sorry I told you of my feelings. It is vital that you know how important you are to me. I don't want you ever hesitating to come to me or confide in me. I will do all in my power to protect you or help you work through a problem. But this is all I can offer you for now. Perhaps it shall always be this way. Only time will tell."

"I know."

She summoned Harriet, and the three of them rode in silence as his carriage made its way through the busy London streets toward the bustling dockside. Berry's maid was so enthralled by this unexpected outing that she spent the entire ride peering out the window to view the streets, which were teeming with activity, and paid no attention to Berry or him.

Gideon could have hauled Berry onto his lap and kissed her senseless, and Harriet would not have noticed a thing.

Of course, he was not going to kiss Berry. Not now or any time in the near future. No matter how desperately he wished to crush his mouth to her soft lips.

He wanted to do the right thing. He *had* to do the right thing for Berry's sake. But he was no bloody martyr.

Resisting her was going to be difficult. She'd asked him to kiss her.

He strained against the leather squabs, suddenly feeling too confined. How was it possible for a man to fall so quickly or so hard for a woman? Did everyone in love feel a similar physical ache from wanting the person they loved so badly?

They arrived at the warehouse, which was one of the largest along the docks. Harriet remained with the coachman, Brent, and the armed footmen while he and Berry walked inside.

The proprietor ran out of his office to greet them. "Lady Berry! A pleasure to see you." Apparently, everyone knew Berry.

"Mr. Dunning, how are you? And your lovely wife and

daughter?"

"Fine, fine. Excellent. How may I help you?"

Berry introduced Gideon to the man who appeared to be in his early fifties, judging by the sparse tufts of white on his balding head. Upon his hearing Gideon's name, his eyes rounded in surprise. "Ah, welcome, Mr. Knight. I did not realize you and Lady Berry were acquainted."

"Yes, he is my new neighbor and I insisted on bringing him here," she said. "Only the best will do for the houses on Duchess Square. We are interested in seeing your malachite."

Dunning led them to the back of his vast warehouse. "Here is my entire supply."

Gideon watched as Berry perused the samples and then charmed the man into reducing his price, although he did not think it was quite the bargain she believed. After all, Dunning had to make a decent profit. And Berry, as sweet as she was, came from money. The man had probably raised his prices in order to appear as though he would then lower them as a favor to her.

But Gideon was not going to suggest this to Berry and disappoint her. She looked so proud of herself.

After selecting the quantity and ordering that it be cut in a particular design, even giving precise measurements that she must have taken at some point when visiting his house, they moved on to the wood flooring. She selected a dozen samples that Dunning assured them would be delivered to Gideon's residence first thing in the morning. "Thank you, Mr. Dunning. And please give your wife and daughter my warmest regards."

"I certainly will, Lady Berry."

She walked out seeming quite triumphant about her accomplishments.

"How do you know Dunning and his family?" Gideon asked as they climbed back in his carriage.

"His wife is one of the orphans from St. Brigid's that my grandfather helped place back in the day. She went to work as a cook in the Dunning household."

"Ah, the way to a man's heart," he said with a chuckle.

Berry grinned. "Yes, precisely. Mr. Dunning fell in love with her cooking and then fell in love with her. It was a small household, and they were a family of tradesmen who did not find it necessary to put on airs. Mr. Dunning's father was not enthralled about the match, at first."

"Because she was an orphan and he had no idea about her family background."

"Yes, but he was not immune to her cooking skills, and she quickly won him over." She cast him a soft look. "I'm glad they found their happiness. They were a love match and still are after all these years."

Gideon was not about to pursue that discussion. Berry was too much of a romantic. Any talk of love, especially one like theirs that was not meant to be, would have her in tears. "You did not mention who was hosting this evening's dinner party."

"The Berwicks and I were invited by Lord Folger in celebration of his birthday. It is to be held at the Claremont Inn."

Gideon's back went up. "The Claremont?"

"Yes." She frowned. "What's wrong? You do not look pleased. It has an excellent reputation. I've dined there a time or two, and the food is quite good."

"I know." He and Bonham had attempted to purchase shares in the establishment and been rebuffed. The owner was an officious prig whose goal was to climb the social ladder. He did not want to be associated with orphans who also ran gaming hells. Gideon knew he would not be welcome there.

Berry studied him, trying to read his expression. "Oh, do not tell me. You own it, too."

"Quite the opposite. Bonham and I had hoped to invest in the Claremont, but the owner took an immediate dislike to us. We would be tossed out if ever we sought to dine there."

"Oh, that is outrageous," Berry said, sounding outraged and wounded on his behalf.

He shrugged. "I can understand his being wary of our gaming

establishments, but it was the fact we were orphans that had him looking down upon us as though we were filth."

"I am so sorry, Gideon."

His heart gave a tug, for Berry spoke with her typical gentleness.

"Not your fault. The problem is, I cannot be there tonight to protect you should Hawthorne attempt to approach you. I suppose I could remain across the street while you dine inside."

"That is ridiculous." She shook her head. "I will be safe enough in Lord Berwick's care. And you have your own affairs to look after. I've taken you away from your work enough today. It is just a supper party. Lord Berwick will see me to my door. Melton and my footmen will stand guard at my home. I shall be fine, and I doubt Lord Hawthorne will attempt to cause a scene at one of London's finest dining establishments, or think to break into my home again tonight. Even a fool like him will know to wait a few days until we are not so watchful."

Gideon still did not like it. "I wish you were going anywhere other than the Claremont."

"Lord Folger is hardly going to change his plans at this late hour. As for me, I shall never dine there again… Not until you own it."

He laughed. "That may be a while yet. The man is a pompous goat, but he knows how to run a business."

"So do you." She sighed, and her shoulders sagged. "I wish I did. I wouldn't be walking around in circles about my doll idea."

He nodded. "I am no expert in selling dolls, either. We'll both be stumbling around blind in this venture."

"At least you understand the pitfalls. I would walk right into them."

"Surely Lord Berwick has taught you plenty about investing."

"Yes, I suppose. Have you ever made mistakes in your business ventures?"

"Other than being cut off at the knees by the Claremont's owner?" He rolled his eyes. "Oh, yes. Fortunately, Bonham and I have only been burned once or twice, and those were small losses in our early days that we were able to absorb even back then. But the lessons were well learned and never to be forgotten."

They set aside their conversation as the carriage drew up in front of Berry's home. Gideon assisted Berry and her maid down.

Melton opened the door as soon as they started up the walk. "All's well, Mr. Knight," he reported. "I've had Somers and Wilbury patrolling the grounds since this morning."

Gideon nodded in approval. "Then I'll take a few minutes to see what is going on in my home before returning here."

Berry took light hold of his arm. "You needn't come back. I am going upstairs to take a nap, and then I'll be readying myself for tonight's party. You needn't fret about me. I'll be all right for these next few hours. Truly. But I don't mind waiting up for you upon my return. As I said, I should be back around midnight. Melton knows to let you in whenever you arrive. Take a turn about the house to satisfy yourself that I am safe. No one will object should you decide to patrol Duchess Square throughout the wee hours until dawn. But I think this evening will pass uneventfully."

"I hope so," he muttered. "Very well, I'll see you at midnight."

"Mr. Knight?" she called to him as he turned to leave. "Thank you for everything. And for every kind word you've said to me." She cast him another of her uniquely Berry smiles that seemed to light up his heart.

She was thanking him because he had told her that he loved her.

He shouldn't have told her. It was too soon. Too hopeless right now.

Perhaps things would change after Lord Stanhope's ball. But he doubted the *ton* would accept him so readily. It would take something more than mere attendance at one ball.

It wasn't even a Christmas ball. Those were special, and it was said that magic happened at Christmas balls.

He thought of Berry and her Snowball Ball. Gad, what a Berry thing to name it. She was such a kitten. He'd tear Hawthorne apart limb from limb if he ever hurt her.

He stopped by his house and found Bonham, Suzanna, and Gwendolyn up in what was to be his bedroom suite, staring into the commode in his dressing room. "What are you doing?"

"Studying your drainage," Suzanna responded, actually sounding excited about it. Odd girl.

"My drainage?"

Bonham glanced up and grinned. "Isn't Suzanna a marvel?"

Gideon laughed. "Yes, and since you seem rapt with this next project, I'll take care of the Musket Club tonight."

He should have insisted on Bonham taking over that duty, but how could he pull his friend away now? Bonham had been even more excited about Gideon's home purchase than he was. Of course, owning this house meant everything to Gideon. But it mattered to his best friend, too.

Perhaps Bonham was building up his own confidence to take the leap and purchase a home for himself. He had to be thinking about it quite seriously, especially now that he was falling in love with Suzanna. And meanwhile, he and Suzanna were wreaking havoc with the guts of Gideon's home with their new ideas.

Well, he'd let them have at it. Suzanna especially had a talent for this sort of thing.

"I'm coming back around midnight. I promised to look in on Berry when she returned from her dinner party," Gideon said.

Gwendolyn looked up at him. "Do not worry about her. Miranda and I have assigned two footmen each to patrol our grounds and Duchess Square. Berry's footmen will do the same. She will be safe with us. And the footmen know to grab that hired carriage if it shows up again. They'll hold its passengers until you arrive."

This ought to have pleased Gideon, but he strode out worried he was overlooking something important.

What was he missing?

CHAPTER FOURTEEN

BERRY CHOSE TO wear a gown of pale-silver silk that shimmered like icicles after a winter's storm. Of course, this was the summertime and it would be months yet before the weather turned cold. She chose a single strand of pearls to place around her neck and another strand that Harriet threaded through her hair.

To complete her attire, she donned kid leather slippers and lace gloves in the same silvery shade as her gown.

Harriet smiled at the end result. "You look beautiful, Lady Berry. I'm sorry Mr. Knight is not here to see you. I think he likes you. I'm sure he would fall in love with you if he caught a look at you now."

Berry blushed. Gideon had told her that he loved her. It was frightening and wonderful.

And also happening too quickly.

He was wise to express caution, although he really could have kissed her. Where was the harm in that? A kiss was not a commitment to marriage.

And marriage was the problem, wasn't it? They had to think this through quite carefully because of the damage it might do to her charity efforts for the orphanage.

Mrs. Bolton knocked at her door. "Lord Berwick is here, m'lady."

Berry shook out of her thoughts. "Oh, I'll be right down." She gave herself a final inspection in the mirror, and then stood at attention while Harriet took a moment to fix the stylish egret feather in her hair before she hurried downstairs.

"Good evening, Lord Berwick."

He cast her a weary smile. "Don't you look lovely, my dear?"

"What's wrong?" He appeared worn out and was unusually quiet as he escorted her to his carriage.

"Lady Berwick slipped on the stairs and sprained her ankle as we were about to leave," he said in anguish. "That's why I am a little late in picking you up. She's at home, soaking her foot in warm water, as we speak. I wanted to send our regrets to Lord Folger, but she put up such a fuss and would not hear of it."

"Oh, poor thing." Berry climbed into his carriage. "Are you certain it is only a sprain?"

"Yes, that much is confirmed. Our housekeeper has some medical knowledge and told me there was no break. But it was such an awkward twist and gave us quite a scare. I am assured she will be fine in a few days. Still, I hate to leave her in distress."

"You have a capable housekeeper in Mrs. Cummings, and a loyal staff who will tend to Lady Berwick. She is right about our not begging out of the dinner party. Lord Folger only invited twenty of his friends, so losing the three of us would be noticed."

Lord Berwick settled across from her. "That is what my wife said."

"And she is right," Berry insisted. "You will simply have to suffer with my company this evening."

He laughed. "You are always a joy. Tell me, what did you do today?"

Berry told him about the dance lessons and her trip to the warehouse with Gideon.

"You are even accompanying him to warehouses?"

"It is more that I am bringing him along. He seems comforta-ble leaving the entire decoration of his home to me."

"Well, you do have excellent taste."

"He seems to think so," she said with a satisfied smile. "But it is his home and he must have complete input, don't you think? He also wanted to stay close to me because of Lord Hawthorne."

She told Lord Berwick about her broken window latch and the hired carriage that had been lurking near Duchess Square.

"Oh, my dear. This is quite troubling. Something must be done at once."

"Mr. Knight has already arranged for the best Bow Street Runners in London to guard me. He insists on bearing the costs, but I will make him see reason. At the very least, I ought to pay half, should I not?"

"He can well afford the full expense."

"As I am coming to realize, for he did not even blink an eye when Mr. Dunning gave him the price for the malachite stone. But about these Runners—they will not be available to start for another day." She then told him about the precautions her friends were taking on her behalf in the meanwhile. "And Melton has my staff on alert, as well."

"Good." He pursed his lips. "You could come and stay with us."

"Mr. Knight suggested it, but I do not like the idea of bringing trouble to your door, especially now that Lady Berwick is indisposed. Anyway, Mr. Knight said he would stop by around midnight to make certain I am safely returned home from Lord Folger's party. Oh, it sounds scandalous, doesn't it? But he intends nothing improper. He is genuinely concerned about what Hawthorne might do. It curdles my stomach to think he might have gotten into my bedchamber while I was sleeping and completely unaware."

Lord Berwick nodded. "We must remain vigilant until that bounder comes to his senses and gives up on you."

"But this morning's incident proves he hasn't changed his mind. I do not think I will sleep at all tonight. Fortunately, it is only for one night. The Bow Street Runners will be on the job by tomorrow and I will be able to sleep without worry, at least for the next few nights."

"Are you certain they cannot begin guarding you tonight?"

"They were very clear about their prior commitments when Mr. Knight asked this very question. It instills confidence to know they are London's best and constantly in demand. Anyway, having them around is merely a temporary fix. It is Lord Hawthorne who needs to be diverted from his scheme, and we need to figure out how to do it."

"Obviously, he needs to be put in the direction of other heiresses," he said. "There are some who would accept him, daughters of wealthy merchants who are willing to trade their fortune for acceptance among the *ton*."

"Yes, and he is in line to eventually become the Marquess of Dundalk. That ought to be an attractive lure. Plenty of families would consider him an excellent catch for their daughters for this reason alone. I don't understand why he is so determined to have me."

"Well, the problem is that Hawthorne is a much-debauched wastrel and may not outlive the current marquess. This is why several wealthy tradesmen have already balked at considering him worthwhile. They would prefer to toss money at a man who already has a title. And I've heard the current marquess is about to remarry. It is merely gossip, but it would explain Hawthorne's sudden desperation. The marquess's bride is rumored to be young enough to give him sons."

"Oh, I see. Drat. This will lower Hawthorne's desirability even further," Berry muttered. "Well, good for the marquess. The world will be better off if Hawthorne never inherits the title."

"But this is why he is so determined to have you. He has his eye not only on your fortune but your family's dukedom. Your granduncle will not live forever, and you are quite possibly next in line to inherit."

Berry snorted. "I'm sure there are a few wastrel cousins who come before me."

"True, assuming they are still alive. No one's heard from

them in years."

"I hope they are alive and have ten children each. That will show Hawthorne," she said with a huff.

"I understand from your granduncle's solicitors that they are searching for two possible heirs now. We'll see what they turn up. In the meanwhile, you seem to be enjoying Mr. Knight's company. Tell me a little more about your day with him."

She stared down at her hands. "There is not much else to tell. He was attentive to me, but only because Hawthorne is such an evil little clot and will not leave me alone."

Lord Berwick frowned. "Was Mr. Knight too attentive? Did he also make a nuisance of himself?"

"Not at all." She glanced up at him. "He was perfectly charming and delightful, and no more attentive to me than to any of the other ladies. Well, of course he had to pay closer attention to me, because I am the one in danger, and did you not appoint him to protect me? He takes his duty quite seriously."

"Berry, do be careful. This man knows his way around women. I did not think he would ever dare try anything with you."

She looked up, startled. "He wouldn't. And he won't ever. You are right to trust his honor. He is one of the finest men I have ever met. I will always be safe with him. I only wish others understood how good a man he truly is."

"You think he is good?"

"Isn't he? You chose him as your successor because of his fine qualities. Will you deny that he is honorable? Trustworthy. Loyal. And smart, too. What is wrong with my agreeing with your opinion of him?"

"Oh, my dear. The difference is that you are in danger of falling in love with him. But you must temper that feeling at once. Nothing can come of it but disgrace for you. I like the man and respect his abilities. However, I will never agree to your marrying him. He came to St. Brigid's as a child wandering the streets. Who is his family? We do not know his background."

"Nor does he, but he's made something of himself despite all his disadvantages," Berry pointed out.

"He runs gaming hells."

"And yet you trust him with my welfare."

"It is not the same thing. One is a business matter. The other is a matter of the heart."

She sank back against the fine leather seat bench, feeling the weight of Society's rules upon her shoulders. "You needn't worry. He hasn't asked me to marry him, nor will he ever. And I am not ignorant of the impediments to a union with him. He has taken pains to point them out to me."

Lord Berwick gasped. "You've already had this conversation with him? Tell me, my dear child, are you in love with him?"

They arrived at the Claremont Inn just in time for her to avoid answering the question.

Lord Berwick was obviously concerned, and Berry knew their conversation would resume the moment they climbed into the carriage for the ride home.

How was she to avoid it? Perhaps she could pretend exhaustion and sleep on the entire ride home.

Since she had hours to come up with a plan during dinner, she set the matter aside and strode forward to greet Lord Folger and the other guests who had arrived before them.

Lord Berwick expressed his regrets and told everyone about his wife's unfortunate accident, a much-discussed topic of conversation as they sat down to dine.

Berry adored Lord Berwick, but she was relieved to find him placed at one end of the table while she was seated at the opposite end. An earl sat to her right and a viscount sat to her left. Both men were bachelors, and Lord Folger must have arranged the seating by design.

It was a thoughtful gesture, but both men were as dull as turnips.

Since Lord Berwick was studying her from the opposite end of the table, she made certain to toss back her head and laugh at their remarks that they considered witty but were mostly inane and occasionally crude, because they were both outrageously flirting with her. These men clearly assumed that a wealthy spinster in her late twenties must have taken a beau or two to her bed by now, and therefore saucy language was permitted.

But Berry hadn't any experience with men. In fact, she did not understand most of their lewd jests. She would ask Miranda to explain what they meant when she next saw her.

Miranda was the experienced one among them. She had been married once and widowed quite young, so was she not the logical one to ask about matters of intimacy? Berry dared not ask Gideon for fear he would march out in a fury, seek out those crude lords, and punch them in their faces.

Lord Folger's dinner party finally came to an end as the hour approached midnight.

Berry had eaten to the point of bursting and imbibed far too much champagne. This was another reason she wished to go home and climb under the covers, for she was sated, bloated, and tired.

Lord Berwick attempted to resume their earlier conversation as soon as they climbed into his carriage and the horses began their sprint toward Duchess Square.

The Claremont Inn was not all that far from Gideon's Musket Club. In fact, they were riding past it as Lord Berwick began to question her about Gideon's intentions toward her.

She glanced out the window and noticed the carriages lined up by the door of his club. The ladies looked so elegant.

How could Gideon possibly desire her over them?

They were traveling at a fast clip, and the club was soon out of sight.

Lord Berwick placed his hand over hers to regain her attention. "Berry—"

Whatever he was about to say was cut short when their carriage came to a sudden, jerking halt that knocked her out of her seat. In the next moment, they heard shots and shouts, and then the carriage door flew open.

Berry screamed as a masked man pulled her out. "Help! Help!"

A large hand clamped over her mouth. "Shut up or we'll kill Lord Berwick."

They could have threatened to kill her and she would have continued screaming. But to threaten this man who had cared for her like a father for all these years? The scream died in her throat.

Although she dared not cry out, she still fought to break free from her assailant's grasp, and had almost succeeded when another man came up from behind her and hit her over the head so hard, it dropped her to her knees.

A blinding pain shot through her temples. However, the blow did not knock her out completely. She was dazed and her eyesight blurred, but she forced herself to blink away the fog surrounding her vision because she needed to make out whatever details she could about her assailants.

"Take them both," the man who had struck her said, and she recognized Lord Hawthorne's voice.

He then grabbed her by the hair and yanked her head back so she was forced to look up at him. He called her a horrible, blasphemous word, and then said, "You won't escape me now, you stupid—"

He suddenly released her and fell to the ground while yelping in pain. He uttered more vile words.

What had just happened? Berry was suddenly free of his grasp.

A young man urgently whispered in her ear, "Quick, Lady Berry. Come with me. I'm Henry. Mr. Knight's man."

She staggered to her feet and leaned on Henry as they ran in what she hoped was the direction of the Musket Club.

She heard footsteps behind them and, suddenly, footsteps rushing toward them as Henry called out, "Joss! Pudge! Help!"

A man told Henry to "get her inside quick."

"Save Lord Berwick," she cried, and then collapsed at the club's door.

Someone picked her up and began to carry her up a staircase. "Berry," came the anguished voice she recognized as Gideon's. "You're bleeding, love."

"Gideon! Oh, Gideon!" She wrapped an arm around his neck and held on tightly while she tried to tell him what happened. The other arm hurt too much when she tried to raise it, so she left it dangling at her side.

"Hush, sweetheart. My men are after them. They'll save Lord Berwick. Just lie still. You're badly hurt. Henry will tell me what happened when he returns. He's leading the others to Lord Berwick."

Another fellow spoke to Gideon. "Shall I have one of the boys fetch Dr. Farthingale?"

"Yes, at once." Gideon shoved open a door and carried her inside. "Berry, I'm sure you know of him. He's treated the orphans at St. Brigid's. He's my doctor now, as well. And he's the best there is in London."

"But he must tend to Lord Berwick first. He *must*." She sobbed against his shoulder. "He's old...and Hawthorne's men were beating and kicking him. How could they be so cruel?"

"I don't know, love. But they'll get what they deserve. Pudge and Joss have gone to rescue him."

"And Henry?"

"Yes, love."

"He's the lad who saved me."

"Yes," Gideon said with a trace of wry relief in his voice. "Seems he was on Hawthorne's trail after all."

"He did not merely rescue me—I think he saved my life."

"I know, love." He set her down on a bed, a big, soft one that held his scent on the pillows. She felt bereft when he left her side. But he only moved away for a moment to issue more instructions to the club's staff.

He was so gentle with her when he returned. "One of my lads has gone to fetch the doctor. My cook is preparing a marrow broth for you. My steward will bring up more blankets for you.

You're shivering, Berry."

She gave a slight nod. "You mentioned someone called Pudge?"

He smiled. "He's one of my best men and will protect Lord Berwick. Wait till you see him. He's the size of a mountain. He'll give Hawthorne a good scare, and a good thrashing if the fool resists."

Berry nodded, but the slightest jostling made her wince. "I know Dr. Farthingale fairly well. He's been looking after Mrs. Garland, too."

"Has he, sweetheart?"

"For many years now," she said, her voice sounding raspy to her own ears, which were still ringing from the blow she had taken to the head. "I have every confidence in him."

"So do I. He provided excellent medical services to the orphans. Mostly after my time, but that's how I learned of him. He's treated several of my wounds over the past few years."

She reached out to touch his face. "You were hurt?"

"Nothing too serious. You'll be in good hands with him. But it could be a while before he arrives. I'll need to stop the bleeding."

"Am I really bleeding?"

"Yes, love. You must have been struck hard over the head with a cudgel."

"It hurts like blazes. Hawthorne is the rat who hit me."

"I'm so sorry, Berry." He plucked the egret feather out of her hair and set it on a night table beside the bed. "I should have stayed with you."

"Not your fault. You couldn't have come with me."

He moved away again and returned with a wet cloth that he gently used to dab the blood away, and then he set another dampened cloth upon her forehead. "I'm going to take off your shoes now, and then I need to have a closer look at your arm and shoulder. Does anything feel broken?"

"No, just bruised. I fell on my knees and then hit my left arm and shoulder when I stumbled to the ground. Oh, Gideon. I suddenly feel ill." She rolled over to the side of the bed and began to heave.

"Bollocks," he muttered, and grabbed the chamber pot from under the bed. "I have you, love. Let it come out. I won't let go of you."

"Don't. Please, don't ever let go of me."

"I'm right here, Berry. Always. For as long as you need me."

She expelled every bit of the delicious supper she had just eaten. When there was nothing left inside of her, Gideon set aside the disgustingly odorous chamber pot and eased her gently onto her back in his bed.

He tucked pillows behind her head so that she was not lying flat, and then dampened yet another cloth and dabbed cologne on it before putting it back on her head. "There, sweetheart. Are you feeling any better?"

"Oh, not yet." She rolled forward again, clambering over him as she aimed for the chamber pot and tossed up more of her supper.

When the heaves finally stopped, she collapsed in a sprawl across his lap. Her bosom rested upon his muscled thighs, and her heart was racing so that she thought he might have felt it beating against his thighs. It was quite scandalous, but she hadn't the strength to move off him yet. "I'm sorry."

"Oh, Berry. You needn't apologize. You have a concussion. Nausea is one of the symptoms." He turned to one of his staff members who must have walked in while she was heaving. "Horace, bring up some apple cider. And some oat biscuits."

"At once, Mr. Knight," the young man said, and hurried away.

"Berry, you might have to spend the night here." Gideon spoke so gently to her and stroked her body to soothe her as she remained limp and exhausted atop him. "You're going to have a wicked lump on your head by morning. Dr. Farthingale might decide it is too dangerous to move you in your present condition."

"But I must go home." Although, how would she manage it when she could not even lift her head and was speaking into his leg? "I'll be ruined if word gets out that I spent the night here. Oh dear. Others have seen me."

"Henry brought you to my club through a back entrance," he said, continuing to run his big, roughened hands over her body with exquisite care. "None of the patrons saw you, and no one on my staff is going to tattle. They would never betray you. But if gossip somehow spreads, then rest assured I will do all in my power to save your reputation."

"How? Nothing short of marriage would remove the scandal."

"Then I'll marry you. Assuming you will have me. As for me, I have been ready to marry you since the day you stormed over to my house to complain about the noise. To bloody hell what anyone thinks. I love you and will always protect you."

She had been hearing love declarations from gentlemen for many years now, but this was the first time the declaration sounded sincere.

Perhaps because it was given under the most unromantic circumstances possible. No moonlit garden. No gentle night breeze. She had just cast up her accounts and was drooling out of the side of her mouth while about to pass out on Gideon's lap.

He must have been thinking the same, because he gave a soft, laughing groan while carefully easing her back onto the pillows. "Not quite how I expected to declare my love for you."

"Worst circumstances ever," she agreed, casting him a wan smile. "Gideon, please tell me this feeling between us is real. Don't say things you think I want to hear because I am hurt and need to be reassured."

"It's real, love. And agonizing. I cannot get you out of my heart. And now to see you wounded like this… I wish I could take all of your pain upon myself."

"You needn't turn into a martyr."

"It is no more than any man would do for the woman he loved."

She burst into tears.

"Oh, Berry. I'm sorry. What did I say? I only meant to soothe you."

"You have. I've never felt such happiness," she blubbered. "These are happy tears because you are the best man in the world and you love me. *Me?* We should not be a fit at all. How can we be so perfect for each other? Yet we are. I love every moment I am with you. My heart is yours forever, Gideon. I want you to know this. Always. To the end of time. And I really think we ought to kiss again. But not until I've cleaned up and my breath no longer feels like a dozen dragons turned my mouth into a chamber pot for their use."

"You'll have your kiss." He wiped her mouth with one of the damp cloths, or perhaps he'd taken another clean one to dampen and use on her. She was going to go through his entire inventory at this rate. "You are such a kitten. That's what you are to me. A sweet, beautiful kitten with big emerald eyes and a tinge of strawberry in your hair. Bonham laughed so hard when I told him. But that's what you've done, curled up in my heart. It is you I want. Only you. I couldn't care less about your money. Give it all over to the orphanage, if you wish. That ought to keep them going for years, even if no one else ever donates another shilling. I'll provide for you, and you will never lack for anything."

She had never heard such ache in anyone's voice. "Gideon, there is one promise I must have from you."

"About your trust fund?" he asked. "I meant it when I said I will never touch your money. I'll put it in writing and have the document witnessed, if that is your concern."

"Not that. I want your promise that you will kiss me before I die."

He inhaled sharply. "You are not going to die."

"I hope that's true." But she ached everywhere, especially her head. And now her stomach was churning again.

"I've told you I would kiss you."

"And you had better make it the best kiss ever given in the annals of time," she said, feeling a more pronounced roil in her unsettled stomach.

"I'll do my best." He cast her a gentle smile as he gave her cheek a light caress, unaware she was beginning to feel nauseated again.

How could there be anything left to come out?

She sat up, hoping this would make her feel better. "Because I will never forgive you if I pass away and you don't kiss me."

His arms came around her, those strong, solid arms that now held her protectively. "I'll kiss you, Berry. I give you my oath."

"And not like that first kiss. I'll hit you if you pick me up by the armpits."

His laugh was mingled with a groan. "I'll wrap you in my arms and hold you tight to my body."

"You have a nice body."

"So do you."

"Yours is spectacular." She rested her head against his shoulder and closed her eyes, for this felt so good.

"So is yours," he said in an affectionate whisper as she nestled comfortably in his arms.

His body felt warm and masculine. She breathed in his familiar sandalwood scent, and especially appreciated the light citrus overtones that seemed to soothe her stomach as she inhaled it on his skin.

He ran his knuckles lightly along her cheek. "Keep talking to me. It is dangerous to fall asleep when you've been hit as hard over the head as you have been."

"I cannot think of what else to say." She had her eyes closed because it hurt too much to keep them open.

"Tell me about your childhood. Did your family always reside on Duchess Square?"

"Yes, mostly. But we often spent the yuletide with my grandfather on his estate. Occasionally, we visited my eccentric granduncle. Everyone would snap to attention and scurry to Broadingham whenever he commanded it."

"Why?"

"Well, he was the duke. No one was going to countermand his orders."

"You are related to a duke?"

"Yes."

Had he just gasped?

"He's a cantankerous old goat that neither my grandfather nor my father ever liked. Nor did they ever trust him, and never considered having him take care of me when he could not even take care of himself."

"Dear heaven."

She eased back a little, still secure in his embrace, and looked up at him. "I haven't seen him since my parents died. He never sent for me, nor did he ever make the slightest effort to come down to London to see me. He was too busy getting married. He's gone through five wives, although I think he never bothered to actually marry two of them. Why are you grumbling, Gideon? What difference does it make? He never wanted anything to do with me."

Gideon gently set her back against the pillows and raked a hand through his hair. "I don't know. I never thought about your ancestry. Not that it matters, I suppose. Dukedoms are not carried down through the female line. It is only the male heirs that matter."

"Um…well…not Broadingham. It is a ducal grant descended from Eleanor of Aquitaine's lineage. It is quite possible that the title will fall to me. It is one of those rare grants allowing a female blood heir to take the title of duchess in her own right. Did Lord Berwick never mention it to you?"

"No," he said sharply.

"Well, if there are no surviving heirs in my granduncle's line, male or female, then I would become the next duchess."

"Blessed saints."

"You sound angry."

"Why should I be angry? I am not angry. Not with you," he said, still grumbling. "Berry, you're a *duchess*?"

"Not yet, and probably never."

"But it is just as probable that you could be?"

She shivered. Why was he getting so worked up over the possibility?

When she asked him, he took a deep breath and let it out slowly. "I was found on a cobblestone street. I have no idea who I am or where I was born. I have been in turmoil, struggling to make myself worthy for *Lady* Berry. And now I am learning you, the woman who has captured my heart, could be the next Duchess of Broadingham. As if that isn't bad enough, you can trace your ancestry back to a queen of England. A *queen*, Berry."

"It isn't my fault."

"No, it is completely mine for thinking it was possible to overcome our differences and make a life together."

She burst into tears. "You said you loved me. I will not allow you to take it back."

"Berry—"

"And what if we were to have children? Would you love them any less because they are in line to become a duke or duchess?"

"Oh, Lord. Berry, that is even worse. A jest for the ages. That my son could be a duke?"

"Or your daughter a duchess," she reminded him. "But a child is a child and deserving of love no matter his or her lineage. Are you now putting up conditions to your love?"

"No, I love you and will continue to love you until I take my dying breath. That hasn't changed and never will. Same applies to any children we might have. But Berry, you are so high above me. You are the stars in the celestial heaven and I am a speck of dust within an abyss. How can I drag you into my dark hole?"

"I would go willingly. Persephone did the same for Hades. *Ow*. My head hurts. I don't want to talk about this. You are sounding too much like Lord Hawthorne now, spouting all these nonsensical rules the *ton* has created to keep us apart."

"All right, love. I'm sorry I've upset you. We'll work it out."

"There is nothing to work out," she said, allowing her thoughts to spill out, since he had told her that she needed to stay awake and talk. Well, she was going to give him an earful. "I am not going to marry some idiot lord because the *ton* has decided he is suitable. Who are they to guide my destiny? Or ever decide the rules of marriage when so few of them ever keep to their vows? Even the patronesses at Almack's are having notorious affairs outside of their marriage bonds. And yet we are supposed to bow to them and beg to be allowed to dance a waltz? Am I to follow the advice of people who do not love, honor, or ever obey the vows they have made to their spouses?"

She took a breath and continued. "And another thing… Once I am a duchess, assuming it happens, everyone in the *ton* will be tripping over themselves to make my acquaintance and curry my favor. They wouldn't care if I married a goat, a real live goat that bleats and butts and gives milk. That goat and I would still be invited to all the balls and social affairs held within the London Season."

"So, I am to be a bleating goat?" he said with mild humor.

"Oh, Gideon. You know what I mean."

"Yes, love. I do."

"If you care for me, you have to fight for me, because I will be fighting so very hard for you. And you should hope I will be that duchess, because no one will ever dare look down upon you for fear of angering me, a powerful duchess. Broadingham is a massive estate. Inheriting it would allow me to take in two hundred orphans with ease. But I am not likely to inherit it, so you must stop making a fuss about it." She started to cry again, not caring she was turning into a watering pot. "Why haven't your men returned yet? Do you think something has happened to Lord Berwick? Oh, heavens! Someone must get word to Lady Berwick. She sprained her ankle and did not join us this evening.

What am I to tell her? She'll be frantic with worry if he does not return home soon. Help me up. We must find him."

"Berry, lie still." He held her down gently when she tried to get to her feet.

"Oh, the bed is lurching. It feels like a boat upon a stormy sea."

"The bed is firmly anchored. It is your head that is reeling."

She tried to get up again, but that only made her want to cast up her accounts, which irritated her because she did not think there was anything left in her stomach to purge. Apparently, she was wrong.

There was more.

Gideon quickly moved the chamber pot in front of her, and then held her until the last of it came out and she had no more left in her.

She fell back onto the bed with a moan. "Where's Lord Berwick? He should have been brought here by now."

Gideon dabbed her lips with a damp handkerchief. "Joss and Pudge will give me a full report the moment they return. If Lord Berwick is injured, they will bring him here, and Dr. Farthingale will tend to both of you. If he was spared injury, then they might be escorting him home as we speak."

"No, he would never leave before seeing that I am all right. Why are they taking so long?"

"It's only been a few minutes, Berry."

"It feels like an eternity."

"Because you are worried about him. But fretting does you no good. It is also possible they are waiting for the magistrate's men to arrive and arrest Hawthorne and the idiot friends he enlisted to assist in your abduction. They won't get away with it. Hawthorne has no privileges of rank. His is only a courtesy title. And I doubt his family will come forward to rescue him from this mess of his own creation."

She cried again because her head really hurt. And so did her arm and knees.

"Berry, will you allow me to look at your knees? And your arm. I can at least clean out the scrapes until Dr. Farthingale arrives."

She was in his bed. Had thrown up in his arms.

And they had admitted their love for each other.

"Yes, do whatever you need to do. All of me is yours."

Someone knocked at the door as he was about to raise the hem of her gown. Gideon left her side and went to answer it. "Horace, thank goodness you're finally back," he said, dragging the young man in. "I need your help. Berry, this is my valet, Horace."

"A pleasure to meet you," she mumbled into her pillow. "Do forgive me if I don't get up."

"Oh my." Horace set aside the cider and biscuits he had brought in and stood over the bed to stare down at her. "I'll bring up a fresh chamber pot and find a change of clothes for you, Lady Berry. You cannot stay in that gown a moment longer, even though it is quite exquisite. Is it one of Madam de Bressard's designs?"

She nodded. "How did you know?"

"It fits you to perfection. She's the best modiste in London. I've brought you this cider, should you be thirsty, and some biscuits to calm your stomach. The club is mad packed tonight and everyone is dashing about like chickens without their heads."

Horace turned to Gideon. "Reggie's trying to handle the crowd at the door until Pudge returns. And Michael's walking the gaming floor handling his tasks and Joss's. The patrons are asking for you. What should I tell them? Will you make an appearance and mollify them?"

"No appearance tonight. Just tell them that I'm here but too busy to come down again tonight. They know I'm around because they saw me earlier, so no need to make up a story. Keep it simple."

"Yes, Mr. Knight," he said, and scurried out.

Once they were alone again, Gideon sat at the edge of the bed and raised Berry's gown to her thighs. "Both knees are badly scraped, love."

He left her side a moment to fetch a handkerchief from his bureau, since he'd probably run out of clean cloths to use. He then brought it over along with a bottle of brandy. The mattress dipped as he settled on it. "This will sting," he warned, pouring the brandy onto the handkerchief and then applying it gently to her right knee and then her left.

She had never experienced so much pain in her life.

It was not only that the brandy burned as he cleaned the blood from her knees—the burning sensation ran up her body into her head, which was already pounding and ready to crack wide open at any moment.

The stinging sensation of the brandy also revived her nausea. Gideon's valet had just returned with a fresh chamber pot when she began to heave again.

"Horace, bring it here!" Gideon cried, getting it under her just as she cast up her accounts again.

This had to be the second worst night in her life, the first being when she had learned her parents had died. No child should ever hear such news. She had never been so scared, only eight years old and suddenly alone in the world. But Lord and Lady Berwick had come quickly to take charge, to take her into their hearts and into their family.

She needed to know that Lord Berwick was all right.

Why hadn't anyone sent word yet?

She finished heaving and sank back against the pillows, struggling not to cry again.

"Berry," Gideon said softly, "take a sip of cider."

"No." She was afraid to drink or eat because she did not think she could hold anything down yet. Where was Dr. Farthingale? "My head hurts so much."

"I know, love. Just lie back. The doctor will be here very soon."

But he sounded worried.

So was she. Not for herself, but for Lord Berwick.

Where was he?

"Gideon, please. Is there something you are not telling me? Why aren't your men back yet?"

Chapter Fifteen

"They must be at the magistrate's office giving statements." Gideon hoped this was enough of a response to Berry's question to calm her. "I'm certain my men and Lord Berwick will turn up soon. These things take time."

But he was worried and grew more so as the minutes ticked by and he heard nothing.

Berry was right. Why *hadn't* his men returned?

He dared not leave her side to find out.

Horace had gone out to scout the streets, but came back to report there was no sign of Lord Berwick, his carriage, the assailants, or Joss, Pudge, and Henry anywhere nearby.

As the night wore on, Gideon knew he could no longer delay reporting the incident to Lady Berwick or Berry's staff. He sent one of his lads off to the Berwick residence with a hastily written note to assure her that they were doing everything in their power to get her husband safely returned home.

He sent another lad to report the same to Melton, and then instructed him to summon Bonham, too. With all the upheaval going on, Gideon needed his best friend to take on his share of the work at the club, at least for the next few hours while he joined in the search for Lord Berwick.

The Musket Club was their headquarters and where everyone reported to him and Bonham, but it was also their practice to personally go to each of their other clubs in the morning to make certain all was in order. He and Bonham had established an efficient routine. While Gideon tabulated the previous night's take and expenses, Bonham would inventory the stock at each gaming hell, taking account of all supplies, such as the liquor, food, linens, silverware, glasses, decks of cards, chips, and the like.

This also kept those in their employ honest. In truth, most already were. But every once in a while someone succumbed to temptation and attempted to steal. Bonham was very good at sensing when something was off.

Gideon now needed him to take over the entirety of the work while he joined in the search for Berry's beloved trustee. Hopefully, it would not require more than a morning before they fell back into their usual routine.

Berry drifted off to sleep while he waited for the doctor and Bonham to arrive. He did not know why his friend had been so keen to guard Gideon's new home. Gideon had intended on being the one to sleep there every night, but Bonham had wanted to do it, even insisted on it.

Perhaps he needed to experience the feel of living on his own before taking a similar leap and purchasing a home for himself.

All they had ever known was the orphanage, where they'd slept twenty boys to a large room. Their quarters at the club were only a small improvement. They each had their own bedchamber and office. But their suites contained no kitchen or library or parlor, just a place to sleep and a place to work above the gaming hall.

Gideon's new residence would now be left vulnerable with Bonham on his way here and no one to guard it, but Gideon did not care. Anything stolen could be replaced. Anything damaged could be repaired.

He glanced at Berry, who was now curled up and softly crying in his bed. He dreaded leaving her for even a moment, but knew she wanted everything possible done to find Lord Berwick and get him safely back home.

Gideon noticed Berry was beginning to shiver. "Blast," he

muttered, wrapping her securely in a blanket before taking her in his arms and adding the heat of his body to keep her warm. She needed the heat, but he also needed to hold her because he was so worried about her. "Berry?"

She would not open her eyes or stop shivering.

He heard a quick rap on the door, and then Horace scurried in with Dr. Farthingale close behind. Gideon let out a sigh of relief. "Thank goodness."

"What happened?" Dr. Farthingale asked, obviously surprised to find Berry in Gideon's arms.

Gideon gently set her back upon the pillows and rose while quickly recounting what Berry had told him.

"Hawthorne? That man is bad news," the doctor muttered, setting down his medical bag and removing a few instruments. He glanced at Berry's arm and knees, frowned because she was still shivering, and then concentrated on her head injury. "Has she been throwing up?"

Gideon nodded. "Four times so far."

The doctor made a noncommittal grunt in response. Gideon looked on as he roused Berry and tested her vision. "How many fingers am I holding up, Lady Berry?"

Horace was standing beside Gideon and muttered, "Thank goodness," when Berry responded correctly. She responded well to the other vision tests, seeming able to follow the movements of the doctor's finger with her left eye and her right.

Dr. Farthingale then proceeded to test her hearing, which also seemed good, except Berry said she still felt a ringing in her ears. "It will pass in a few days," he assured her. "I have some exercises that will work if it doesn't. But there'll be no exercising for you just yet. I do not want you moving about at all."

He then tested Berry's memory and ability to concentrate. She was a little foggy but managed to come up with the answers to his questions, some of which required memorization and retention skills.

The doctor seemed pleased and assured Gideon that she had

done very well.

"Even if it took her a little while longer than usual to respond?"

"Yes, even so."

"What do we need to do to care for her?" Gideon asked.

"Very little anyone can do. Just keep her warm and comfortable. Watch her to make certain her symptoms do not worsen. Summon me immediately if they do. She needs to rest. That is the best medicine for her. Do not allow her out of bed. No walking around until I check on her again. She hasn't gotten her balance back yet, and might not for several days. No lifting heavy objects—no lifting even *light* objects for her right now. No reading, because even that will strain her eyes and impede her brain's recovery."

Gideon was surprised. "Even reading?"

"Yes, complete rest is the most important thing her brain and body need to recover."

"Then should I keep her here?"

Dr. Farthingale winced. "I understand your concern. Remaining here is not ideal, but I dare not have her moved just yet. The effort of getting dressed and taking a carriage ride might cause her more damage, and she's quite fragile right now. I think it will be at least two days before you can safely take her home."

"All right. My staff and I will do our best to keep her whereabouts quiet. Will you stay a little while longer, doctor?" Gideon then explained about Lord Berwick. "I'm worried he was also hurt. But I have no idea where he is or where my men have gone. Hawthorne may have hijacked his carriage and could be holding him hostage. My men are likely chasing after them. But who knows? I'd bring reinforcements if I knew where to start looking."

"You mentioned hiring that Bow Street investigator, Homer Barrow. I think this is an urgent enough matter to summon him immediately. He makes it his business to know everything that is going on in London."

Gideon nodded. He had contemplated calling upon Barrow,

especially as the hour passed and he had still heard nothing from Pudge, Joss, or Henry. But as diligent as Homer Barrow was, would he be in his office in the wee hours of the morning? And the man was due to call upon Gideon at eight o'clock this morning to start guarding Berry anyway.

It was only a matter of a few hours. But every minute counted now that Hawthorne had attacked Berry and Lord Berwick.

Bonham arrived as he was discussing the situation with Dr. Farthingale. Gideon quickly filled his friend in on all that had happened.

"Blessed saints! I'll kill that vile Hawthorne with my bare hands."

Gideon nodded. "You may have whatever remains of him after I am through."

Since the doctor agreed to stay on and watch Berry for a few more hours, Gideon left Bonham in charge of the club and wasted no time in seeking out Barrow. It was still the middle of the night, but he thought it was possible someone might be in the Bow Street office, since much of their investigative work entailed night surveillance.

Besides, he had no idea where Barrow resided. If the office was closed, Gideon would have no choice but to wait until morning to meet with him.

He had Brent bring him over in his carriage. If there was searching to be done, they might as well tear around London in his conveyance. Both he and Brent were handy with weapons, and he hoped the villains and scoundrels they encountered in the more dangerous areas would recognize his carriage and not cause trouble as he rode through their territory.

Gideon breathed a sigh of relief upon noticing a light burning in Barrow's window. As it turned out, Barrow himself was there with the two men he had mentioned would be put to the task of guarding Berry.

All of them turned in surprise as Gideon walked in. Barrow rose to greet him. "What has happened to bring you here at this hour, Mr. Knight?"

Gideon quickly told them what had occurred. "And now my men have vanished and I don't know how to track them."

"Well, it's Hawthorne we need to find, and that's where we'll come upon the others. Any idea in which direction he might have fled?"

"No, not a clue."

"Well, let's see." Barrow started thinking aloud. "Hawthorne is a leech, and has no place of his own. He relied on his family, but they've now thrown him out and would certainly never condone his actions tonight. He dares not go to them, for they'll turn him straight over to the magistrate and wish him good riddance."

"He travels with a group of unsavory friends," Gideon mentioned. "Although Lady Berry could not make out their faces, she recognized Hawthorne's voice and was certain there were three other men with him. Possibly the three wastrels he is known to keep company with."

Barrow nodded. "Oh, I am quite familiar with that lot. Lord Pullingham is one of those little rats. The man has money, the only one of Hawthorne's friends who does. It is his wife's money, of course. Pullingham has never worked a day in his life and had to marry a rich tradesman's daughter to maintain his style of living. Her father purchased a townhouse for them in Belgravia."

Gideon arched an eyebrow. "That's serious money."

"As I said, all the wife's. And her father keeps tight rein on it, all bound up in trusts and such. Pullingham might be aiding Hawthorne, but he would never allow the man to hide Lord Berwick at his residence. Besides, his wife happens to be in London now. She would be screaming bloody murder and every constable in London would have been called to her home by now. She will never allow that sneaky rat of a husband and his friends to embroil her in this nefarious nonsense."

"Then where? Somewhere outside of London?" Gideon asked.

"No, Hawthorne does not have the resources for that. I'm sure he meant to grab Lady Berry and carry her off to a prelate who could be bribed to overlook her protests and marry them fast right here in London. It is common knowledge that the prelate at St. Simeon's Church of the Revelations in Southwark is on the take."

"But I have Lady Berry safely at my club, so why would he bother to go there now?"

"In the hope that crooked prelate might hide Lord Berwick for him."

"Truly? Would a man of the cloth be that stupid?"

Barrow rolled his eyes. "You, of all people, should know how stupid *and* venal people can be. Has your upbringing not taught you as much?"

Gideon grunted in acknowledgment.

"If he were willing to lie about Lady Berry's consent to marry Lord Hawthorne, is it a stretch to think this prelate would lie about hiding Lord Berwick and holding him hostage? This assumes there will be a ransom demand for his return. That man is going to grab a share of whatever is paid over for Lord Berwick's return." Barrow paused and shook his head in dismay, his prominent jowls wobbling. "Let's hope they choose to ransom him. We are now dealing with frightened men. It is also possible they will decide to kill him and toss his body into the Thames."

"And the *ton* considers me low and unworthy," Gideon muttered, grunting in disgust.

"Well, Pullingham's home and St. Simeon's Church are the two places I will start asking questions. Keep in mind, Hawthorne probably has not planned for any alternatives and could still be driving around London in a panic while he decides what to do next. Your men are hopefully following him and this is why they have not returned to your club yet."

Gideon admitted that this was likely.

"If I were a betting man, I would place wagers on Hawthorne ultimately deciding to make for St. Simeon's once he manages to lose your friends. It is familiar ground, and he thinks no one will figure out the connection between him and that prelate."

"Makes sense. I'll come with you."

"And I'll nose around the Pullingham residence," one of Barrow's men, the one called Mick, said.

The other man, whose name was George, also rose. "I'll stop by the magistrate's office to see if anyone has reported a disturbance. As the complaints come in, we may be able to deduce where Hawthorne is fleeing, or at least the direction in which he is fleeing."

"Consider us on the case, Mr. Knight," Barrow said with a nod. "But I suggest you return to Lady Berry. You do not want to be caught up in any nasty business, especially if Lord Hawthorne resists capture. No, you do not help Lady Berry by confronting that villain and possibly getting hurt yourself. And you dare not get caught up in an assault charge. He is a lord, after all. Even if it is just a courtesy title. Let us handle it. I'll report back to you at your club before noon today."

Gideon was not the sort to sit around and do nothing. Dr. Farthingale was still with Berry, and Horace was there to carry out his precise instructions. Bonham would take care of the club and any other business that arose. "I'm coming with you, Mr. Barrow. I'll stay back and let you take the lead. Otherwise, you would be one man alone against Hawthorne and his rabble. Also, if Lord Berwick is badly hurt, you'll require my assistance and my carriage to get him to safety."

Barrow did not look pleased, but nodded. "All right, Mr. Knight." He then turned to his men. "My gut tells me they are heading to Southwark and the church. Meet me there as soon as you have checked out Pullingham's residence and the magistrate's office."

Gideon always carried two weapons on him, a pistol in the lip of one boot and a knife in the lip of the other. He watched as Barrow also armed himself. "I rarely ever have to use force, Mr. Knight. It is all in how one talks to the accomplices. Few of them are willing to hang for a friend's mad idea. As they sober up, they will realize the mess they have gotten themselves into and scurry off like rats abandoning a sinking ship. You must let them. Our objective is to rescue Lord Berwick first. The magistrate's men will apprehend Hawthorne's accomplices later."

"And what of Hawthorne and the prelate?"

"Apprehending them is secondary. Lord Berwick is much respected by many important men of power. He'll see that Hawthorne is duly punished. And do you think the Bishop of London will ignore him when he demands punishment for the prelate? Frankly, I am surprised that nothing has been done about him yet. I suppose his misdeeds have been too small so far for the bishop to pay attention. But this incident will not be swept aside and ignored."

Gideon did not comment, for the Bow Street investigator obviously had more faith in religion and the judicial system than he. "Got it, Lord Berwick first."

In truth, this was what Berry would want most of all.

Brent had the carriage waiting out front. "Mr. Knight, what's happening?"

Gideon quickly apprised him of their plan.

"To Southwark it is," Brent said eagerly.

Gideon opened the carriage door. "Climb in, Mr. Barrow."

It was not long before they were across the Thames and headed toward the church. The streets of Southwark were dark and mostly empty at this late hour, for most of the taverns had shut their doors by now. Torchlights illuminated the streets, but barely, and most of their ride was in darkness or cast in deep shadow.

Brent knew these streets better than anyone, and capably guided them to St. Simeon's without problem.

The air was dank and fetid, the night breeze doing little to chase away the foul odors of Southwark or those wafting off the Thames. Gideon ordered Brent to pull over as they neared the church, for it was wiser not to announce their presence. To his surprise, Lord Berwick's captured carriage was quietly standing in front of the church. "Are they idiots?" he muttered, for who would be so foolish as to make no attempt to hide themselves, especially after absconding with the carriage and its owner?

"Yes, they are idiots," Barrow replied.

The driver, obviously not a professional man but one of Hawthorne's friends, was perched in the driver's seat and looking ill at ease as he glanced around furtively.

"He's alone," Barrow remarked after watching him for a minute or two. "No one is in the carriage."

"I can take care of him," Gideon whispered with marked impatience, for he was eager to get inside the church and rescue Lord Berwick. It would not take much to knock this man out and do the same to his wastrel friends. Gideon was a street fighter. Hawthorne and his circle of friends were lazy dolts who probably could not even shoot straight should they withdraw pistols and attempt to kill him.

"You'll do no such thing," his Bow Street companion grumbled. "Leave this to me."

Barrow picked up a stone and hurled it at one of the pair of horses. It struck the horse in the rump, startling the beast, and both took off at a gallop.

The unsuspecting lord almost fell off his perch.

The last Gideon saw of him and the carriage, he was clinging to the driver's seat for dear life as the frightened team headed back across the river, no doubt toward Lord Berwick's home, because this was what horses did when unguided—they embarked on the path that would lead them back to their familiar mews and the comfort of their stalls.

Gideon smiled at the Bow Street Runner, duly impressed. "Well done."

"You see, it is best to avoid confrontations," Barrow replied. "Now comes the hard part. Stay behind me, Mr. Knight. If Lady Berry's count is reliable, then we are dealing with two more accomplices, Hawthorne and the prelate. Four men, and an injured Lord Berwick that we must ensure is not harmed once they discover our presence. I cannot caution you enough. Rash actions will endanger his lordship."

Gideon nodded, for he understood this very well.

They walked silently toward the rear of the church, looking for a discreet access point, for the front door turned out to be barricaded at this hour. Gideon thought churches remained available to the cold and hungry at all hours, but what did he know? "Look, this side door is ajar."

"That's likely the way they went in," Barrow said. "Hush now, the church walls will echo our voices if we speak once inside. Have your eyes adjusted to the darkness?"

"Yes." In truth, this was one of Gideon's strengths. Bonham often declared he had the eyes of a night predator.

They crept in and made their way toward a back room whose door was closed, but there was light slipping through the cracks.

As they approached, they heard raised voices.

Gideon hoped this was a good sign, for it could mean the accomplices were sobering and realizing what a mess they had made of Berry's abduction.

"Get him out of here!" they heard someone, presumably the prelate, shout at Hawthorne. "How could you bring him here, you fool? This was never part of our agreement."

"Well, our agreement has now changed," Hawthorne replied, sounding scared and petulant. "Where's the risk? He's bound, gagged, and blindfolded. He won't know where we've taken him."

"But he's seen *you*," the prelate countered, his voice cracking, as he was obviously infuriated. "He knows you were the one to abduct him. How are you going to stop him from implicating you? And now, you've implicated *me* in your mess."

Gideon's heart stopped.

Were they going to kill Lord Berwick?

One of the accomplices suggested it, but the other pointed out that Berry had seen them too. "And possibly the lad who rescued her can also identify us."

This second accomplice, whose voice Gideon recognized as Pullingham's, must have been sobering and finally understood the consequences of what they had done. "We'll hang for sure if we harm him."

The prelate groaned. "Get him out of here. Find someplace else to hide him until you figure out what to do. I want no part of this."

"You officious bastard," Hawthorne snarled, and must have lunged for the prelate, because both of his accomplices shouted, "No!" and then something thudded to the floor.

There was more panicked chatter between Hawthorne and his friends.

"That's it, I'm done," Pullingham said, his bombastic voice once more easily recognized. He had used that imperious tone quite often when demeaning the stewards in Gideon's establishments.

Gideon and Barrow ducked into an alcove just as both accomplices abandoned Hawthorne and stormed past them. However, with the carriage chased off, Gideon knew the pair might be too scared to walk the streets of Southwark at this hour and decide to return.

They had to act fast.

As soon as the two accomplices left the church by the same side door they had entered, he and Barrow burst into the room.

Gideon went straight for Hawthorne, who had just drawn his pistol. Gideon feared he intended to shoot Lord Berwick and then reload and shoot the unconscious prelate. He tackled Hawthorne and knocked the pistol out of his hand, possibly breaking that fiend's hand when he resisted, for Hawthorne shrieked in pain.

"This is for Berry," Gideon muttered, and landed a blow to Hawthorne's twisted, enraged face.

He was about to hit him again, but Barrow placed a beefy hand atop his fist to stop him. "No, Mr. Knight. He is unconscious. You'll kill him if you hit him again."

"Who will care?"

"I will," the experienced Bow Street Runner said with a surprising amount of compassion. "And so will Lady Berry. Do not beat this man to death."

Gideon realized he was right.

Berry had fallen in love with the chivalrous orphan side of him, not the ruthless gaming hell owner who lived by a brutal code of the streets.

In truth, he had never killed anyone. There was never a need. Everyone knew he was not afraid to defend himself, and few were strong enough or smart enough to defeat him, although some had tried and suffered the consequences. But those consequences were a loss of business advantages or the usual injuries one might incur after a fight. He had never turned those fights into death matches.

He tempered his rage, although it was a close thing, and he silently vowed to kill Hawthorne if the churl roused and began tossing insults about Berry.

He would not care if Hawthorne insulted him. But if he demeaned Berry? Those would be his last words spoken.

"Mr. Knight, *please*," Barrow said with calm authority.

Gideon lowered his arm, knowing this was the gentlemanly thing to do.

But Hawthorne had hurt Berry. The cur was possibly mad enough to have killed Lord Berwick now that everyone had abandoned him and he could not possibly pull off a ransom scheme on his own. Should he not face some consequences beyond a punch to the face and a possible broken hand?

The prelate, who lay sprawled beside a bound-and-gagged Lord Berwick, began to moan. Hawthorne must have used the heavy candlestick lying beside the man's head as a weapon to knock him out.

Gideon set it back on the table where it belonged, wanting to keep it out of the prelate's reach, lest this man of the cloth think to use it against any of them.

He would not stop the man if he intended to strike Hawthorne, however.

While he watched over Hawthorne and the prelate, Barrow removed the blindfold from Lord Berwick's eyes and the gag from his mouth, and then unbound him. "Can you walk, Lord Berwick?" he asked gently.

"With assistance," Lord Berwick replied, his voice raspy. He was noticeably in pain.

Gideon shook his head. "No, I'll carry you." Berry had seen the poor man being kicked and beaten by Hawthorne and his friends. Gideon could not be sure how severely they had hurt him. "My carriage is just down the street."

"Praise heaven." Tears began to flow down the old man's face. "How is Berry? Did that beast Hawthorne hurt her?"

Gideon winced. "I'll take you to her. Dr. Farthingale is tending her. He believes she will make a full recovery. But that devil Hawthorne struck her hard across the head."

"Oh, my poor Berry!" Lord Berwick said with a sob. "I must see her."

"Yes, I'll take you to her right now. The doctor should still be with her, and now he will tend to you."

"Knight, I may need you to take over trustee responsibilities for Berry for a while."

Gideon nodded. "No need to think about it tonight. Let's see how you are feeling in the morning. You've just experienced one of the worst nights of your life and must rest, my lord. But I am at your service, and will do whatever you need me to do to protect Berry."

"Seems you've done plenty already."

Gideon wished he had done more.

The urge to kill Hawthorne arose within him again, but he tamped it down. He would be of no use to Berry while facing a murder charge. And killing an unconscious man would be viewed as cold-blooded murder.

"Get Lord Berwick out of here, Mr. Knight," his Bow Street

companion said, using the rope that had bound Lord Berwick to now bind Hawthorne. "I'll wait for Mick and George right here. They'll be along soon, possibly with a few of the magistrate's men. They're going to take his lordship's abduction and the attack on Lady Berry very seriously."

Gideon supposed this was for the best. The ever-alert Barrow meant to get him out of here before Hawthorne revived.

"See you in a few hours," Gideon muttered. "Thank you for getting right on the task. You saved Lord Berwick's life, Mr. Barrow."

Brent helped Gideon settle Lord Berwick in his carriage and they soon returned to the Musket Club. As instructed, Brent led the team to the rear entrance, although it might have been safe enough by now to pull up in front of the club.

All was quiet as dawn broke, and most of the patrons had returned home. The sky had gone from darkest black to lighter shades of gray. The sun would be up shortly.

Pudge, Joss, and Henry were back and immediately assisted Gideon in getting Lord Berwick upstairs. Bonham came running out of his quarters when he heard the commotion. "Put Lord Berwick in my bed for now. Thank goodness you are alive, my lord. We were so worried about you. Dr. Farthingale's still here. Probably drifted off to sleep for a few minutes. He's been keeping a watchful eye on Lady Berry."

"Berry," Lord Berwick said, and tears welled in his eyes once more. "How is she? I must see her first."

Gideon nodded. "But only for a minute, my lord. She needs her rest, and you need to be examined by the doctor. We do not know the extent of your injuries, so you are best off—"

"Yes, yes," Lord Berwick said, ignoring all cautions the moment Gideon opened the door to his quarters and he saw Berry sitting up in bed and being spoon-fed marrow soup by Horace. "Berry!"

"Lord Berwick!"

Gideon had never seen a happier reunion or more tears shed

and hugs exchanged.

Dr. Farthingale came to his side. "Well done, Mr. Knight. I was quite worried this incident would not end happily."

"So was I," Gideon admitted, his gaze on Berry, who now looked at him as though he were her knight in shining armor. She graced him with a smile that would linger in his heart forever.

He was also pleased to see her having been changed out of her damaged gown and put in one of his nightshirts that was far too big for her slight frame.

She looked quite delicious in it.

The pins had been taken out of her hair, and her silken tresses were in a gloriously loose tumble down her back. Gideon gently brushed a few curls off her lovely face.

Horace cast him a triumphant smile. "You did it, Mr. Knight."

The others were hovering by the door, Joss, Pudge, Henry, and Bonham, all eager to hear the tale. Gideon was eager to hear theirs, as well.

But first, Dr. Farthingale insisted on having Lord Berwick settled in Bonham's chamber so he could examine the man.

Horace handed the soup bowl to Gideon. "Here, you help Lady Berry. I'll assist the doctor. Lord Berwick will require a fresh nightshirt, too. And he'll need to wash the filth off him. I'll give him the musk soap you foolishly refused to use. Cook made a fresh pot of marrow soup. I'll have some sent up for his lordship if Dr. Farthingale approves."

Gideon chuckled. "Thank you, Horace. I see you gave Lady Berry the best care."

"Of course I did," the valet said with a sniff. "And when I'm finished settling Lord Berwick, I'll return to take care of you. You not only look like a mountain troll, you smell like one, too."

Joss and Pudge burst out laughing.

Berry did, too. It did Gideon's heart good to see her in fine humor.

"How are you feeling?" he asked Berry, an eyebrow quirked in hopeful question.

"In the pink." She held out her arms to him.

They were the arms of heaven to him.

"I don't care if you smell like a mountain troll," she said with a wealth of feeling. "You saved Lord Berwick's life."

"And Henry saved *your* life," Gideon said, relieved to see her looking better.

He called the lad over and gave his hair a ruffle. The lad was beaming as brightly as a lighthouse torch. "She already gave me my hug, Mr. Knight. But I expect she has a very special one saved for you."

Gideon sat on the edge of the mattress beside Berry, his heart beyond full, and took the tray holding the soup bowl off her lap.

"I'll take that for ye, Mr. Knight," Henry said.

"Thank you, lad." Gideon handed it over to the boy, whose chest was still puffed up with pride. He then leaned forward to embrace Berry, whose open arms still beckoned him.

"I love you," she whispered.

"Same," he said, careful to hold her with exquisite care.

He felt such a fierce longing for her, but hardly dared touch her while she was hurt and in such a delicate condition. Despite her claiming to be in the pink, he knew she was not.

However, she was on the mend, and this relieved him greatly.

"Same," he repeated, hoping she understood how much he loved her.

She had become so important to him. He wanted so desperately to marry her.

How was it possible for her to have such an impact on him in so short a time? He could not ever see himself without her. They hardly knew each other, and yet it felt as though she had always existed for him and always been in his life.

In a way, she had.

The Thane family had been so closely bound to the orphanage. He must have seen Berry, a sweet child by her mother's side, once or twice while he still resided there. Of course, he had been working through the anger of being abandoned, and too caught up in his own concerns to pay attention to the little angel who sometimes accompanied Lady Thane on her weekly visits.

He might not have been aware of her at the time, but his heart had known.

Yes, his heart had known and remembered. This had to be why he felt that immediate recognition upon their meeting again as adults.

He ached to marry Berry.

However, he dared not propose to her before speaking to Lord Berwick. Was he mad to hope this man she loved and trusted like a father might approve?

Not that Gideon required it. But this wise old man who had almost died tonight while attempting to protect Berry was owed this measure of respect.

"Are you ever going to tell us what happened?" Bonham asked, reminding Gideon that he and Berry were not alone.

Under normal circumstances, all his friends would have disappeared and shut the door behind them. But there was nothing normal about this night, and everyone was eager to learn what had happened.

He eased away from Berry with the greatest reluctance, but first plumped her pillows to make certain she was comfortable.

She cast him an impatient smile. "I am achy but very happy. You needn't fuss over me. Won't you tell us how you saved Lord Berwick? And what did you do with Hawthorne?"

"Or to him," Bonham added. "Is he still alive?"

CHAPTER SIXTEEN

THE OTHERS NOW gathered around Gideon and listened intently as he told them everything he and Homer Barrow had done. "I cannot take credit for this good outcome. It was Mr. Barrow's deductive brilliance that won the day."

Joss nodded. "Pudge, Henry, and I followed those fiends as far as we could. They had taken Lord Berwick's carriage, tossed the poor driver off it, and then attempted to race off. The driver's all right, but no thanks to those miserable curs. He assured us he would report the abduction to the magistrate."

"He probably has done. Mr. Barrow sent one of his men to the magistrate's bureau to find out whether anything out of the ordinary had been reported. He sent another to Lord Pullingham's home because he and Hawthorne were partners in crime, so to speak."

"We were on foot," Joss continued, "and managed to keep them in sight for a while. But we lost them once the traffic thinned. Still, we kept up our search in the hope we might come upon them."

"But we never spotted them again," Pudge said, raking a hand through his hair. "We finally gave up and returned here. It did not occur to us to look in Southwark. We thought for certain he was hiding out somewhere along Curzon Street, since that is where many of the Upper Crust are known to keep their mistresses. Beggin' your pardon, Lady Berry."

"Quite all right, Mr. Pudge," Berry replied. "I am aware of such discreet arrangements."

Gideon smiled.

Mr. Pudge?

Pudge's real name was Albert Smith, but no one ever called him that.

Gideon shared a grin with his friends, including Pudge, who all thought it quite a sweet mistake. None of them would ever correct Berry.

"But there wasn't a trace of them on Curzon Street," Henry said, continuing the story. "So we looked around Covent Garden and then Bloomsbury."

"We did not know what we were doing," Pudge admitted. "But we wanted to give it our best for the sake of Lady Berry."

She smiled at all of them. "I am honored, and thank you from the bottom of my heart for all you did for me and Lord Berwick."

Dr. Farthingale returned while they were still talking about this evening's incident. Everyone turned to him in worried expectation, for the doctor was frowning.

"He is bruised, but nothing is broken."

"Thank heaven," Berry murmured.

"However, he also needs to be kept under close observation, because there might be internal bleeding that is not yet apparent. Those bounders kicked him viciously."

Gideon reached over to take Berry's hand, knowing this news would have her crying again. "Should he stay here for the next few days, too?"

The doctor nodded. "Yes, if you do not mind turning your club into a temporary infirmary. He has been jostled too much already, and I fear moving him again may set off that bleeding before his body has time to recover. Also, it will make it easier for me to check on both of my patients if they remain here."

"Consider it done," Gideon said, although he was worried that having both of them here would make it impossible to keep their presence a secret. The magistrate's investigators were certain to come by the club to question the pair.

He exchanged a glance with Bonham, for they both knew having the authorities come around might hurt business. No patron wanted to find themselves face to face with a sharp-eyed constable.

Well, he and his partner would deal with the matter if it became a problem.

After a few more minutes of discussion, his friends left to retire to their own quarters.

Bonham remained behind. "I'm going to return to Duchess Square once I've finished checking on our other clubs. But I'll have their accounts sent over here for you to review. You are far better at numbers than I am. Do you mind?"

"Not at all," Gideon replied. "That's fine." It would keep him close to Berry and still enable him to attend to business matters while she rested.

Bonham closed the door behind him, a highly improper thing to do. But Berry did not seem concerned.

Gideon took her hands in his once more. They were cool to the touch, but felt far warmer than before.

"I've been holding down food for the last few hours," she said, looking quite cozy in his bed and casting him a kittenish smile.

He grinned. "Is this your way of asking me to kiss you? Even though I smell like a mountain troll, if Horace is to be believed."

"Horace is prone to exaggeration, isn't he?" She laughed softly. "And I must look as hideous as the Minotaur with all my lumps and bruises."

"You look beautiful," he said, his voice husky with the ache of wanting her. "Are you ready for your kiss?"

She looked up at him with her big eyes and a big smile just for him. "I have been ready for *you* since the day I was born."

"All right, kitten." He resumed his seat beside her on the bed and placed an arm on either side of her as she lay propped against her pile of pillows.

He brought his mouth close to hers.

Berry's lips were just the right amount of plump and soft, and had the perfect amount of give against his own. Her breath was sweet and held a trace of mint and the marrow broth she had just eaten.

He gently pressed the weight of his body against hers, only lightly because she was bruised and he did not want to hurt her.

"Close your eyes, love." His voice was still husky because he was as eager for their first *real* kiss as she was. "This one is from me, straight from my heart."

She squeezed her eyes shut. "I am already melting."

He smothered a smile. Whatever little heat she was feeling was nothing. He was going to make her burn for him.

"I love you, Berry," he whispered, and captured her mouth in a kiss that was meant to ignite that sweet body of hers.

Yes, the kiss was meant to devour her, conquer her, but also be exquisitely deep and gentle.

But gentle did not mean tepid. He wanted her to feel the scorching intensity of it.

After all, he had a reputation to uphold. A bad reputation. He knew how to seduce women.

Berry was clutching his shoulders and surrendering with delight.

What he had not expected was *his* reaction to her innocent response. She had him burning, too.

A sharp knock at his door brought their kiss to an abrupt end.

Gideon drew off her just as Horace burst in. "Make yourselves decent," he whispered urgently. "And this door must stay open."

"Why?" Gideon rose to stride across the room and toss Horace out. The lad could be quite irritating at times, especially right now. Gideon had just started kissing Berry and did not appreciate the interruption.

"Lord Berwick is fretting and insists on getting out of bed to speak to Lady Berry."

"Whatever for?" Berry asked.

Horace shook his head. "I don't know. Just make yourselves presentable. I stalled him by telling him I would find a robe for him to wear."

Gideon stepped to his wardrobe and withdrew a black banyan. "Here, have him put mine on. Foolish old man. The doctor told him to stay in bed. He was quite clear in his instructions."

"Well, he isn't listening, is he?" Horace turned toward Berry. "He insists there is something important he must tell you."

Gideon's heart sank.

Was it to warn Berry not to involve herself with him? Would Lord Berwick maintain this class distinction even after all Gideon had done for them? Well, he hadn't done it with the expectation of any reward. He had done it because he loved Berry, and she was all that mattered.

"Uh oh. He didn't wait for me. I think I hear him coming down the hall," Horace said, and dashed off to assist Lord Berwick...and slow him down to give Gideon and Berry time to look as though they had not just been in the throes of a hot kiss.

Gideon knew he looked fine. But Berry?

Gad, that kitten. She had that just-kissed look on her face.

Well, there was no help for it. Lord Berwick was not going to be fooled even if Berry managed to look expressionless.

Gideon smiled at her. "Sorry we had to cut it short."

She blushed. "Was there more to the kiss?"

"Yes. Much more. I was just getting started."

"Oh my." Her eyes widened. "Well, the sample I got was awfully good."

She had the sweetest way of making him smile. "Then you liked it?"

"Tremendously."

He nodded in approval.

"What do you think Lord Berwick wants to tell me? I am not going to listen if he's just going to bluster again about the importance of bloodlines and family connections. You are the right man for me, and there can be no doubt of it after tonight."

"Again?"

She sighed. "We spoke of you tonight while on our way to Lord Folger's party."

"And he warned you against liking me?" Well, he should not have been surprised. Business was one thing. Love and marriage were quite another.

"Gideon," she said softly, for he was not hiding his irritation very well, "I am a grown woman and know my own mind. I spoke out of turn. Lord Berwick is an intelligent man. There's no need for either of us to get worked up before we know what he intends to say."

"But is it so difficult to figure out? I am good enough to risk my life for you, but I will never be good enough to be your husband. So, after all this, we are right back where we started. Do you think he would cause problems for the orphanage if you ignored his concerns and married me?"

"No, never. He cares for those children dearly."

Gideon shook his head. "But he might influence your donors. St. Brigid's will be harmed if the donations dry up."

"Let's hear him out first."

Gideon rubbed a hand along the back of his neck. Berry believed that love could triumph over everything, but Gideon was too cynical to hold out such hope.

He realized she was struggling to hold back tears. He silently cursed himself for getting angry before even hearing the old man out. "I am upsetting you. This is exactly what the doctor ordered me not to do. Ignore me. I am just mouthing off. I love you and I am not going to stop loving you or striving for the right to earn your hand in marriage. We'll figure it out. I am not going to lose you. I'll fight heaven and earth, if this is what it takes. I will always fight for you."

Lord Berwick, with Horace's assistance, now stood barefoot at the threshold of the bedchamber dressed in Gideon's nightshirt and banyan, which were taut around his belly. "You can stop fighting, Mr. Knight. Sit down and stop looking as though you want to strangle me. I've been bruised enough for a lifetime after tonight."

Gideon felt ashamed of his stupid rant. "My apologies, my lord. Have a seat." He carried one of the larger chairs to the bedside. "I'll leave you and Lady Berry to speak in private."

Lord Berwick settled in the chair with a grunt, for he was obviously in pain. "No, Mr. Knight. Stay. This concerns you, too. I could not rest until I had spoken my mind."

Gideon motioned for Horace to get out and shut the door behind him. He then stood beside Berry and the man who had taken care of her for almost two decades. "Go ahead," he urged, knowing he owed the man enough respect to hear him out.

Lord Berwick took Berry's hand. "My dear, I know we had this conversation and I told you that I could never give my approval to your marrying Mr. Knight."

Gideon's heart twisted. Was he now going to remind Berry and insist on her looking elsewhere for a husband?

She sat up stiffly, obviously just as riled as he was. "With all due respect, Lord Berwick, I do not need to hear this again."

"I know. This is why I must tell you that if you do have sincere feelings for Mr. Knight, then I will not disapprove. In fact, I will support you wholeheartedly if you wish to marry him. That is…" Lord Berwick turned to Gideon. "I heard the last of what you said just now. Will you give me your oath that you love Berry?"

"You have it. Upon my honor. I cannot breathe for loving her so much." Gideon gave a pained laugh. "There is no one for me but Lady Berry. She has my heart and will always have it. I will remain true to my marriage vows to love, honor, and protect her for all of our days."

"Yes, I thought you might be feeling this way."

"I feel the same," Berry said, tipping her chin up.

Lord Berwick shed a tear as he said, "I think facing death puts priorities into proper perspective, doesn't it? Adversity brings out the worst in some men and the best in others. And this horrible incident with Lord Hawthorne made me realize how wrong my outlook has been. It shames me to admit that I might have once considered Hawthorne the worthier man. And why? Simply because of the fortune of his birth?"

Berry looked aghast. "No! You could never have thought so."

Lord Berwick shook his head. "Well, never seriously. I dismissed him as soon as I realized what a sneaky little rat he was. But I still had my objections about Mr. Knight. Although I liked him, I still worried about what the *ton* might think if you were ever to marry him. But he has been dealing with adversity and overcoming it with valor for all his life. Not only overcoming it, but helping others and raising them along with him. He protects the weak. He is one of the most honorable men I know."

"Being raised in St. Brigid's gave me the chance to improve my life," Gideon said. "Who knows what my fate might have been had I ended up in a workhouse? Or put to work as a chimney sweep's monkey? Those poor boys rarely survive beyond the age of six."

"There is a special quality about you, Mr. Knight. One I saw while you were being raised in that orphanage and later as you made your way in the world. I placed some of Berry's investments with you to test you, and you proved my faith in you. But it was sheer stupidity and narrow-mindedness that prevented me from understanding you would make her a good husband, too. Even now, I am worried about how you will be received by the *ton*. It is no small matter."

"Then you still have concerns?" Gideon asked.

Lord Berwick nodded. "Not about you, but about how you will be received by others. Well, that is something we will work out later. What is most important is that if I do not wake up tomorrow, I wanted Berry to know that I approve of her choice in a husband."

Tears flowed down Berry's cheeks. "You *will* wake up. You *must*, for me and Lady Berwick, and your children, and everyone else who loves you. You are much beloved and we would be bereft without you."

He held out a hand. "Help me up, Mr. Knight. I had better return to bed or Dr. Farthingale will box my ears. So will my wife. I expect she will be running over here shortly and not leave my side until I am able to return home. My daughters might do the same. I apologize in advance if we inconvenience you."

"No inconvenience, my lord," Gideon replied.

"Well, I still do have some concerns for you and Berry. May I suggest you both say nothing until after Lord Stanhope's ball, and then we can assess the situation? The *ton* may need to absorb you in small doses, but I will do my best to ensure they will accept you."

Berry had a stubborn look on her face. Gideon did not think she was going to wait to marry him. Nor did he wish it, either.

But this was not about their instant gratification. If they could end up married and the orphanage contributions were ensured to continue, then where was the harm in waiting a few weeks for this best outcome?

He assisted Lord Berwick back to his bedchamber and left him under the watchful care of Horace.

As for Gideon, he was exhausted and could do with a few hours of sleep. He would manage it in one of the large chairs in his bedchamber, or simply stretch out on the carpet if the chair proved too uncomfortable.

But before he slept, he needed to finish that kiss he and Berry had started.

He strode back to his quarters with that intention and was surprised to find a woman standing by the bed, staring down at Berry.

He thought it might have been her maid, Harriet, who he expected would come over here shortly to tend to her mistress. But the woman was dressed too finely.

Bloody bollocks.

Jasmine.

Who in blazes had let *her* up here?

CHAPTER SEVENTEEN

BERRY HAD CLOSED her eyes a moment, for she was exhausted but also exhilarated by Lord Berwick's admission that Gideon might be the right man for her. He would give his blessing if they chose to marry, and that was all that mattered.

Upon opening her eyes, she had expected to find Gideon returned to her side. Instead, she saw one of those beautiful ladies Gideon had escorted to the Covent Garden theater shortly after they had first met.

Up close, she did not look quite so pretty. In fact, she looked haughty and held malice in her eyes.

Berry realized this woman was not meant to be here, for Gideon would never have allowed someone like her anywhere near her or Lord Berwick.

"He is mine," the woman spat. "He'll drop you now that he has bedded you. You were nothing more than a challenge. The high and mighty Lady Berry. Well, he's had you now and will soon lose interest."

"*Had* me?" Berry wanted to laugh at the notion, for were her lumps and bruises not obvious enough indication that something other than a tryst was going on?

Gideon walked in just then—a relief, because Berry thought this woman was capable of putting a pillow over her head and suffocating her. "Get out, Jasmine," he said harshly. "Who let you up here?"

"I know my way well enough. After all, I am quite familiar with your bed," the woman purred. "You used to enjoy my company once."

"Dear heaven," he muttered, approaching her. "That was in the past." He cast Berry a pained glance, no doubt mortified about what she was thinking.

She made no effort to say anything.

What *could* she say? He obviously had an imperfect past, but was he any different from other bachelors who sought out ladies for casual encounters or took on a mistress?

What mattered was his conduct since meeting *her*, and had it not been exemplary? Whether he would revert to his past ways and past dalliances was a question yet to be answered, but Berry was ready to wager her heart on his being faithful. She did not think that a man who valued loyalty as dearly as he did would ever be disloyal himself.

Gideon groaned. "You've had several benefactors since that time, Jasmine. Do not pretend there is anything between us."

Jasmine placed her hands on Gideon's chest with proprietary familiarity. "But none were as good as you, my love. Why did you take me to the theater the other night if you did not wish us to get back together?"

"As a favor to you and Chloe, that's all. Nothing more to it. Come downstairs with me." He took her by the elbow and attempted to steer her out of his bedchamber.

"No, I will not go. Get *her* out of here."

"Do not make it more embarrassing for yourself," he warned. But she was intent on causing a scene.

"I am not leaving!" Jasmine glared at Berry. "*She* is the one who must leave!"

"Are you that blinded by jealousy?" Gideon spoke softly, but Berry could tell he was seething. "Do you not see she is injured? Lord Berwick was also hurt tonight and he is now settled in Bonham's bed. They almost died. How could her gashes and bruises have escaped your notice?"

"Hah! Too bad they didn't die. They don't belong here. *She* doesn't belong with you. Her sort will never accept you."

Gideon frowned. "What is wrong with you? Why aren't you with Haverstock? What brought you here at this hour? Come downstairs and talk to me. You have been acting oddly lately, and I am very worried about you."

"You think I am demented? Isn't that a laugh," she said harshly. "Perhaps I am. But it is men like you who have made me this way."

Berry was listening intently to this exchange.

"No," Gideon said firmly. "I offered you a respectable position, but *you* chose this life for yourself. Do not blame me for the path you now regret."

"I do not regret my choices!"

"Then why are you here?" Gideon appeared to be struggling to understand what was going on in this lady's mind. "Why rage at Lady Berry when she has never done you any harm?"

"Because she does not need to lift a finger and has everything. And now, she even has you. Or is it the fact she is an heiress that attracts you?" She laughed once again. "Beware, Lady Berry. He can be quite persuasive when he wants to be. But do not be fooled by his charm. Beneath it all he is ruthless in getting what he wants, and in disposing of whoever he no longer desires. Run away from him while you can, because he will destroy you once he has you in his grip."

"And yet *you* would return to me. Why, if I am as ruthless as you say?" Gideon asked.

The question seemed to confuse Jasmine. Unable to respond, she broke free of Gideon's grasp and started toward Berry with her fingers curled into claws.

Gideon immediately stepped between them and drew her toward the door.

"You'll both regret this! I'll tell the gossip sheets all about you and her. Your precious Lady Berry will be ruined."

"Then *your* precious Gideon will be forced to marry me to

protect my reputation," Berry pointed out. "Is this what you want? You will chase him straight into my arms."

Jasmine cursed Berry and ran out.

Gideon followed, but Berry suspected it was only to make certain the woman left the premises and was never permitted to return.

He strode back in a few minutes later and sank into the chair beside her bed.

"Well, that was restful," Berry remarked.

He shook his head. "There are no words… I cannot apologize to you enough. Please believe that I was never one of Jasmine's benefactors. Not that I am blameless, for I did not reject her occasional advances. I was no celibate monk. Perhaps I should have taken more care in the past. I've had nothing to do with her in *that* fashion for some time now. Not that I am proud of my actions back then, but I am no liar. I have always been honest about my intentions. I never claimed to love her, nor have I ever treated her cruelly."

"But she is in love with you. To see you in love with someone else must be quite a heartbreak for her."

"You are being too kind. She never cared about me, and never thought twice about sharing herself with other men if there was something to be gained by it. She valued expensive gifts above all. She has always put her own interests first, being faithful to Jasmine and no one else. I think she is angry because she thinks her allure is fading. She's had two benefactors in short succession. I've tried to tell her that it isn't her looks that are the problem but her volatile temper. Who wants to face her tantrums every night? But she won't listen."

He took a breath and continued. "That night you saw me at the theater with her and Chloe, she had wanted to see that play and her benefactor refused to take her. Of course, he could not be seen in her company, since he was married. Similarly for Chloe and her benefactor. So I escorted them. We saw the play and nothing more happened afterward." He buried his face in his hands. "Not that this excuses any of my past. She's going to cause problems for you. She'll sell the information to the gossip rags. I'll do what I can to keep your name out of print."

"You won't be able to stop any of it." Berry knew how those scandal sheets operated. The shock value was what sold papers, so why should they care to dig beyond the apparent scandal to get at the truth? "But I think she may keep quiet."

Gideon glanced up at her. "Why would she keep it a secret? What is in it for her?"

"As I mentioned to her, and I hope she takes it to heart, you will be forced to marry me in order to protect me from the scandal if people learn I slept here tonight. Once she calms down, she will think it through and not do anything that will bring us together."

"Or she will see that I have already lost my heart to you and do whatever she can to pull us apart. It is my dearest wish to marry you, but not under a cloud of shame. You deserve better."

"So, you would not marry me if the gossip rags report what she tells them?"

He gave a mirthless laugh. "I would crawl on my knees to marry you. Walk through brimstone and fire. Yes, I would marry you today, tomorrow, or any day if you agreed to it. Will you have me, Berry? All I meant was that you deserve a proper wedding and a proper courtship."

"Oh, I think I deserve *you*. Whatever happens, you are still my knight in shining armor. I think our tale can be spun quite romantically, especially as you will have Lord Berwick's blessing and support." She cleared her throat. "Assuming he has not heard Jasmine's ranting just now. That might give him pause in embracing you wholeheartedly."

"And you? Did she scare you off?"

"No, although perhaps that scene she caused should have. But I am not sophisticated and do not have any experience with men. Not that I think it matters. Lord Berwick taught me early on to look at a person's actions, not their flowery speeches or ardent declarations. Your actions speak for you, do they not? I am not talking about your prowess with women. That is a given. Even my dear friends turned into lusting beasts as we all shamelessly spied on you."

He cast her a wry smile.

"But what Lord Berwick saw in you, and what you have also shown me, is the heart of a lion. The valor of a man who cares deeply about people and wishes to rescue as many as he can. My family cared for the orphans brought to St. Brigid's, but you have been caring for many of them *after* they were forced to leave. It is no coincidence that you were the one to save Lord Berwick, or that it was one of your lads who got me away from the carriage and brought me to your club where he knew I would be safe and protected by you. See, you are that knight in shining armor."

"Then you still wish to marry me? No doubts? Not even the fact that I own these gaming clubs?"

"You and Bonham were already in the process of selling them, weren't you?"

He nodded. "Yes—in fact, I was thinking of buying into warehouses along the London docks. Mr. Dunning has a fine operation going with his lumber and fancy tiles. Worth looking into, I think. But that is for a later discussion."

She smiled. "I think Lord Berwick will love the idea."

"Berry, do you think this awful evening can be spun into something acceptable to the *ton*?"

"Yes, for you are a genuine hero."

He leaned forward and gave her a soft kiss on the lips. "And you are the love of my life. I shall spend the rest of my days proving it to you. Oh, tears again?"

She nodded.

"Why are you crying?"

"Because you've turned this horrible night into the best one of my life."

His regard turned tender. "Is that a yes to my proposal?"

She cast him a glowing smile. "That is a fervent yes. I will gladly marry you."

CHAPTER EIGHTEEN

T HE SCANDAL DID hit the front pages of the gossip rags, but not quite as Gideon had expected. Jasmine was not going to be pleased with the result, for the story unfolded just as Berry had predicted: Gideon was made to be the hero who rescued her and Lord Berwick, never mind that it was Homer Barrow who was the true hero.

But a jowly Bow Street Runner who was an old, happily married man did not sell papers. Gideon was deemed the hero because the ladies thought him to be a very handsome bachelor and readily believed he was a valiant knight.

They were in raptures upon learning that Berry had fallen in love with him. Since everyone adored her, both the morning editions and the afternoon extra editions sold out when it was reported Gideon had also fallen in love with her and proposed marriage.

Are wedding bells about to chime for one of the ladies on Duchess Square? was the latest story.

No one raised an outcry when the gossip rags printed confirmation the following day that Lord Berwick had given his blessing to their union.

A fairy tale, one paper wrote.

A love story for the ages, said another.

Everyone had been swept away by the romance of it.

The fuss was still going on three weeks later, and Gideon

gave silent thanks every one of those twenty-one days that Berry and Lord Berwick had survived the incident and were now recovered.

He climbed down from his carriage as it drew up in front of Berry's residence on the now-quiet Duchess Square. She was hosting the Ladies Tea Society meeting in her home.

He could understand the need to hold it here in the first week after her abduction. Berry had been in delicate health, and the only trip Dr. Farthingale would allow her to take was the one home after she had spent two days in his bed. Two glorious and yet agonizing days for Gideon, because there she was, clad in nothing but his overly large nightshirt, her golden hair spilling over her shoulders and her smile radiant, but he could do nothing about it.

He shook out of the thought and returned to the present. Gideon strode to her door as the meeting was about to break up. "Good afternoon, Melton."

"Good afternoon, Mr. Knight. Lady Berry is expecting you."

He had promised to show her friends the results of all the work done on his new home. Of course, Suzanna and Gwendolyn Carstairs, as well as Miranda and Gwenys Lawson, had been popping in throughout the renovations and were familiar with the progress. But the other ladies were keen to see what Berry had designed for him.

They gathered around him when he walked in and followed him out like ducklings all in a row as he led them next door. Berry then led them on a tour of his home.

Upon the tour's end, Gideon joined them as they stood in his ballroom, *oohing* and *aahing* over the chandeliers that had recently been installed.

"How beautiful!" Lady Alice exclaimed, and wished him many years of happiness in his new residence.

Lady Mabel did the same. "Oh, now *I* must redecorate! Berry, will you help me? What a beautiful job you have done here."

Berry cast her friend a heartwarming smile. "Of course. It

would be my pleasure."

Maude Harcourt shook her head in dismay. "You will need to spend a fortune on a staff to properly maintain this house, Mr. Knight."

"He can well afford it," Miranda intoned. "Be happy for him."

Maude frowned. "But there's no furniture yet."

Berry laughed. "It will take several months before all of it arrives and is put in its proper place."

"Well, it shall be winter by then, and I shall probably be abed for most of it with a lung infection," Maude declared.

"That's looking on the bright side," Gwenys teased.

"You lucky dog," Bonham said, joining Gideon once the ladies had returned to Berry's home to bid their farewells and arrange for their next meeting.

"I know," Gideon said, surveying a home that had yet to be furnished, just as sourpuss Maude had indicated. But the rooms were all painted, the chandeliers and sconces were installed, and the dark oak flooring had been laid in every room of the house, save for the kitchen and the entry hall, which were tiled.

The cherry bookshelves in his study and library had been set against the walls and secured. They looked quite splendid as the afternoon sunlight shone upon them and brought out their rich red tones.

All that was needed were books to fill them. He knew Berry would enjoy this task, and intended to ask her to join him when he went to the London booksellers to select the ones to complete what he hoped would be an impressive library.

Berry's malachite stone, shaped in the form of a star, had become the focal point of his entry hall, the exquisite dark green standing out amid sparkling white tiles. The hall would look even more magnificent in the evenings, for the malachite seemed to come alive under the amber glow of candlelight.

Of course, this was exactly the effect Berry had hoped for.

"Is Suzanna talking to you yet?" Gideon asked Bonham.

His friend winced. "Not yet, but she is warming up to me. I'm sure she is ready to forgive me. She's coming back in a few minutes to help me put the finishing touches on your drainage system. And I rue the day I ever bothered with your shaft. How is it my fault an innocent lift system is called the same thing as a man's vital male organ?"

Just yesterday, Miranda had explained to Berry and Suzanna the double meaning of the word *shaft*, over which they were properly horrified and refused to call that shaft mechanism anything but a pulley system. Then Suzanna overheard Bonham jest with Gideon that Suzanna could *pull-ey* on his system anytime she wished, which earned him a resounding slap from her.

But Gideon thought it must have all worked out, because as he wandered upstairs twenty minutes later to see how his friend was progressing on the drainage pipes, he came upon Bonham and Suzanna in a heated embrace.

Who else but Bonham would kiss a girl with all his heart and soul beside a commode and sink in a water closet?

Perhaps they were meant for each other. Suzanna did not seem to mind at all.

Well, who was Gideon to pass judgment when he had given Berry her first true kiss not an hour after she had thrown up into his chamber pot four times?

He heard Berry returning after seeing the last of her friends off. "Gideon! Gideon! They all loved your house!"

He hurried downstairs to greet her. "I missed you, love."

She laughed. "For all of five minutes that I was gone?"

"It was a bit longer than that. Your friends are leaving impaired. It takes at least half an hour to get them to the door once they stand up and declare they *must* leave. But come with me." He led her into his study, closed the door for privacy, and then backed her against the wall.

She looked up at him, her eyes sparkling in expectation. "What are we doing in here?"

"Nothing yet, but I am going to kiss the daylights out of you and do not wish to be interrupted."

She smiled. "That is excellent thinking. I love you, Gideon."

"I *really* need to marry you or I am going to expire," he said as he took her hands in his and gently held them to the wall. He pressed the weight of himself lightly atop her and kissed her breathless.

But for weeks now, all he had done was kiss Berry. The restraint required was agonizing. If it were up to him, they would both be shedding their clothes right now and exploring each other's bodies as they coupled like wild monkeys. On the floor. Against the wall. Against the bookshelves.

Everything about her ravaged his senses and brought out his primal urges.

However, he had waited this long and would wait until they were husband and wife to complete this union.

Anyway, Berry was still on medical watch and restricted from heavy exertions.

Tonight was the night of Lord Stanhope's ball and the first time they would be seen together at a *ton* function since their courtship had become public knowledge. This was the night that would determine whether he truly stood a chance of being accepted by the *ton*.

He did not care for his sake, for he still had no desire to become one of them. But this was important for Berry and her work on behalf of St. Brigid's.

Horace made certain Gideon was dressed impeccably in his formal white cravat and coattails when he returned to the Musket Club to prepare for the ball.

Joss, Pudge, Bonham, Henry, and even William, the troubled lad newly sent to him from the orphanage, were there to look him over. He had placed William under Henry's mentorship now that Henry had truly come into his own.

Saving Berry had changed Henry's life, given him a sense of pride and an appreciation of his own worth. The incident had brought out his valiant nature, which might have stayed dormant forever had it not been for that fateful night.

There would be no cheap pilfering again. Henry was a reformed young man. He was a hero.

Horace frowned at Gideon when he complained about the stiffness of his collar. "And the cravat is too tight."

"If you have the breath in your lungs to endlessly gripe at me, then you can manage just fine. Leave it alone," the irritating lad commanded, and would not let him touch a single fold. Horace even had the audacity to yell at him when he happened to sit down on his coattails. "Get up! What are you, a barbarian? You'll wrinkle the jacket!"

"Bloody blazes!" Gideon shot to his feet. "Must you fuss? I hired you as a valet, not an alewife."

"Fine, be that way. Why should I care? Just because this is your first ball and the most important moment in Lady Berry's life? But go ahead and ruin it for her. Leave her in tears because you do not know how to properly protect your clothing. It isn't as though she is the kindest, sweetest, most darling lady in all of London. It isn't as though she deserves better than an oaf of a betrothed who walks around in wrinkled clothes."

His friends were all laughing, which only encouraged Horace.

But Gideon did not mind. Horace adored Berry, and he was right. This evening was very important for her. His every step was going to be watched and every misstep reported in all the papers. He was even wearing fancy evening shoes that pinched his feet tighter than the deuced cravat that was strangling his neck.

"You must tell me what Lady Berry is wearing," Horace pleaded, folding his hands as though praying. "Take down every detail."

Well, that wasn't going to happen. What did Gideon know about gowns other than how to slip them off ladies?

But he nodded. "Sure, Horace."

Since Lord Berwick's carriage had been damaged during the abduction, Gideon collected him and his wife in his own carriage, after which they rode to Duchess Square to pick up Berry.

"Blessed saints," he murmured when she greeted him at the front door.

She looked like a dream in white silk and lace. Only the trace of a bruise could be seen on her forehead. Gideon was surprised she had not tried to cover it up with powder.

"Oh, no," she said as he assisted her into the seat beside Lady Berwick. "I want people to notice the bruise and remember what Lord Hawthorne did to me."

"The wretched cur is in prison now," Lady Berwick said with a satisfied nod. "Where he deserves to be for the next fifteen years. I am certain his family had a say in his sentencing, because he would have been placed under house detention otherwise and received a shorter term."

"He is such an odious man," Lord Berwick muttered. "He got what he had coming."

"He ought to have been hanged for what he did to you, my dear." Lady Berwick cast her husband a loving look. "And to you as well, my dear Berry."

"Unfortunately, he will be released sooner if he becomes a marquess," Berry pointed out.

"One can only hope that will never come to pass," Lord Berwick grumbled. "And speaking of inheritances, I have news for you about Broadingham's heirs."

Berry leaned forward in her seat. "What have the duke's solicitors found out?"

Gideon tensed. He had yet to accustom himself to the possibility of a child of his being in line to become a duke or duchess. Not to mention, Berry herself might become a duchess.

"There were two potential heirs that we knew of, but one has died without leaving any surviving issue. The other heir has been found…"

"And?" Gideon and Berry asked at the same time.

"The poor man is on his deathbed and not expected to last the year."

"Oh dear," Berry said with genuine concern. "Any children?"

"Yes, he has three children...but they are stepchildren. Not blood related."

Gideon let out a breath. "What are you saying?"

Berry's eyes were wide as saucers as she awaited the impossible response. "No, it cannot be."

"Berry, it seems you will soon be Duchess of Broadingham, my dear." Lord Berwick turned to Gideon and laughed softly. "Prepare yourself, Knight. You may not know who your parents are, but your children are going to have no such doubts. With the Lord's blessing, you are going to sire the next little Broadingham duke or duchess."

Gideon's heart was in his throat. Was this not the greatest irony? Him. A nobody. Siring the heir to a dukedom?

Lord Berwick shook his head. "Broadingham's solicitors would like us to meet with them at some convenient time in the upcoming weeks. No rush, but they would like to get things in place, since the heir is on his deathbed, as I said. The man lives on some small island off the coast of Brittany, so word of his demise might be delayed. But it will reach us soon enough, and his solicitors want to be prepared for this eventuality. Brittany? Who would wish to live in such isolation?"

"I'm fairly certain Hawthorne is wishing for it right now," Gideon remarked. "Anything must be better than the confines of his prison cell."

"As ye sow, so shall ye reap. No one is going to come to his rescue," Lord Berwick said. "His friends who were with him that night have all fled the country. I called upon the Bishop of London today. The prelate at St. Simeon's is no longer there."

"Where have they put him?" Berry asked.

"He's been sent off to one of their foreign outposts to convert the populace. I don't think we shall ever see him in London again."

"Lady Miranda told me that Pullingham's father-in-law sent him off to Italy without Lady Pullingham," Berry remarked.

Lady Berwick smiled as she nodded. "Yes, it is true. Lady

Pullingham has packed up their townhouse and is selling it, so I think she expects he will stay gone for good. She got what she wanted out of the marriage, a title and children, one of whom will eventually inherit an earldom. So there's no more need to put up with that wastrel."

They arrived at the impressive Stanhope residence, which was awash in torchlight. Carriages were lined up in a queue that stretched around the corner. Gideon estimated it would take them another ten minutes to reach the head of the line.

But he had settled his coattails just as Horace instructed and had no concerns about his appearance as their carriage moved closer to Lord Stanhope's porticoed entrance. The evening might go completely amiss, but Gideon could proudly report to Horace that his coattails were free of wrinkles.

As it turned out, he need not have worried about his reception. Lord Stanhope greeted him warmly.

"Ah, London's hero. First saving the British Museum's priceless statuary, and mere days later saving the lovely Lady Berry and my dear friend, Lord Berwick. Who will you save next, I wonder? Welcome to our home, Mr. Knight."

"A pleasure, my lord. I appreciate the invitation."

"Everyone is eager to meet you," Lady Stanhope said, smiling broadly. "Having you attend is quite the coup for us. You have made our ball *the* event of the Season."

After greeting their host and hostess, Gideon joined Berry and the Berwicks as they made their way into the ballroom. Berry laughed softly when she noticed him counting the chandeliers on the ceiling and taking note of the paint colors.

He winked back at her and smiled.

Footmen briskly walked around balancing trays of champagne-filled glasses in one hand as they made their way through the crowd of lords and ladies who would never think to mutter an apology if they bumped into them and almost spilled the trays. Gideon had worked as a footman at such elegant *ton* affairs back when he and Bonham were scrambling to earn whatever they could.

It struck him as odd that he was on the other side now. But he made a point of being considerate to the footmen and thanked the young man who had offered him a glass of champagne. He took one for himself and another for Berry.

It was not long before guests surrounded him and Berry, for they were the talk of the ball and everyone wanted to be introduced to him. She was completely in her element, charming everyone with her dazzling smile and gracious comments.

The Stanhopes opened the ball with a quadrille.

All eyes were on Gideon as he led Berry onto the dance floor. He hopped about with lordly perfection and performed his glissades with the best of them.

He managed the waltz with supreme ease, for all felt right with the world once Berry was in his arms.

Miranda, Gwendolyn, and Suzanna were in attendance, so he danced with them, too. Only Gwenys was missing, because she would not make her debut until next year. The ball was a crush, and he could see how someone as young and naïve as Gwenys might have difficulty at such an affair. It overwhelmed *him*, and he had years of experience out in the world.

Berry did not dance with anyone but him because Dr. Farthingale had not given her permission yet. Gideon did not think she minded having to sit out most of the dances, and no one was going to question her medical excuse. While he danced with the ladies of Duchess Square, she spent much of her time chatting with several other young ladies, who turned out to be Dr. Farthingale's nieces.

Berry introduced him when he rejoined her. Apparently, the nieces had married quite well.

It turned out Daffodil Farthingale was one of Berry's good friends. She had married the Duke of Edgeware. "I call her Duchess Daffy," her husband teased.

"Because he is an oaf and a scoundrel," she said with a gentle laugh. "It is Duchess *Dillie*, and I am pleased to meet you, Mr.

Knight." Dillie then introduced Gideon to her other sisters and their husbands. He tried to keep them all in order but knew it was an impossible task. Rose Farthingale was married to a viscount. Laurel had married a Scottish baron. Daisy's husband had been awarded an earldom for his valor during the war. Dillie had an identical twin, Lily, who was married to the grandson of a duke.

Miranda came over and whispered in his ear. "See, they are a tradesman's daughters who all made love matches with peers of the realm. Times are changing, Mr. Knight, and many of the younger peers are all for these changes. As for family, do not think having one is always ideal. Edgeware's parents hated him—I mean, really hated him—ever since he was a child. His mother wished him dead. Dillie was his salvation. She is his heart and soul now, and has gone a long way to repairing the severe damage his despicable parents caused him. So, having a bad family is sometimes worse than having no family at all."

He nodded, but made no further comment. He still harbored anger over being cast off by his parents, for they had tossed him aside with as much concern as one might give a pair of old boots.

Just like Edgeware's situation, he knew Berry was going to fill that gaping hole for him.

Miranda was asked to dance by a slightly inebriated Scot who complimented her red hair while drawing her away to partner him in a quadrille. "Are ye sure ye are no' Scottish, Lady Miranda? Ye certainly look Scottish to me."

"Perish the thought," she said, smiling sweetly at the man as the insult flew over his head.

Berry appeared at Gideon's side. "Oh, poor Miranda. He's going to step on her toes, for sure. He's one of the Duke of Solway's relatives down from the Highlands. They are known to be a bit wild. Not in an evil sense, like Hawthorne or his friends. They are just keen on making noise and having a good time, mostly while drinking too much."

Gideon did not know the Duke of Solway or his kin because they were not regulars at his gaming clubs. He supposed their vices were drinking, brawling, and wenching. But these Scots were known to be thrifty, so he was not surprised they did not frequent his gambling establishments.

He watched Miranda dance with the Scot, ready to step in if she appeared to be in distress. But Miranda smoothly handled the man, who was a bit clumsy but did not step out of line with her.

Berry tugged on Gideon's jacket sleeve excitedly. "Fiona and her husband are here!"

The pair noticed Berry bobbing up and down while she tried to grab their attention.

Fiona hurried across the room and hugged Berry fiercely. "What a month you have had! Rob and I have been reading the gossip rags that are filled with stories about you. May I congratulate you?"

"Oh, yes," Berry replied. "I have never been happier."

Fiona turned toward Gideon with a smile. "I had hoped you and Berry would be good neighbors, but I did not realize quite how good a fit you would become."

Gideon arched an eyebrow. "She is hard to resist."

Fiona nodded. "Yes, isn't she wonderful? And what a wretch Lord Hawthorne turned out to be."

The Duke of Durham clapped him on the back. "Good work, Knight. Glad to see Berry and Lord Berwick are well recovered from their injuries."

"I am still under caution," Berry said, pointing to the bruise on her forehead. "Only two dances allowed this evening, which is fine, because I did not care to dance with anyone but Gideon. Oh, look. Another of the Duke of Solway's relatives has taken Gwendolyn onto the dance floor."

"You had better hope they do not start coming around to Duchess Square with their bagpipes," Durham teased.

Berry laughed. "Oh, I think Miranda and Gwendolyn will chase them off if they dare. Are you staying in London for the summer?"

Fiona shook her head. "No, just for a few more days, and

then we will return to Shoreham Manor for the rest of the year. It is more pleasant to raise our newborn son and entertain our friends there in the countryside. You and Mr. Knight are most welcome to visit us if you are ever near Brighton. Rob's duties to the Durham properties will have him traveling often to London and the north. I will try to join him whenever possible, but for now it is best that I stay anchored at Shoreham Manor while our son is so little."

Berry's eyes turned watery. "I am so happy for you."

Fiona gave her another hug. "As I am for you. Grab your happiness and to blazes what anyone else thinks. Whatever problems you may encounter, work them out together. I almost lost Rob for my own stubbornness. Good thing he was even more thickheaded than I was."

It was nearing sunrise by the time the ball ended and the guests made their way home. Gideon had survived his first *ton* affair without making a complete fool of himself, and had received several pats on the back and promises of more invitations to come.

In truth, he hoped no one would follow through on those invitations. He wanted to be accepted for Berry's sake but did not actually desire to attend more of these *ton* affairs.

After all, he was a working man and actually had to *work*.

Berry and the Berwicks could hardly keep their eyes open by the time they all stepped into his carriage for the ride home. Gideon instructed the ever-reliable Brent to drop Lord and Lady Berwick off first. Now that everyone had seen how serious he was about Berry, nobody was going to pass a remark about their riding in his carriage without a chaperone.

Could anyone doubt their marriage was in the offing?

As the carriage rolled on toward Duchess Square, Berry curled up against his chest. "You make the perfect pillow."

He chuckled. "Have I already grown soft?"

"No, you are all splendid muscle and heat. Just perfect."

He wrapped his arms around her, feeling a contentment he

had never known before. They planned to marry soon, but had not yet set a date because Berry and Lord Berwick were insistent on making no official wedding pronouncements until after the Stanhope ball.

It was now over and had gone well. Gideon did not wish to wait another day to finalize their wedding plans. Were it up to him, he would take her to the closest church and have the vicar marry them this very morning.

But that was unlikely to happen, as Berry and the Berwicks were going to sleep through the entire morning and possibly into the early afternoon.

However, he could obtain the license today. This would give them thirty days within which to marry.

Wasn't this enough time to take care of any outstanding issues?

There were some things yet to be resolved, the terms of the betrothal contract, for one. He did not see this as an impediment, because he was ready to give Berry whatever she wanted. Knowing her, she would put the orphanage first.

But he fully intended to give her enough to leave her a very wealthy widow. Of course, he hoped to be around for a long time, but he meant to keep her safely independent should he no longer be there to protect her.

Of course, if she did inherit the Broadingham dukedom, she would be one of the wealthiest peers in England.

Another matter to be discussed was where they were going to reside. They had two homes on Duchess Square and needed to decide which one they would occupy. Both were more than he had ever thought to obtain in this lifetime. His preference was to reside in the one he had just purchased and been spending the summer fixing up to his ideal specifications.

It wasn't just a house to him. It was the realization of a dream. Something of his very own.

His sanctuary.

But perhaps Berry felt the same about her home. Well, they

would come to some agreement on it. Ultimately, he would go along with Berry's wishes. He was marrying *her*. She was the one who would make whichever house they chose a true and happy home.

But what would they do with the other townhouse?

CHAPTER NINETEEN

"I've asked Suzanna to marry me," Bonham said, obviously waiting up for Gideon when he returned to the Musket Club after the ball. "I figured if you could take the leap and propose to marry someone who was obviously too good for you, then so could I."

Gideon had just walked into his chamber and was ready to toss off his formal attire, but stopped and turned to stare at his friend. He shook his head and laughed heartily, for Bonham's smile was as wide as an ocean. "Did she give you an answer?" He had just seen Suzanna at the Stanhope ball, and she had not said a word.

"Do you think I would be floating on air if she hadn't? Yes, she accepted me."

They were both laughing now, amazed that any refined lady would ever have anything to do with them, much less actually agree to marry them. Gideon understood exactly how his friend felt, for he was experiencing the same elation. "Congratulations. She's a fine lady."

"So is Berry," Bonham said with all sincerity.

They embraced each other as brothers would, for they had been on this life journey together. Brothers in friendship since around the age of three. Growing up together, leaving the orphanage together, and building a successful business partnership. In all those years, never once had they considered ending up married to actual *ladies* whose fathers held titles and were peers.

In truth, Gideon could not recall their ever talking about marriage at all, because it simply had not been a consideration. Perhaps it was a result of growing up completely on their own that they had expected to die that way, too.

But his business brain began whirring, and an immediate solution to his and Berry's issue of having two houses presented itself. Bonham and Suzanna would require a marital abode, would they not? Bonham could not bring Suzanna to live above the Musket Club, nor would Gwendolyn appreciate the pair setting up residence in her home. But Gwendolyn would be thrilled to have them as her neighbors on Duchess Square, would she not?

This was the perfect solution. Gideon and Berry would have to choose which one of their homes to keep, and then they could offer the other to their friends.

He would discuss the idea with Berry when he saw her later today. He could not think of a better outcome, although it saddened him to think he might be giving up this new home of his. She had done such a beautiful job of turning it into an inviting abode. Much of the furniture had already been purchased, as well as drapes for each room.

Well, they would figure it out. He would not mind so much if Bonham ended up with his home. After all, Bonham had helped repair the guts of the house, upgrading the shaft mechanism and putting in the drainage pipes that were extremely convenient to have.

But Gideon would sorely miss the new ballroom, the refurbished study with that glorious cherry shelving, and that malachite entry hall.

Truly, it was a pity he might have to give it up.

Ah, but he would gain Berry, and that was worth everything.

Anyway, Berry had not voiced her opinion and might surprise him with her choice.

He and Bonham were still chuckling when Gideon asked,

"How about we leave the inventory and accounts to Joss and Pudge tomorrow?"

"All right, but why?"

"You and I are going to obtain marriage licenses."

Bonham clapped him on the back. "Excellent plan. I am going to bust if I don't marry Suzanna soon. What a mind that girl has."

Gideon looked at him askance. "Her mind? Seriously?"

"Yes, it is all part of the package. Beauty and brains. She's a lot smarter than me, isn't she? Look at the way she picked up those mechanical concepts as though they were as simple as darning a worn pair of socks. I'm sure she will have some interesting ideas on our wedding night, too. She is quite knowledgeable about the laws of physics. You know, bodies in motion. Forces of attraction."

"Gad, Bonham. I have no idea where you are going with this, nor do I wish to know."

"My point is, the wait is going to kill me. Do you think Suzanna and Berry are going to insist on lavish *ton* weddings?"

"Lord, I hope not. But it is one of the things Berry and I will be talking about today."

Bonham nodded. "I'll wait to see what you two decide. Suzanna has a mind of her own, but in this I think she will be influenced by Berry's decision."

Gideon slept later than usual, enjoying the unexpected morning of leisure while Pudge and Joss took care of the tasks normally left to him and Bonham.

But he was also eager to get the marriage license, so he made no fuss when Horace walked in and opened the drapes wide to reveal a sunny day. "Rise and shine, Mr. Knight."

"Botheration, must you be so cheerful in the morning, Horace?"

"Did you remember every detail of Lady Berry's gown? Did she look spectacular? Was she wearing a tiara or just gems threaded through her hair?"

"Yes, she was wearing a gown. It was white. She looked like

an angel. I wanted to ravish her."

"Because you are a naughty devil. May I say, that report was completely unhelpful. I'll just have to wait for the fashion articles in the gossip rags. And I see you are alive and breathing, so your cravat was not too tight and did not strangle you."

Gideon chuckled. "But I might strangle *you* if you don't stop talking now."

Of course, Horace ignored him and continued to chatter while Gideon washed and dressed. "See, Mr. Knight," he said, turning Gideon toward the mirror so he could look at himself once Horace had finished. "Is that a duke or is that a duke?"

"Neither, actually. But you did a fine job of making me look like a gentleman, as you always do. Thank you, Horace. I am most grateful."

Horace beamed. "My pleasure, Mr. Knight."

Gideon then grabbed a bite to eat before he and Bonham walked out of the club together, on their way to St. Mary's, the Mayfair church that the ladies on Duchess Square attended.

They hadn't gone far before they saw Chloe and Pudge helping someone who appeared to have fallen and was in distress.

"Blessed saints," Gideon muttered. "Is that Jasmine?"

Bonham followed his gaze. "Dear heaven, it is. Come on, we had better help."

They ran toward them. Jasmine seemed weak and on the verge of fainting.

"What happened?" Gideon asked.

"Oh, Mr. Knight!" Chloe was trying to hold back her tears. "She wouldn't tell you, but she's dying."

"What? How?" Bonham asked.

"Something about her pancreas, Dr. Farthingale told her. Jasmine said it was the same disease what killed her mother."

"Oh, hell," Gideon said with a groan. He knew Jasmine's mother had died young, and that was why Jasmine was brought to St. Brigid's.

"Hell, indeed," Bonham muttered.

Gideon's heart sank, for he would never wish this outcome on her. "She looked fine when the three of us went to the theater a few weeks ago. Did she know then?"

Chloe nodded. "Yes, but I had no idea. She told me later that night, after you had escorted us home. I wanted to tell you, but she wouldn't let me. She didn't want word getting around. I think she was in denial. If no one knew, then it could not be happening. Haverstock dropped her as soon as he realized something was wrong. The cur told her to leave the townhouse he had let for her."

"Typical nob," Pudge muttered with disdain.

Chloe nodded. "She's been staying with me this past week, but my benefactor does not want her around."

"Arse," Bonham said under his breath. "They're all alike."

Chloe was more practical about it. "He's paying for *my* services and *my* attention. He wants privacy. Discretion. He does not want a sick woman in the bedchamber next to ours. I would rather he were the one to leave, but he's paid for my lodgings. The lease is in his name, not mine."

Pudge cast Gideon a pleading look. "She's one of us. Even if she has turned into a witch this past month. I understand why now. Can I have an advance on my wages? I'll find comfortable lodgings for her close by and do what I can to make her comfortable in her last days."

"I can also help tend her," Chloe volunteered. "Frankly, I don't care if my *services* are terminated by my benefactor. He's no prize, anyway."

Gideon shook his head. "I'll pay for Jasmine's lodgings and care. Chloe, would you be willing to look after her in the way she needs? Or should I hire a caretaker with some medical knowledge, a companion to live with her and attend to her night and day?"

"I'll do it. She's my friend. But if you wouldn't mind, it would help to have someone come by for a few hours a day to show me what to do for her." She looked up at them with a pained look on her face. "I know Jasmine has been awful to you lately, Mr. Knight. But she is the closest thing I have to a sister. She was often vain and insufferable, even as we were growing up. But can you understand why I must take this upon myself?"

"Yes," Gideon said. He well understood this feeling of kinship, for none of them had anyone but each other. Those in the Musket Club were their family.

"I'll kick in my share," Bonham said, giving Gideon a look he well understood.

Family needed to take care of each other.

Gideon had been so angry with Jasmine, but it was senseless now. He could not condone her jealousy when coming upon Berry in his bed at the club, but he understood the grief and fear she must have been feeling. She had just been given a death sentence, and there was Berry being given everything poor Jasmine had always wished for.

Including him.

Perhaps Jasmine had loved him. In her own selfish way, of course. Theirs had never been more than a casual relation. She dropped him whenever a rich benefactor came along and returned to him whenever she was bored or between men.

He was not going to remember her as a saint, for she was far from it. But if they did not look after her, then no one else would. As irritating as Jasmine could be, she did not deserve to die forgotten.

He and Bonham lost several hours in getting her comfortably settled in a pleasant apartment close to the club. Pudge, Henry, and William helped Chloe move her belongings out of her benefactor's Curzon Street love nest and into the new place. Joss made certain to send over plentiful food and supplies for them.

"I'll stop by daily to look in on you both," Pudge said. "Let me know if you need anything, Chloe."

She nodded, and then took Gideon and Bonham aside. "This disease kills fast, says Dr. Farthingale. You offered Jasmine employment as a hostess at the Musket Club once. Would that position be open for me afterward?"

Bonham nodded. "It is yours whenever the time comes, if you want it. Greeting responsibilities only. If any patron makes improper advances, he will be tossed out. Your role would be to present a smiling face, an occasional sympathetic ear, and ensure our patrons promptly receive the drinks they have ordered. That's it. No bedding our patrons. The club has never been that sort of place, and we will not have it turned into something other than an honest gaming establishment."

"I am done with that, I assure you." She nodded. "Thank you."

With Jasmine now looked after, they went to obtain their licenses.

Afterward, they rode to Duchess Square, Bonham heading to the Carstairs residence where Suzanna and her cousin, Gwendolyn, were no doubt eager to see him.

Gideon strode to Berry's home.

Melton greeted him at the door. "Good afternoon, Mr. Knight. Lady Berry informed us you were a stunning success last night."

Gideon grinned. "Thank you, but we know it was Lady Berry who made me look good. Where is she?"

"Seated on the terrace." The butler led Gideon out to her.

Berry was all smiles as she rose to meet him. "Mrs. Garland was so eager to hear all about the ball, so I spent the last hour telling her how marvelous you were. She's sleeping now, and my throat was so parched from doing all the talking that I thought to sit out here and enjoy a glass of lemonade. Care for some? Or would you prefer a stiffer drink?"

"No, I'm good."

She took a closer look at him. "Oh, I don't think so. You look troubled. Is something the matter?"

He told her about Jasmine. "That's why I was late in coming over here."

Berry put a hand to her throat in obvious dismay. "I am truly sorry. Is there anything I can do for her?"

"For the woman who wanted to scratch your eyes out?" He knew it was not in Berry's nature to be malicious, but was surprised that she would actually extend a hand to help out Jasmine after the woman had been so insulting while Berry was struggling to recover from her own injuries.

"Oh, I did want to see her get her comeuppance in that moment. But holding on to anger and resentment serves no purpose. I do not wish ill on anyone, not even her. I am terribly sorry for her. It is a very cruel outcome."

Were the roles reversed, he doubted Jasmine would have shown her the same kindness. But this was the reason he had fallen in love with Berry, for her soft heart and generous nature. "I got the marriage license."

He then told her about Bonham and Suzanna.

She squealed and clapped her hands. "Oh, Gwendolyn predicted this! She knew it the moment they set eyes on each other. She predicted the same for you and me, but I dared not believe her. I only dreamed of the possibility, but expected the reality to be quite different. I was preparing myself for heartbreak, never expecting this happiness."

"Same for me." Gideon shook his head. "Berry, I still cannot believe you and I are a possible match. That is, *I* know we are. But I never thought you would deign to accept me when I am everything reviled by Society's elite."

She cast him a gentle, admonishing frown. "I did not spend years holding out for love just to refuse it when the perfect man came along. That you and Bonham are hardworking is an asset, not something to be frowned upon. The *ton*'s rules about this are ridiculous. Who wants a lazy dolt for a husband? I would prefer a gentleman in trade any day. I know Suzanna feels the same. She never cared what others thought and was ready to accept Bonham if he ever proposed."

"But that's just it—we are not gentlemen. We've worked hard to build up our business, but we have none of the elegance one expects in a gentleman."

"And Hawthorne and his friends did?" she remarked with a dismissive shake of her head. "They were given every advantage, given allowances, courtesy titles, the best schooling, and squandered it all."

"Still, you had to give thought to what I represented because you had the orphanage to worry about."

She nodded. "Even so, if you loved me, I was going to do all in my power to make both work. It simply was not an option to do otherwise. I was not going to give you up or the orphanage without a fierce battle. After last night, that is no longer a concern."

He was not so certain it would all be easy sailing from here on out.

However, they had been given this precious chance to make a life with each other, and he wanted to grab on to it as much as Berry did.

"We have some things to talk about," he said.

She motioned for him to sit in the chair beside her. "Yes, several important matters to resolve before we marry. I'll leave the betrothal terms for you and Lord Berwick to negotiate, but do let me know if he gives you a hard time," she said with a light laugh. "You will have access to all my funds anyway as trustee. And the law gives a husband broad powers over a wife's assets."

"I am interested in *you*, not your wealth. But setting aside trusts and laws, Lord Berwick needs to know that you will have access to all I own in return. You will, Berry. I am always going to protect you."

"I know. You always make me feel safe."

He smiled.

"Then we have the problem of two houses," she said. "I have a suggestion that might resolve this."

He leaned forward, hoping she might be thinking the same thing he was. "Go on, tell me."

"Suzanna and Bonham will need a home of their own."

He let out a breath. "Yes. That had come to my mind, as well."

"Do you think he would consider purchasing my home? Suzanna loves this place, and it would be perfect for her in so many ways, not the least of which is to remain close to Gwendolyn."

"You would give up your place?" In truth, the notion surprised him, because she was very sentimental, and this home was a connection to her parents.

"Well, I would ask a fair price. I don't think Lord Berwick would allow me to simply gift it to them."

"Bonham would insist on paying for it. He isn't looking for charity. But I know he would be in favor of the idea. He and I have not discussed the possibility. I wanted to discuss it with you first." He shook his head. "I thought for sure you would ask me to sell mine."

"I love your house." She cast him an impish smile. "After all, I designed it exactly as I would wish my home to be. And you have that lovely ballroom. After last night's triumph, people might actually attend our parties if we ever hold any."

He laughed. "I'll try not to behave like an arse and have everyone hate me again."

"They'll adore you, especially the women."

He took hold of her hand. "As long as *you* still like me."

"Oh, I do not think you need ever worry about that." She turned toward the stone wall that separated their homes. "We could throw some splendid holiday parties in your enormous ballroom, and even hold some special events for the orphans. Why not bring them all there for a musical recital or yuletide festivities? And wouldn't the Ladies Tea Society love to hold their weekly meetings there?"

He groaned in jest. "We are not going to have a quiet life, are we?"

"Occasionally noisy, but we can always cut back on entertaining if it gets too much for you. This is to be your home and sanctuary, after all."

"And yours, Berry. It is important that you are happy."

"I will be." She edged forward and kissed him softly on the lips. "I still wonder whether we met when you were growing up at the orphanage. Perhaps when I was six or seven and you were nearing fifteen years old."

"I don't know. Would you have noticed a brooding, angry boy who often went off on his own? As I've told you before, I doubt you would have liked me back then. You are such a kitten. And I walked around with a gigantic chip on my shoulder because I resented my parents for abandoning me."

"We may never know what happened to you, but I cannot imagine your mother ever purposely abandoning you. Yet, you turned that anger toward a good purpose. No matter your motives, you made something of yourself."

Ah, yes. His motives. He wanted to shove his success in the faces of his parents, wanted them to live to regret their decision.

"Perhaps you needed that anger to become the man you are today, but there is no need to hold on to it," she continued. "We'll raise our own family, have our own children, and create our own memories. Precious ones."

Blessed saints.

Would he be a good father?

Berry, of course, would be the perfect mother.

As she said, it did him no good to hold on to his anger. How could he remain bitter when he had such a promising future in his grasp?

Yes, time to move forward. No looking back.

Of course, he would never forgive those who had abandoned him. He was not anywhere near as nice as Berry was.

But he would push the hurt and seething grudges far down in importance. Life was too short to dwell on the bitter.

"Berry, I would like to talk about something else important. A thing that is within our control—the wedding. Any chance you might agree to keep it simple and marry me tomorrow?"

"How about a compromise? I agree to marry you next week and we hold our wedding breakfast at the Denby Arms? Plan on about fifty people. Forty for me and ten for you?"

He laughed. "Done."

After all, she could have insisted on inviting two hundred and fifty of the *ton* elite and making him wait a year for the wedding. Other than Bonham, Joss, and Pudge, whom did he care to invite? Well, he supposed Horace and Henry, too.

He placed his hands behind his head and relaxed back in his chair. "Anything else to discuss?"

She nodded. "One more thing."

"What is that, love?"

She cleared her throat. "Sleeping arrangements. Are we to share a bedchamber?"

"And a bed?" He had not considered any other possibility, although this was foolish of him. These lords and ladies often had separate sleeping arrangements. "Do you wish for separate quarters?"

"No. I want to sleep beside you every night."

He nodded. "Then we share."

She released a soft breath and smiled.

He smiled back.

This marriage thing was going to be quite easy, wasn't it?

CHAPTER TWENTY

BONHAM AND SUZANNA had married two days before them, and Berry had to admit to being envious. Suzanna could now share a bed with Bonham, and appeared to enjoy this very much. So did he. The two could not stop grinning at each other and whispering sweet nothings in each other's ear.

This was what Berry ached to have with Gideon.

It was only another hour until the ceremony, and then she and Gideon would be husband and wife. They would belong to each other.

She had to stop being so sentimental about this, but it was overwhelming and wonderful. They had been two souls alone throughout their lives.

Now they would be two souls *together*.

Harriet assisted in styling her hair while her friends, the ladies of Duchess Square, looked on. They were going to ride over to St. Mary's in a row of carriages. She was to ride with Miranda and Gwenys while Gwendolyn, Suzanna, and Bonham followed in Gwendolyn's stylish barouche.

Gideon had wanted to pick her up in his carriage, but Lord and Lady Berwick needed a ride, so he agreed to be the one to bring them to the church.

After all, Lord Berwick was essential. He would perform the fatherly duties on Berry's behalf, the ceremonial gesture of handing her over to the new husband who would now assume the role of protector and provider. It was only right that he be given the honor after taking care of her for all these years.

Of course, she had more than enough to provide for herself. But protecting herself from all the predatory wolves like Hawthorne had come to be a problem. She still shuddered to think what might have happened had Gideon not found Lord Berwick in time.

She shook out of the thought. This was a happy day.

Her own driver was designated to bring Harriet, Melton, and Mrs. Bolton to the church in her carriage. Unfortunately, Mrs. Garland would not be joining them, for she was too weak to get out of bed.

Once ready, Berry took a moment to stop in Mrs. Garland's bedchamber to show her the wedding outfit she had chosen. The gown was silk, of course, and in the palest shade of rose, with a lace overlay at the bodice in the same hue. "Berry, dear, you look beautiful. Thank you for showing me what you've chosen. I am so sorry I must miss your wedding. But I am not important. Enjoy your day, and I am sure I will hear all about it from Mrs. Bolton and Harriet when they return."

Berry kissed her and then joined her friends downstairs.

Miranda's was an open carriage, and Berry inhaled the scent of the roses she'd had planted in the little park within their square of elegant townhomes. The day was already warming, but the sky was a surprisingly vivid blue marked by soft tufts of white clouds floating by. "And you'll never guess who paid a call on us yesterday," Gwenys was telling her, chattering away like a magpie.

Berry tried to follow the conversation even though she was completely distracted. "Um, you had a visitor? Who?"

"Those Scots who danced with Miranda and Gwendolyn at Lord Stanhope's ball! Can you believe it? Oh, they are so handsome. I wish I had been at the ball. I would have danced with every last one of them. And their accents!"

"It is called a brogue," Miranda corrected her niece.

Gwenys put a hand over her heart and let out a swooning breath. "Oh, couldn't you just die to hear them talking? I did."

Miranda rolled her eyes. "Honestly, Gwenys, you must not encourage those Highlanders. Do you wish to be carried off to the wilds of Scotland? You are not even out yet. Be patient, for your turn will soon come."

"Maybe yours and Gwendolyn's, too. Why not? Now that Suzanna and Berry have made love matches for themselves, maybe it is a sign that you shall both do the same. The love gods are shining down on Duchess Square."

"Nonsense, we are quite content as we are," Miranda insisted.

Berry said nothing, for she had to agree with Gwenys.

Having found her happiness, she silently wished for love matches for Miranda and Gwendolyn. Miranda had been left a young widow and Gwendolyn had never been married. Miranda's marriage had not been a happy one. In truth, it had been more of a sad mistake.

Gwendolyn had been betrothed, but the fellow had died before the wedding and she had never truly recovered from the loss, for theirs had been a love match.

Berry now fully understood how devastating a loss it had been for her dear friend. But were not Fiona and Rob, the Duke of Durham, the perfect example of a second chance at love?

She silently wished this for her friends.

It was a short ride to the church, and Gideon was already pacing in front of the massive doors while waiting for her to arrive.

Her heart fluttered upon her seeing him, for he looked so very handsome. Truly, he could be mistaken for an elegant duke.

Or the perfect knight.

He strode over to help Gwenys and Miranda descend, and then wrapped his hands around Berry's waist to lift her out of the carriage. He kissed her lightly on the lips as he set her down. "You look divine."

She grinned. "So do you."

He placed her hand on his arm, and then lovingly wrapped his hand over hers. "Horace is waiting inside and cannot wait to see what you are wearing. He's been driving me mad all morning, blathering on and on about your perfect sense of style and how I cannot stand at the altar beside you while looking like a mountain troll."

Berry laughed. "Horace and I shall become the best of friends. I suppose we will have to work out the finer details of our dressing arrangements. Much as I enjoy him, he cannot be strolling into our bedchamber while I am dressing, nor can Harriet be in there while you are dressing. But that's a worry for later, I suppose."

"An easy fix to provide each of us a distinct dressing area. We'll be mostly going our separate ways while attending to our daily duties. But at night, I want you in my arms."

She nodded, feeling quite the same.

Miranda stuffed a handkerchief in her hand as the guests were about to take their seats in the pews. "I know you, Berry. You are going to cry throughout the ceremony."

"Nonsense, I shall be fine," she insisted, and was met by doubtful glances from all around her. "I am not a watering pot."

Gideon grinned.

Miranda chuckled.

And Berry was glad she had taken her friend's handkerchief, because her eyes now began to tear as Horace, Pudge, Joss, Henry, and Bonham took seats in the front pew. They were Gideon's family.

She and Gideon took their positions in front of the altar. More tears welled in her eyes.

"I love you, kitten," Gideon whispered, and took her hand in his, which was not at all the thing to do. But they had already broken so many *ton* rules, so who cared if one more was broken?

He did this for her benefit, wanting her to know he would always be there for her. She knew it, and loved having this warrior by her side.

The tears streamed down her cheeks as soon as the vicar uttered the first sentence of the wedding ceremony. They did not stop until she and Gideon exchanged their "I dos" and their friends began cheering upon the vicar's last words. "I now pronounce you man and wife."

The vicar may have said something more, but everyone was up and clapping, whistling, and stamping their feet, so no one heard his final remarks.

Indeed, the cheers were resounding. Completely shocking and disorderly. But even the staid Lord Berwick was whistling and clapping. Lady Berwick and their daughters tossed rose petals at Berry and Gideon as they marched down the aisle toward the front doors.

After more rounds of hearty congratulations, everyone rode over to the Denby Arms for the wedding breakfast. This time, Berry rode with Gideon in his carriage while Miranda took Lord and Lady Berwick in hers.

"Alone, at last," Gideon said with obvious relief, and scooted her onto his lap as they made their way along the bustling London streets. He wrapped his arms around her. "I cannot believe this day has finally arrived. We are husband and wife, Berry."

"Isn't it wonderful?"

He nodded.

"Well, what are you waiting for?" She wrapped her arms around his neck. "Care to do something naughty about it?"

He laughed. "Oh, yes."

His mouth closed over hers with crushing need, and she realized he must have been holding back his ardor all this time. Not that his prior kisses lacked anything. They were all marvelous and had her swooning.

But this was more intimate, his hands roaming freely over her body, claiming possession of her while at the same time showing her that she had possession of his heart. She probably had possession of his body, too. For was this not the entire point of a marriage ceremony? To pledge heart and body to each other.

One of his big hands came to rest upon her breast, and he seemed to like its ampleness, because he was suddenly paying extraordinary attention to it.

The light squeeze and gentle flick of his thumb across the bud had her body suddenly in flames. She arched into him, uncertain what was happening to her, although the way she responded to his touch was very much the way she had when watching him work on his ballroom while shirtless in the heat...all that glistening skin and those coiled muscles.

Yes, so much heat was flowing through her right now.

She moaned.

"I love the way you fill my hand," he whispered, then gave a husky, groaning laugh and removed his hand to rest it around her waist instead.

"Why did you stop?"

"We're almost at our destination. I dared not start something I could not finish in time." His smile held the promise of pleasures to come tonight.

He made certain their clothes were properly restored before they reached the Denby Arms, although Berry knew her face revealed that they had not been merely holding hands in the carriage.

Well, no matter. Being husband and wife excused their mis-behavior.

The wedding breakfast was enjoyable and probably lasted longer than expected because everyone was having too much fun to leave. But it finally came to an end, to Gideon's obvious relief.

Berry was relieved as well, for that kiss in the carriage had felt wonderfully different and she was eager to experience more under Gideon's guiding hand.

They had decided to spend the night at the Denby Arms, since it was one of London's finest hotels and also provided them privacy. While she adored her friends on Duchess Square, she preferred to put a little distance between them for one night. Not to mention, having poor Mrs. Garland in the bedchamber only a few doors down from her own would have put a decided damper on their wedding night. Horace and Harriet had packed an overnight bag for each of them, and those were already sent up to their room.

It turned out to be an exquisitely appointed bedchamber, no doubt the fanciest guest room available at the Denby Arms, perhaps at any hotel in London. Gideon was sparing no expense.

A steward brought up a bottle of the finest French champagne and a tray of fruits and cheeses, among other delights.

Berry's heart beat faster now that they were finally alone.

Gideon's smile was wickedly appealing as he approached her and took her in his arms.

And then it was as though a dam had burst and all their feelings flowed out in a rush amid sighs and moans and ardent kisses.

She had never experienced passion before, but it all came naturally and without hesitation under Gideon's guidance. There was no shyness between them, for it felt as though they had known each other forever and perhaps even beyond forever.

Their clothes flew off. She studied Gideon's body, surprised by how closely it resembled those Greek statues in the British Museum, for it was firm and finely chiseled, every muscle and sinew magnificently sculpted, including that male part of him that ought to have put her delicate sensibilities in a dither.

She was eager to see what he would do with that male organ.

Of course, she was not completely naïve and knew the basics of how a husband and wife coupled.

Gideon unpinned her intricately styled hair and ran his fingers through it as it tumbled down her back. "Beautiful. Silky," he murmured, kissing her deeply while carrying her to the bed.

He laid her down on it and then stretched out beside her, the solid length of him warm and reassuring.

She traced her hand over the dragon depicted on his arm, almost expecting it to come to life and breathe fire on her. There was something beautiful about the broadness of his shoulders and the masculine power of his arms.

And when he held her, she felt cherished.

He introduced her to passion that night, a feeling that tore through her body like an inferno as Gideon touched her, licked and teased her, first with his roughened hands, which always caressed and stroked her with gentle precision, and then with his lips and tongue, which left her with a yearning ache that only he could quench.

This was his prowess, this ability to slowly claim every part of her body, to scorch her and seduce her into surrendering herself and hungering for more.

He was no less affected. Whatever he took from her, he gave back of himself.

He rested his head against her bosom when they had both sated their burning urges and collapsed in a joyful but exhausted heap entwined in each other's arms. "Your heart's beating wildly," he murmured, and then glanced up to smile at her, no doubt feeling the pride of a conquering hero.

She ran her fingers lovingly through his hair. "That was quite some ride we just took."

His laughing breath tickled her breast. "Berry, it was the best. I love you, sweetheart."

Dear heaven.

She was having that urgent feeling again, that need to be enveloped by him, to feel his hands and lips on every inch of her as he led her to pleasure.

Apparently, he felt it too.

Groaning, he moved over her once more and resumed their feasting love. It was a deep hunger, a craving for each other, their senses heightened to such a point of sensitivity as they breathed each other in, tasted each other, and saw an infinitely happy future when gazing into each other's eyes.

"I love you so much, Gideon," she whispered as passion overwhelmed her, and she cried out his name again and again while coming undone.

They shared the bottle of champagne and the fruit and cheese after their second coupling, after which they spent the night in each other's arms talking. Well, she talked, and he did not seem to mind listening or answering her questions, because this experience was new and fascinating to her.

She woke up before he did, opening her eyes shortly after the break of dawn, and looked upon his face in repose.

She wondered whether these few hours were the first truly restful moments of sleep he had received in all his life. Until now, he had been guided by resentment and bitterness over his abandonment. So much explosive anger, but thankfully directed, compelling him toward the path of good instead of toward a path of destruction.

He now had her and the possibility of children of his own.

Perhaps it would take more than one night for him to fully accept the changes in his life, to plan for a future with the new family they would make together.

There was an edge to him even as he slept, an aura of power.

But this was Gideon. He was a force that could not be ignored, not even in sleep.

For the moment, he seemed to be at peace.

She closed her eyes and snuggled against him, breathing in the lovely sandalwood scent of his skin and seeking comfort in his warmth. The man was a furnace.

She drifted back to sleep for another hour, and this time when she awoke, he was looking at her. It was the softest look, a completely loving look. "Good morning, kitten," he said, propping himself on one elbow as he stared down at her stretched out beside him.

She smiled at him.

This was going to be a wonderful day.

And a wonderful life.

He rolled her under him and they set about creating a little duke.

EPILOGUE

Duchess Square, London
June 1828

"UNCLE BONHAM! AUNT Suzanna! Come quick," little Archibald George Knight, the seven-year-old Marquess of Brent—also known as Gideon's son—shouted over the stone wall separating their properties. "Mama's going to have a little girl!"

Gideon ran downstairs and out into his garden to pick up his son and bring him back into the house. "Archie, we don't know yet whether you'll have a brother or a sister."

"Oh, no. I am sure it is a little sister," said his son, who looked like a miniature of himself with his dark hair and penetrating gray eyes. "I talked to her in Mama's belly, and she said she was a girl."

Bonham now climbed onto the wall and hopped over to Gideon's side. "Suzanna's running around to the front with our Millie," he said, referring to his daughter, who was a year younger than Archie—but you wouldn't know it, because she was such a bright little thing. "I thought I'd take the shortcut. Archie, your sister talked back to you?"

The boy nodded earnestly. "I put my hand on Mama's belly and told her to move around if she was a girl, and she did. We're going to name her Lucinda…Lucy for short, but Papa said we would have named her Lucifer if she was a boy."

Gideon burst out laughing. "No, I was just teasing your mama about that. Your brother may be a little devil, but he'll have a saintly name because your mother is a saint to put up with me."

Archie cast him a stubborn look. "But she's going to have a little girl."

Gideon indulged the lad. "All right, it's to be a girl. But if it's a boy, we are going to name him Raphael."

"It's to be a girl," Millie said, breaking away from Suzanna and running toward them. She had an impudent, upward tip of her chin as she supported Archie's statement. The two children were thick as thieves and always defended each other, much as Gideon and Bonham had always done for each other as children.

Gideon laughed and held up his hands in surrender, for a six-year-old girl had to be far wiser than the dense adults around her. "Fine, Millie. If you say so."

Suzanna joined them in the garden. "Good morning."

Archie gave her a hug. "It's going to be a girl. Her name will be Lucy, not Lucifer. We're naming her after my grandmother," he said, referring to Berry's mother, who had passed on so many years ago.

"How wonderful. Would you like to spend the day with me and Millie and Uncle Bonham? Your mama and papa are going to be quite busy and it might get dull for you around here. Perhaps we can go for ices or have a picnic in the park?"

Archie nodded.

"Good, and we ought to bring along Miss Jergens," Suzanna said, referring to Archie's capable governess.

"I'll get her." Archie ran off into the house before Gideon could countermand the plan.

Of course, he was going to do no such thing. His heart was aching with fear for Berry, who was about to deliver their second child.

"And I need my Brigid," Millie insisted, referring to the doll Berry had created several years ago that had proven to be extremely popular, even to this day.

Gideon had wanted to name the doll after Berry, but that suggestion was not so well received. They had ultimately settled on Brigid as a compromise, in honor of the orphanage. Lord

Berwick had been adamant that Berry's name ought not to be used—and he was probably right, because there was still a lot of bias among the elite toward anyone in trade.

"Brigid is going to put on her 'going out for ices' outfit," Millie said, tugging on Suzanna's hand to lead her back to their house that formerly belonged to Berry.

Gideon watched them disappear next door.

"She loves that doll," Bonham remarked.

Gideon nodded. "And the clothes. You've spoiled your daughter rotten. Her doll has more clothes than Millie, Suzanna, and Berry combined." Berry had created an entire collection of clothing for the Brigid doll that little girls throughout England adored.

Bonham laughed. "I won't deny it. Care to wager on whether Brigid and Millie will be wearing matching outfits?"

"No, that is a sucker's bet. They are going to match, of course. As I said, you are even more of a doting father than I am, and have spoiled your daughter shamelessly."

"I know," Bonham admitted. "She gets everything she wants. But she has Suzanna's intelligence and kindness, and will always be a sweet girl, even if her fool of a father is ridiculously indulgent."

Gideon raked a hand through his hair, his humor suddenly fading. "Bonham, I hate this."

His friend let out a long breath. "Berry's strong. She'll get through the delivery."

Gideon shook his head. "I don't know what I'll do if I lose her."

"Don't think like that or Archie will pick up on it immediately. Say no more. He's returning with Miss Jergens."

Bonham remained steadfast by Gideon's side and made idle conversation to take the pressure off him while they all waited for Suzanna to return with Millie.

"Are you sure you'll be all right?" Bonham quietly asked him once his wife and daughter rejoined them. "Do you want company while you wait? I'm sure Suzanna won't mind my staying with you. She and Miss Jergens don't need me around to amuse the children."

"No, I'm not fit company. Go with your wife. I prefer to deal with this waiting agony on my own." Gideon glanced worriedly at his bedchamber window. "The midwife is up there now. Dr. Farthingale will stop by shortly. I'll be mad with worry until Berry gives birth. She had a rough time with Archie. How is she going to manage if it is another big, bruising boy?"

Bonham patted him on the back. "She may look delicate, but she's a fighter. Unfortunately, it is all her fight. There is nothing you can do but stay close and pray hard. Ah, I am being summoned by Suzanna. We'll keep Archie with us overnight if that's easier for you and Berry."

Gideon nodded. "Much appreciated. We'll see what happens in these next few hours."

He ruffled his son's hair, kept smiling as he waved them off, and then strode into his study and began to pace like a caged lion.

He was never more relieved than when Dr. Farthingale arrived to check up on Berry. Gideon was leaping out of his skin to hear what the doctor had to say after he had seen her and spoken with the midwife.

"She's fine. All is going smoothly. I'll stay around for a cup of tea, if you're offering."

"Yes, of course. I'll have Melton bring refreshments in here." They had brought over all of Berry's staff, who'd quickly adapted to their new home. One would never know that Melton or Mrs. Bolton had spent an entire lifetime next door.

Still, it had to feel a little odd to them that new servants were now walking the halls they had been walking for over two decades.

Well, change was good…wasn't it?

Bonham and Suzanna were very happy in Berry's old home. Berry did not seem to miss it very much, but Gideon supposed it helped that she and Suzanna had a close friendship to the point she could stop by her old home any time she wished.

Horace, of course, had come with him from the Musket Club and continued his duties as valet in his home on Duchess Square. Gideon was a little surprised by how easily Horace had managed to fit in, because the lad was a decidedly odd duck. But Berry's staff embraced him warmly.

Only Mrs. Garland was pensioned off, and that was done shortly after Gideon and Berry married. She was now residing in a cottage outside of Oxford and being well cared for by her sister.

"Doctor, it's been hours since Berry went into labor," he said after they had finished their tea. His breaths were ragged and uneven, and his hands were shaking because he truly was terrified something might go wrong.

Dr. Farthingale regarded him calmly. "Everything has been proceeding normally. I would have told you if she were in any distress."

Gideon buried his face in his hands. "I cannot lose her."

"You won't."

The doctor had just finished reassuring him when Gideon heard the midwife shout for them. Well, she had called out only for the doctor. But Gideon had no intention of being left behind. No two beings ever moved faster as they tore up the stairs to his and Berry's bedchamber.

Gideon expected to be kicked out shortly, but there was no way he was not going see Berry for himself and make certain everything possible was being done for her.

He ran straight to her side while the doctor went immediately to the bundle in the midwife's arms. "She isn't breathing," she whispered, but he and Berry heard her.

Gideon took Berry's hand and held it gently. "She's stubborn, just like her father, and did not want to come out of her comfortable abode yet."

Berry's eyes were wide with worry and she looked exhausted.

"That's right," Dr. Farthingale said with confidence, giving the baby a few light taps. "Just a stubborn little beauty. Aren't you? She just needs a little…nudge. And there we go."

They heard a gurgle or two, and then the baby let out a healthy but indignant cry.

Gideon hugged Berry, both of them relieved.

"Thank goodness," she said tearfully.

Gideon felt his own tears welling up.

"Would you like to hold your daughter?" the doctor asked him.

He nodded, drying his eyes off on his sleeve.

When had he ever cried?

Well, perhaps when Archie was born, because that was another time when he feared losing Berry. In truth, he could not imagine his life without her, for she was his heart and the very soul of their family.

"Looks like Archie was right. We have a girl, my love. Yes, doctor. I'll take her."

He settled on the bed beside Berry and leaned closer so that she could see their daughter, who was mostly bald but had a soft tuft of strawberry-blonde hair atop her head.

"Our daughter, our Lucy," he murmured.

"She's beautiful, Gideon."

He laughed and gazed upon the squashed little face that was a deep purplish-red from crying. "I think you are looking at her through the blurred lens of a mother."

"No, I see her clearly." Berry smiled as she rested her head upon his shoulder.

The midwife allowed their cozy scene for a few minutes then ordered Gideon out. "I'll take the babe, and then we need to take care of your wife."

He frowned. "What's wrong? I'm not leaving her side."

Dr. Farthingale placed a calming hand on his shoulder. "Nothing is wrong. But there's blood to clean off her after this delivery. Also, I want to make certain everything has come out cleanly. It won't take long. I'll call you back in as soon as we're done."

Gideon was too much on edge to return to his study, so he spent the next few minutes pacing up and down the hall.

He wasn't the only one hovering close. Mrs. Bolton, Harriet, and Horace also found reasons to walk by. Even Melton found an excuse to walk upstairs. Gideon allowed them all to stay, for they loved Berry, too.

They all held their breath when the door opened and Dr. Farthingale stepped out carrying little Lucy in his arms. "Give the midwife another minute with Duchess Berry. In the meanwhile, let me introduce you to the newest little Knight."

He handed Lucy to Gideon.

The others cautiously peered at his daughter and gushed with compliments even though she still looked like a squashed little thing. But she was squawking and already making demands to be fed or changed, or just wanted more attention.

Gideon returned to Berry's side with their daughter upon the doctor's nod.

The servants returned to their stations, and after another quick check of Berry and the baby, the doctor left. The midwife was going to stay on for another few hours, but took the opportunity to go down to the kitchen for a meal.

Gideon liked being alone with Berry and the little bundle he now placed in her arms. Berry looked better, for her hair was now neatly brushed back and she had on a clean nightgown. She still looked so tired, however.

"I think our daughter is hungry," she said, lowering the sleeve of her nightgown in order to allow their child to suckle her breast.

"My turn next," Gideon teased, for he adored Berry's bosom, which had only grown bigger after two children.

"She has green eyes like mine," she said with delight when Lucy squinted her eyes open for a moment.

He arched an eyebrow. "She'll be as beautiful as her mother in every way."

Berry chuckled. "Oh, I doubt I look attractive just now."

"No, love. You are the most beautiful woman in all the world to me, and shall always be."

As he sat on the bed beside Berry and their squawking daughter, he realized something that perhaps he ought to have realized when Archie was born. Well, he *had* thought about it when Archie was born but set the painful thought aside just as quickly as it had popped into his head.

The thought now nagged at him.

He watched Berry nurture her daughter and realized she might have been right when she insisted his mother would never have just left him on a London street without a care. He had two spectacular children now, and a wife who was his very heart.

Perhaps it was time to put aside the anger and resentment.

He had turned over his orphanage file to Homer Barrow after Archie was born because if anyone could figure out where he came from, it would be this man. Also, Archie was a marquess, and shouldn't a child with such an exalted title know something about his paternal ancestry? But there truly were no clues, and not even the clever Bow Street Runner could come up with a single lead after scouring newspaper records for any reported murders, scandals, and kidnappings in and around London and other areas of England.

Whatever had happened to leave a three-year-old child wandering around a London street would always remain a mystery.

But Gideon could now forgive his mother because she may have done this to save his life. He did not know if his father had any role or had merely been a one-night fancy.

None of it mattered anymore, for Berry and their children were his family, *his* to love and protect, and would never suffer his fate. With the success of the Brigid doll and her ever-expanding line of clothes, they had been able to extend the orphanage to house two hundred, which meant two hundred children who would be protected from the workhouses and chimney sweeps.

Even if the Brigid doll lost popularity, the orphanage funding was secure because Berry was now the Duchess of Broadingham, and that title came with a vast, entailed estate. He and Lord Berwick were managing it for her while she devoted her efforts to the orphanage's expansion.

He settled Berry so that she reclined more comfortably in his arms, for she and the baby had drifted off to sleep, the little squawker now quite comfortable with her mouth at her mother's breast—and a little hand also on her breast to make certain no one would move her away from that position.

Gideon kissed the top of Berry's head. "Love you, kitten."

"Love you so much, Gideon," she purred, stirring awake to smile up at him. "My knight in shining armor."

He kissed her again.

He had been a restless, troubled orphan.

But he was now a happy husband and father.

Those were the titles that mattered most…husband and father.

But it suited Berry to now be a duchess, for she had always been quality, and it showed in her every graceful movement and compassionate actions.

His very own duchess of Duchess Square.

He thought back to his decision to purchase this house, the tormented doubts he had felt when first putting in his offer and the shock when it had been accepted. He'd then wondered how he would be received by his neighbors, and whether he was fooling himself into thinking he could ever amount to anything or ever be considered someone worthy of love.

Then he'd met Berry.

And she loved him.

And had married him.

Truly, this marriage thing was working out quite well for him. Perhaps there was love in the air around Duchess Square.

Who would be next?

THE END

The Journey of Love
The Treasure of Love
The Dance of Love
The Miracle of Love
The Hope of Love (novella)
The Dream of Love (novella)
The Remembrance of Love (novella)
All I Want For Christmas (novella)

MOONSTONE LANDING SERIES
Moonstone Landing (novella)
Moonstone Angel (novella)
The Moonstone Duke
The Moonstone Marquess
The Moonstone Major
The Moonstone Governess
The Moonstone Hero
The Moonstone Pirate

DARK GARDENS SERIES
Garden of Shadows
Garden of Light
Garden of Dragons
Garden of Destiny
Garden of Angels

SILVER DUKES
Cherish and the Duke
Moonlight and the Duke
Two Nights with the Duke
Snowfall and the Duke
Starlight and the Duke
Crash Landing on the Duke

LYON'S DEN
The Lyon's Surprise

Kiss of the Lyon
Lyon in the Rough

THE BRAYDENS
A Match Made In Duty
Earl of Westcliff
Fortune's Dragon
Earl of Kinross
Earl of Alnwick
Tempting Taffy
Aislin
Genalynn
Pearls of Fire*
*also in Pirates of Britannia series

DeWOLFE PACK ANGELS SERIES
Nobody's Angel
Kiss An Angel
Bhrodi's Angel

About the Author

Meara Platt is a USA Today bestselling author and an award winning, Amazon UK All-star with over seventy books published. Her favorite place in all the world is England's Lake District, which may not come as a surprise since many of her stories are set in that idyllic landscape, including her award winning, fantasy romance (romantasy) Dark Gardens series. If you'd like to learn more about the ancient Fae prophecy that is about to unfold in the Dark Gardens series, as well as Meara's lighthearted, international bestselling Regency romances in the Farthingale series, Book of Love series, and Silver Dukes series, or her more emotional Moonstone Landing series and Braydens series, please visit Meara's website at www.mearaplatt.com.

www.ingramcontent.com/pod-product-compliance
Lightning Source LLC
Chambersburg PA
CBHW050659070726
47595CB00014B/456